The Festival

LOUISE MUMFORD

ONE PLACE. MANY STORIES

HQ
An imprint of HarperCollins*Publishers* Ltd
1 London Bridge Street
London SE1 9GF

www.harpercollins.co.uk

HarperCollins*Publishers*
Macken House, 39/40 Mayor Street Upper,
Dublin 1 D01 C9W8

This paperback edition 2024

1

First published in Great Britain by
HQ, an imprint of HarperCollins*Publishers* Ltd 2024

Copyright © Louise Mumford 2024

Louise Mumford asserts the moral right to be
identified as the author of this work.
A catalogue record for this book is
available from the British Library.

ISBN: 9780008589974

Praise for Louise Mumford

'Thrilling . . . Frighteningly inventive' John Marrs

'A brilliantly original premise which is horrifyingly believable'
Catherine Cooper

'An original and action-packed thriller, with a perfectly
unnerving premise that hooked me from the start'
Philippa East

'A twisty, action-packed plot makes
this intriguing thriller unputdownable' Roz Watkins

'Perfectly realised' Trevor Wood

'Tense, claustrophobic and oh-so addictive' Penny Batchelor

'A compulsive and tightly woven thriller' Karin Nordin

'A captivating and distinctive thriller' Sarah Clarke

'A complex, clever novel with memorable characters . . .
A truly gripping rollercoaster ride' Vikki Patis

Author photo: Nigel Brown

LOUISE MUMFORD was born and lives in South Wales. From a young age she loved books and dancing, but hated having to go to sleep, convinced that she might miss out on something interesting happening in the world whilst she dozed – much to her mother's frustration! Insomnia has been a part of her life ever since.

She studied English Literature at university and graduated with first-class honours. As a teacher she tried to pass on her love of reading to her students (and discovered that the secret to successful teaching is . . . stickers! She is aware that that is, essentially, bribery).

In the summer of 2019 Louise experienced a once-in-a-lifetime moment: she was discovered as a new writer by her publisher at the Primadonna Festival. Everything has been a bit of a whirl-wind since then.

Louise lives in Cardiff with her husband and spends her time trying to get down on paper all the marvellous and frightening things that happen in her head.

Also by Louise Mumford

Sleepless
The Safe House
The Hotel

For Jason, always.
For my mother Carol (1944–2024).

Chapter 1

The standing stones had once been women, so the story goes.

These women had been healers, helpers, the kind a family called on to aid with birth, with illness, with death. Often a little unusual, they knew things that others didn't, for example, which herbs soothed pain, or aided the breaking of a fever, advice that villagers revered, needed ... until the mood, fleeting like fog, changed and that knowledge was no longer a blessing but a curse. As witch hunts gripped the country, into the women's lives came a man called Eurig Swain and at his heels followed rumour, whispers and fear. Swain would not rest until the scourge of witchcraft was eradicated from the village, and so committed to that task was he that he swore to wear a hair shirt until every witch in the country had been tied to a stake. It was said his skin became so sore people would often see blood seeping from his cuffs, and that he left these drops of red behind him wherever he went. He was a man marked by gore.

The women might have been sisters, might have been friends, might never have known each other properly until Eurig got them in his sights. He bound them together. Without him, they may have remained unremarkable. Because of him they became legend.

Across the country fingers were pointed and words and

whispers became kindling, igniting fires that peeled flesh from bone. In the shadows of those flames, the five women of our story agreed on a plan, luring Eurig out to the oak tree and killing him there, burying him under its branches. Knowing they would never get away with such an act, they arranged themselves into a circle around the oak tree and turned to stone, escaping the petty, cruel vagaries of men, and creating a sacred spot where magic was the dew that clung to them, the breeze an electric tinge in the teeth of the night air.

The Grey Sisters became their name.

It is said that on Midsummer's Eve the stones shrug off their hard carapaces and turn back into women, dancing in their own moonlit magic circle until morning comes and they return to stone.

It is said that, at that time, people ask things of them. People who need luck. There are ways of asking for it, forgotten ways that the land understands. Respects. And these ways, they require something from the person on their knees.

An offering.

It is just a story, of course.

Chapter 2

Libby Corrigan could smell death on her. An antiseptic odour, it was sweet with rot, collecting into the corners of her eyes like crusted sleep, itching itself into her hair and trapped tight in the weave of her best blouse.

She should not have come.

It had been Dawn's idea. Most things were Dawn's idea. Dawn was an aeroplane, gliding in one strong line across the blue sky, firmly programmed to a destination, and Libby was a vapour trail caught in the wake, liable to haze to nothing.

'What'd you say?' A man leant in close enough for Libby to feel his breath on her neck. She jerked away, the loud club music a beat that made her skin vibrate, like she could just shrug it off, snake-like and free.

'I wanted her dead.' She said the words in the man's general direction, but they weren't meant for him. They just needed to be said.

He frowned a little, his eyes slipping from her, glassy from the alcohol or the drugs. 'What?'

She guessed she was dancing with him because he was moving around her, one of those birds puffing out their feathers and bob-dipping to impress their mate. She stood still. Around them the warehouse thrummed to a rhythm that made the people inside throw themselves into it, arms flailing, sweat flipping from the ends of their hair. It was the kind of music that possessed a person, a demon that needed exorcising. Lights skimmed over the crowd in a wash of colour.

Libby remained still.

Only a few hours ago she had watched as the coffin had been lowered into the hole. There hadn't been many mourners and her mother had set aside no money for limp sandwiches and beer someplace with a sticky carpet, so Libby had simply planned to go home. Until Dawn had grabbed her by the arm.

'My mother.' She didn't lean closer to the man but made the words loud enough to hear. 'I wanted her dead.'

And then Dawn was next to her with a drink that was cool in her hand and she had whisked her away to a quieter spot in a corner, one where those sly, sliding lights couldn't reach them. The music was still trapped in her chest, however, thumping under her ribs, the powerful wingbeat of a bird trying to break free.

'Is this too weird for you tonight, y'know . . . after today?' Dawn peered at her, her hair a tangle of blue and pink, her skin sweaty and glittered. She was dressed in hot pants and a crochet top over a T-shirt with a picture printed on it for 'The Holy Trinity': Dolly, Beyoncé and Taylor. Libby had nearly ended up coming in her funeral outfit of sensible blouse and pencil skirt until Dawn had put her foot down and switched out the skirt for a pair of Dawn's jeans, ripped so wide at the knees they looked like flapping mouths.

Libby shook her head. 'No.' She meant it. Though she would never have picked this as the place to spend the evening after her mother's funeral, as usual Dawn had chosen the perfect thing for them to do. The thud of the music beat its way into the dark whispers in her mind and bludgeoned them into silence. Despite being friends with Dawn since they were little, she had never until now wanted to come with her to a place like this, and she tugged at the holes in her jeans, feeling as if she were in fancy dress. It was a new club, Dawn had told her as they'd queued to get in, an opening night Dawn had been invited to as a thanks for signing up to some festival newsletter.

Rubbing at the stamp on the back of her hand, she took a sip of her lemonade. She could hardly remember how she got that ink on her skin at the beginning of the evening, though it must have been from a doorman stamping her hand as proof of entry. The print was now smudged by sweat, and she tried to work out whether it was meant to be a spider or an octopus.

'Mine is different,' Dawn placed her own hand next to hers.

'What is it?'

Dawn peered at her own stamp in the shifting light. 'I don't know . . . an arrow? A snake? A worm? Who cares?'

Libby's next words were a rush of feeling as she clasped her friend's hand in her own. 'I'll miss you when you go back to college.'

Dawn pressed her glittery cheek to Libby's, deliberately making sure the glitter rubbed off on her, making her giggle. 'I know, Libs. But we've got a whole summer yet. And you don't have to stay here; you can do anything now. Live anywhere. You're only twenty. Get your own college degree if you want. Yeah?'

'Yeah.' But it was a word with cracks in it.

Dawn raised her bottle of beer. 'A toast!'

'Huh?'

'A toast. To the witch. The witch is dead.'

Libby did not tap her glass against the neck of Dawn's waiting bottle. 'Dawn.' There was a warning in her voice.

'What?' Libby didn't need to say anything. Dawn sighed. 'It's fucking true. Having cancer doesn't change the fact she was a total witch. Having cancer doesn't make someone a saint.'

And that was all it took. The world around Libby was paper-thin and the heat of her memories burned straight through it. Suddenly she was back in that room and there was the laboured, rattling sound of her mother breathing, reminding Libby of a dying snake, the kind with just enough venom left in its wasted bite. Two years she had cared for her, two years of that dim room, the sick sheen on her mother's skin, watching as the flesh sunk into hollows creating a new face but one with the same harsh eyes, always watching for something with which to find fault.

Those two years ended in the watery light of a Monday morning. As the street around them had begun to fill with the bustle of people starting their week, her mother had grasped her, nails digging into the soft part of Libby's forearm and dragged her down so she could whisper her last words to her, breath foul from the rot within.

No.

Libby would not think of those words.

Instead she danced, awkwardly at first, moving side to side with her eyes fixed firmly on the middle distance as Dawn flailed and swayed and lunged and lurched around her in wild abandon. But soon that pounding beat hammered the embarrassment from her and she began to dance more freely, each step stomping on the memory of that sickroom, each flick of her arm pushing it further away.

She tried to smile.

That was when Dawn screamed.

Chapter 3

The music stopped.

Cheering began.

And then suddenly Libby was moving fast, faces flashing past her as Dawn, still yelling something, dragged her through the crowd. Inexplicably the word she was shouting, over and over again was: 'Tree!'

'What?' Libby tried to wrest her arm from Dawn's grip so she could slow down and work out what was going on, but Dawn held firm and kept moving, pushing through the crowd towards the DJ stage.

'Tree!'

The people around them seemed to understand this. She could see smiles and feel people clap her shoulder as she was jerked past them. Was this some kind of song request for a track Libby didn't know? Did everyone just really appreciate foliage? Had she fallen whilst dancing and hit her head and this was all a hallucination as she bled out on a sticky dance floor?

Dawn reached the stage, grabbing someone's arm to help lift her up, hauling Libby with her, who banged her shins on the edge. There was no time to give them a rub as Dawn yanked her arm up high and stood with her facing the crowd like a winning coach with their boxer. Except Libby didn't know who she had fought, or what she had won.

More cheering. The DJ, a broad-shouldered man with dreadlocks who wore his headphones around his neck, gestured for a quiet of sorts.

'Do we have a contender for the prize?' he asked, taking Libby's hand and peering at the back of it.

A hush fell as the crowd waited for his next words.

'It's definitely a tree,' Dawn said eagerly.

At last Libby half-realised what was going on. The spider/octopus that someone had stamped her with was not either of those animals; it was a tree, its branches full over a stubby trunk. She saw the DJ glance to the side of the stage where a figure waited, a dark outline against the lights. The figure nodded.

'People! We have a winner!'

There was a roar then and Libby was thrust forward as around the room screens flickered to life in a burst of orange.

'What have I won?' She turned to Dawn who stood at her side still grasping her hand.

'Shh! Watch!'

On the screen a sun rose from behind a hill, the sky behind it going from violet to a deep pink through to a clear bright blue as the sun burned brighter and brighter, until Libby's eyes watered. As it rose higher in that perfect sky, the hill below it sprang to life with a river winding its way along the bottom and a farmhouse building itself brick by brick until a roof popped neatly onto its walls. Finally in one corner, facing the house, five standing stones pushed their way out of the earth, stone teeth in soil gums, until in the centre of them a tree unfurled its branches. Across the whole scene came one word:

SOLSTICE.

Then the music slammed back into Libby, the screens died and the crowd moved and swayed below her like possessed coral in a haunted seabed.

'I don't understand . . .'

Dawn clasped her hands together and smiled at her, her fringe sticking to her forehead with sweat. 'You've won tickets to Solstice – the coolest bloody music festival of the summer! Actual bloody tickets, Libs! I've wanted to go for *years* . . .'

Solstice. The word popped into Libby's brain like a soap bubble. A music festival. She had seen pictures of those though she had never gone to one herself. Fields stuffed with drunk people wearing shorts and wellies, wrecked Portaloos and nowhere to get a shower. Camping. Dancing. Sunsets. Stars over a blazing stage. Whenever Libby had hesitantly mentioned doing anything of which her mother did not approve she had always got the same sneered question: *'Why would you want to do something like that?'* Most times, Libby had had no answer, certainly not one that would have made sense to her mother.

'This is a dream, Libs – a total dream!' Dawn could hardly stop herself bouncing up and down.

Libby stood on the edge of the stage, feeling a trickle of blood run down her leg from the shin she had bashed earlier, and she looked into the pulsing, shifting, rhythmic lights that lit up the people below.

A festival. It was not the kind of thing she did.

Behind her, in the shadows of the small space to the side of the stage, a still, hooded figure watched her for a few moments before quietly slipping away.

Chapter 4

'No.'

That was the only word she had said for the past half an hour, not that it was making much difference.

'Oh my God, Libs – *please*! I've wanted to go to Solstice since forever . . .' Dawn draped herself over the returns trolley in a pose meant to show abject sadness.

Libby had worked part-time at the library for the past two years. She had managed to arrange the hours around caring for her mother and, increasingly, as her mother had worsened, Libby had appreciated the chance to leave the house and escape into different surroundings. Of course, the books were a bonus. The ones she borrowed had got her through many long rattle-breathed nights. She flicked a glance towards the reception desk where Neil, a middle-aged man whose wardrobe was exclusively corduroy and a rotation of lightly stained shirts, stamped books for one of their elderly regulars.

'Get off the trolley, Dawn. You'll get me in trouble.'

Dawn slithered to the ground and sat with her back propped against the trolley leg, grabbing a book on her way, a Catherine Cookson, its plastic cover beginning to split a little. Dawn flipped its pages as she spoke, 'You have to go.'

'I can't just disappear for a weekend. I've got stuff to arrange after . . . y'know . . .'

This was not strictly true. There really wasn't much to arrange. They had never had a mortgage on the flat, her mother having bought it outright using an inheritance, and so there was only an old savings account that Libby would need access to, as well as her current account. That inheritance must have originally been quite a sum because it had kept them afloat for Libby's entire life without her mother having to do much more than the odd intermittent part-time job when the mood took her.

'It's one weekend, Libs! You could still do all that shit! I'll help!' In Dawn's hand the Catherine Cookson book was flopping about like a freshly caught fish. Libby gently rescued it, smoothed its cover and placed it on the correct shelf.

'You can have the tickets,' Libby said, picking up a stack of new titles. 'I don't want them anyway – you take them and get someone to go with you.'

'No, it's got to be you – see?' Dawn hauled herself up and took the tickets from Libby's cardigan pocket, her 'old lady get-up' as Dawn called it. The library only had two temperatures and each of those were directly opposite to what the season required: boiling in summer and freezing in winter. As it was June, Libby was already regretting choosing the cardigan that morning. She tugged it off and hung it over the back of an available chair before peering at the metal discs in Dawn's hand, the two tickets she had won three nights ago at the club. Each one was in the shape of a brass sun the size of her palm and, in the middle of it, there was a QR code. Dawn scanned one with her phone.

The same video they had seen on the big screen at the club played once more: the sun rising, the farmhouse popping up like a cut-out in a children's book, followed by the river and the standing stones and finally the tree. But after that, a page of text filled the screen:

Congratulations! You have won two coveted tickets to Solstice for this year, a music festival unlike any other set deep in the Welsh countryside. Now in its twentieth year, the festival is an experience like no other, bursting with fun, music and spirituality designed to welcome in the solstice, the longest day of the year and the beginning of summer, sunshine, harvest and bounty. Your ticket gives you the full experience with a camping spot and an exclusive VIP tour of the whole site with the chance to meet the festival's founding father, Abel Blake. Please do remember that the festival is a screen-free experience – you are welcome to bring your phones but there will be no mobile signal on-site. This ticket cannot be swapped or gifted and only the ticket holder and one friend is invited. See you in the sunshine!

'There!' Dawn pointed to the screen. 'Only the ticket holder and one friend is invited. You've got to come!'

From his post on the reception desk, Libby could see Neil glance over to them and frown before stamping his next book with perhaps more aggression than was strictly needed.

'Shh!' Libby put her finger to her lips, forgetting she still held a ticket and spiking her lip on one of the sun's rays.

Dawn looked around her. 'There's literally . . .' Libby gestured again and Dawn lowered her voice to a whisper that managed to be just as loud. 'There's literally no one in here, Libs. Apart from Mrs Knotts over there at the desk and she never wears her hearing aid. I know – I serve her on the tills over at the shop.' Dawn was working the summer at the local corner store before heading off for her final university year. 'You have to go!'

'No!'

'But *why*?' Dawn's whisper took on a hectic edge.

Why? Libby paused for a moment. It was a clear no. Of course she wouldn't go. Some festival out in the sticks with nowhere to shower, camping in a muddy field with a truckload of drunk

12

people. She wasn't trendy enough, cool enough, she didn't know the names of the bands and she didn't wear the right clothes.

Her mother's voice: '*Why would you want to do something like that?*'

Why?

'Umm . . . Libby, can I have a word?' Neil's reedy voice floated over to them as he put the stamped books in Mrs Knotts' battered bag for life, an optimistic name for such an abused thing.

Libby sighed. 'See? You've annoyed Neil.'

'Being Neil annoys Neil . . .' Dawn muttered as she pulled out a *Fifty Shades of Grey* and skipped straight to the turned-over pages.

Neil ushered her into his office, which was in fact a small walk-in cupboard just off reception. He kept the door open to 'keep an eye out', so he said, but really it was because with two of them in the room the door wouldn't close anyway. When they sat down, their knees touched.

'Look, I'm sorry about my friend. She's leaving soon . . .'

Beyond the reception desk they could both see Dawn, who had abandoned Mr Grey and moved to the children's play area to thumb through a pop-up book whilst sitting on a small dino-saur chair.

'Well, she seems quite settled now . . .' Neil angled his knees away from Libby's and rubbed at a spot on his shirt cuff. 'But that's not why I called you in.'

'It's not? Oh.'

'No. You see Maureen from mid-week is retiring.' Libby had never met Maureen from mid-week, the only sign of her was a distinct smell of fish left in the staff microwave the next day. 'So I had a discussion with Head Office and we've got an exciting opportunity for you.' Libby imagined Head Office in a room as small as the one she was in, people stacked in like books on an overstuffed shelf, little men and women clinging to the edges and lying sideways on top of each other whilst still maintaining a serious Head Office expression. Then she realised Neil had finished speaking.

'Yes?' Libby said.

'Brilliant! I knew you'd be the right person for the job.'

'Uh, what? What job?'

'Full-time, here at the library.' She had never seen Neil grin so widely before. He had surprisingly neat white teeth. 'It's quite the promotion for you!'

He was right – it was. Libby forced a smile. She told herself she was pleased. It was all very sensible, the level-headed kind of thing she should do. She now had a flat and a full-time job and her life, previously slack like poorly made jelly, was all set. But the more she thought about it, the more she didn't picture jelly, but concrete instead, herself trapped tight within it.

As she smiled, her fingers found the sharp spikes of the brass ticket in her pocket.

Chapter 5

Back home that evening Libby considered the black bags containing what was left of her mother's existence.

It felt like she had been a wind-up toy her entire life, one where her mother's hand had held firm to her key, but now that hand had disappeared and off she clattered, reckless and with no direction.

After the funeral she had got to work clearing out her mother's belongings and now only one room remained: her mother's sickroom, left almost exactly as it was, as if waiting for her to come back.

Most of the bags were filled with clothes, designer stuff in delicate fabrics that couldn't be machine-washed. Every morning, until she got really sick, Libby's mother had met the day in a well-chosen outfit, her hair set and styled, her make-up expertly applied. She worshipped no God except Max Factor. There were lots of framed photos around the flat, all of them studio shots of her in various poses: glossy hair, a confident gaze, leftovers from a failed modelling career. That was probably the main reason she had not believed in a just and righteous God because, if one had existed, she would have lived in a world of film premieres and designer dresses, of her face on magazine front covers, not in a two-bed flat with a daughter who had not inherited her fine bone structure.

Of Libby, there was only one photo in the entire flat, taken when she had been a baby, her mother filling most of the shot, bending over her with a Holy Mary serene expression. Until Dawn had pointed that out one day, it was a fact that Libby hadn't ever really thought about, that maybe other families had photo walls or picture frames on mantelpieces that didn't just have one face on them.

Medicines and the general hospital paraphernalia were cleared out next, and then Libby stripped the sheets, intending at first to wash and reuse them but somehow her hands had a different idea and into the bag they went. She would have dismantled the bed frame itself if she had known how – the smell of antiseptic, of rot and death and bleach had seeped into the wood of its headboard, into the now bare mattress. Next came the things on side tables and windowsills and of these there were few: some floppy, yellowed books – true stories about horrific childhoods involving abuse and pain and fear, strange ornaments made of cheap wood and metal, stretched into painful-looking shapes. Into the bag it all went.

The jewellery she put to one side. There was more of it than she had realised her mother had possessed and it looked to be real gold, not plated, though she couldn't be sure about the gems. Libby had no eye for that kind of thing – they might have been priceless or paste. She would have to get them properly assessed.

She knew she was meant to keep some of it. Most daughters would. They would save a bracelet, or a ring, something to remember the woman now gone. Libby didn't need any of that. The woman was not gone, after all: she was lodged in her brain. Every time Libby let her hair loose about her shoulders she heard her mother snipe about its lankness, how badly it compared to the thick locks she'd had in her youth. When she switched on a television programme she heard that same voice sigh and call

16

her lazy. When she laughed she covered her mouth because that voice told her that her teeth were crooked and stained.

Libby tied up the final bag and looked around her. She could do anything with this room now if she wanted. She could make it an office, or a home gym or a hobby room where she could craft things at a workstation filled with neat drawers and cupboards.

That voice in her head made a tutting sound.

'Why would you want to do something like that?'

The feeling of disappointment had been as natural to her mother as breathing. Her life hadn't worked out the way she had planned. Libby knew she'd started as a model but she had never been given a break and her career hadn't taken off. And then her daughter had to go and continue the trend, never being the child she deserved – too tall, too ungainly, too bookish, too plain.

She could sell the flat. Move out. It was now hers, and though she had lived in it with her mother her entire life, she didn't particularly feel much attachment to it. That was a big idea though, too big for a Monday evening when she hadn't even given any of those bags to charity. Her stomach rumbled and she realised she hadn't had any dinner yet so she stretched out her legs in front of her, rubbed some life back into her calves and stood, heading for the kitchen.

Her mother greeted her. From the bookcase, from on top of the television, at the side of the armchair, on the wall, her smug smile in photo upon photo seeming to patronise her daughter at every turn: *'See how beautiful I was? See how beautiful you will never be . . .'* It did not take long to deal with them. Not into a bin bag this time but piled face down in the corner of the room, defeated Medusas no longer able to turn her to stone with one glance. As Libby stirred a saucepan of tinned soup in the small kitchen that made up one corner of their lounge, she gazed around at the furnishings. All of it – the sofa, the nest of tables, the chair, the coffee table, even the plates and cups – they should all go into that black bag. She didn't want any of it.

17

Especially the painting over the mantelpiece. That painting had been a particular favourite of her mother's, depicting a woman dressed in Victorian garb, slumped on a chaise longue in a pose suggesting defeat and disappointment, her surly gaze fixed squarely at the viewer, a gaze that did not just follow a person around the room but positively stalked them. Vera, Libby had named her.

That needed to go too. Libby could feel Vera glaring balefully at her as she stirred the soup. Leaving the pan to simmer she went over to the wall and considered the miserable painted woman.

'Come on, Vera, time to turn that frown upside down,' she said as she grasped the edges of the frame to give it a firm tug and then watched in amazement as an old photo floated free from where it had been tucked behind.

There was nothing written on the back, no helpful clue in her mother's handwriting, the oversized curves of her 'y' and 'g' which became almost hooks, making even a blameless note into a weapon. Libby peered at the two young women in the picture who gave each other a one-armed hug whilst their other arms were thrown out towards the vista behind, a rolling view of hills. There was her mother, a poised elegance to her stance but the hint of the child in the chubbiness of her cheeks, her hair Eighties blow-dry huge. Next to her was a woman Libby didn't recognise, more wobbly in her pose, a bit less wide of smile, her hair a fraction more straggly and blown almost over her whole face.

They looked carefree and in a silly mood and Libby stopped to stare at seeing her mother this way because the woman she had known had always had a permanent bitter downturn to her mouth. It was a candid, happy shot. Why go to the effort of hiding it?

As Libby poured the soup into a bowl and then rinsed out the saucepan, she could see in the stainless steel of the sink tap a distorted version of her face, her own unsmiling mouth, her frown.

Her mobile phone pinged and an email notification appeared on the screen.

Don't delay! Your invite to accept your FREE Solstice Festival tickets expires at the end of the day! Don't miss your exclusive free pass to the UK's hottest festival. All you have to do is follow this link and register your details so we know you're coming. See you in the sunshine!

At the bottom of the email was a picture from the festival, a blur of arms waving, faces turned upwards to the camera and on each one of them – the kind of smile Libby wanted for herself.

Sunshine.

Fun.

The festival.

'Why would you want to do something like that?'

She was only twenty years old. This could be the start of a whole new her, one who could maybe work out what to do with a life that was emerging from the shadow that had always been cast by her mother. One who did the kinds of things twenty-year-olds did, like dancing in a crowd of people in a summer field, a little sunburnt, a lot happy. One who smiled properly. Who didn't care about the opinions of a dead woman.

She messaged Dawn.

Chapter 6

(An excerpt from the documentary entitled
Field of Dreams: The Solstice Story, first aired one year ago.)

The man and woman settle on chairs at either side of a massive oak tree.

The older woman sits straight, knees together, her long plaid skirt pooling at her feet, which are clad in the kind of wellies that don't just do dog walks in the odd muddy park on a weekend. These wellies are scuffed and caked in dirt with splashes of grime covering the toes. Her long grey hair is coiled into a tight bun and she smooths the tendrils near her temples in a self-conscious way. There is no hint of a smile on her sun-worn face, instead she coolly considers the camera with a frown as if it is a toddler about to misbehave. The words 'Ma Blake' appear on the screen.

All the smiles come from the man next to her. Golden-haired, tanned skin, light-coloured trousers and shirt, he is a retina glare against closed eyelids. Even though no one has said anything yet, he smiles as if he has just heard the most amusing dinner-party story and is ready to tell his own, one arm flung out in a relaxed position against the back of his chair. Under him appear the words: 'Abel Blake'.

The female interviewer's voice can be heard off camera: 'So who came up with the idea of Solstice?'

It is as if someone flicks a switch within the woman and she beams as she turns to the man. 'Abel, of course. He always was a clever boy, much cleverer than me or his father. Without the festival, I don't know what—'

Abel cuts through her words and lays his palm tenderly on the trunk of the oak tree. 'No. Without *Ma* there would be no festival – that's the important point. I might have come up with the idea but she helped make it reality. There is no Solstice without her.'

Ma waves a hand as if she can bat his words away, her previous sunny expression now cloud-choked. 'I hardly did anything.'

'Sanctum though . . .' Abel prompts.

'Oh, well – yes. Sanctum was something I very much wanted to do – a space within the festival for spiritual and mental healing, for the real magic to happen . . .'

Abel turns his spotlight smile onto his mother and, mirror-like, she tries to reciprocate but hers comes out a weak and fleeting thing.

The interviewer's voice: 'Did you expect it to continue to be this successful, so many years on?'

Abel still has his hand on the tree trunk and he smooths its bark as he speaks. 'That first festival . . . it was chaos in a field. I'm right, aren't I, Ma?'

Here Ma nods, biting her lip. 'Well, it was a bit.'

'A lot! But there was a magic there, yeah? I could feel it, the bands could feel it, the crowd too. We had this beautiful weather and I remember walking through the field, and it was just one field back then, and thinking to myself, *I love this, I love how this makes me feel.* Calm. Relaxed. Happy. Even though all the toilets were blocked and there was this godawful cloud of midges at the campsite and we didn't have enough firewood for the bonfire and one of the music acts nearly broke the stage!'

'We always wanted it to be special – to be different, didn't we, Abel? It saved us.'

'It saved a lot of people, I think. There's music, of course but it's also . . . a place to find yourself. Summer solstice, you know – the longest day, bathing in all that light. It's a magic time, always has been. That's where Sanctum comes in, our festival within a festival. We always wanted the heart of the whole thing to be here amongst the stones on Midsummer's Eve.'

The picture widens out so the viewer can see the stones that ring the tree where Ma and Abel sit. There are five of them, grey and narrow, some leaning towards each other, like friends whispering a secret. A voiceover explains:

These ancient stones have stood on this land for centuries and, as Ma Blake has said herself, were the reason the Blakes bought their farmhouse when she was a newlywed. They feature as a focus of the mysterious Sanctum, the festival within a festival that takes place during the revelry. Some mistakenly call this a VIP event, but Abel tells us that, in reality, invitations to Sanctum are issued during the event on what is a totally random basis. What happens there remains secretive, the stuff of rumour and speculation.

The footage cuts to Abel once more. 'Anyone can buy a ticket to Solstice – but Sanctum is priceless.'

There is a pause and then the interviewer says in a calm, quiet voice, 'Can we talk about Tess Sanderson?'

Ma's face is now as stone-like as the standing circle she sits within.

'No,' she says.

The scene cuts out.

Chapter 7

It was now Dawn's turn to say it.

'No.'

Both of them considered the bed. On it was a neat pile of folded clothes and a small leather suitcase, the kind last sold in the Sixties complete with a gold clasp and a top handle.

'But it might get cold.'

'Well, that's when you'll wear your fleece . . . and your other fleece . . . and, is this another fleece?' Dawn held up the offending article. 'One fleece, Libster. It's going to be sunny.'

'But—'

'In fact – here. I'm doing it.' Dawn shoved Libby aside, upended the case and began to rummage in a swift, confident movement. She had freshened the pink and blue dye in her hair and wore a baggy T-shirt tied in a knot above denim shorts so frayed one snagged thread could unravel the entire thing.

Libby had been ready when Dawn arrived at her flat. The problem was she had been a little *too* ready. She had the one rucksack Dawn had told her to pack but she also had the small suitcase, a duffel bag, a golf umbrella and she had been wearing two jackets over her own plain top and cargo shorts. Dawn had taken one look at everything and sighed. 'I mean, where do you think we're going – for a week in the Arctic?'

Libby knew where they were going. They were camping in the countryside, actual camping in a tent, at night. She had tried to imagine it and found the limits of that particular brain muscle.

As Dawn tossed aside a smart blazer, a blouse, two of the fleeces and a spare set of wellies she turned to Libby. 'I'm going to go out on a limb and guess you've never been camping before, yeah?'

Libby shook her head. Of course she hadn't. She had been raised by Ann Corrigan, a woman who kept the windows firmly shut even during the hottest summer months, living in fear of flies getting in, who believed nature was something boring people watched in documentaries and who only went for a walk in the park when she had wanted to show off a new outfit.

'I'll need that!' Libby made a grab for the object in Dawn's hand.

'A hairdryer? Tell me – where do you find plug sockets *in a field*?'

'I thought there were shower blocks—'

'Yeah but they don't have plugs in them – they aren't bloody spa retreats! And the queues will be massive. I'm just going to wet wipe myself down each morning.'

Libby blinked. That was a whole other conversation that she did not have the courage to get into right then and there. She watched Dawn ditch the hairdryer, the dressing gown, the slippers, the pillow and half of her toiletries with a leaden sinking feeling in her stomach.

One rucksack was all she had left by the time Dawn finished. Granted it was a large rucksack with a lot of pockets and an expanding middle but there was just one. She tried to swing it onto her back and nearly toppled over.

'But what if I need—'

'You won't,' Dawn firmly said, shoving her into her boots and pushing her to the door. 'Now move it – or we're going to miss our train!'

* * *

During the two-hour train journey Libby became mesmerised by the landscape slipping past, a rolling view of green fields and hills and hedges. It reminded her of a television toy she'd had as a child, the kind you wound with a handle to make the picture appear to move, a loop of the same thing, over and over again.

When they alighted onto the train platform it was small and suspiciously empty. Only a pigeon neck-bobbed towards them in a desperate run, eager to greet probably the only humans it had encountered in months.

'Are we early?' Libby once again tried to swing her rucksack onto her shoulders. Once again the rucksack defeated her. She had expected a certain hustle and bustle in the train station closest to the festival.

'Well, it's a day before the whole thing starts but lots of people arrive now to, y'know, soak up the atmosphere . . .'

They looked around at the one platform, the neatly painted scrollwork on the awning and the total lack of any other festivalgoers or any of that atmosphere that Dawn had mentioned. The pigeon strutted around their feet, pecking closer and closer to their shoes.

'I think we're meant to change here for the final bit of the train journey to Solstice?'

There was a screen to their left, which would have told them the next few trains due but instead simply said 'Station now closed.'

'What?' Dawn began tapping angrily on her phone. 'But this is the Solstice station! The festival has its own bloody train station so you'd think it'd be open!'

'It's Sunday though, I guess . . .'

That was one of the many things that set Solstice apart from other summer festivals – it did not always happen on a weekend. The longest day was tricky like that: it didn't take into account the easiest time for people to get to a farm in the middle of nowhere, otherwise known as Mid Wales. If you wanted to go, you had to be prepared to miss work and travel at odd times of the week. This year Solstice fell on a Wednesday.

'But it's the Solstice train station – it shouldn't matter what day it is!'

'Is it though?' The train they had alighted from began to chug slowly out with a grinding of metal. Dawn bit her lip as Libby moved to point to the neat black letters on the sign above their heads. 'Because this says Grey Sisters. And there's not even a poster about the festival . . . in fact, there aren't any posters at all.' The noticeboard was a blank of information, just a few pins huddled in solidarity under clear plastic. 'Dawn . . . y'know when you woke me up and said we'd arrived . . . had *you* just woken up too?' Dawn bit her lip harder. 'Dawn?'

'Okay, okay! I must've, like, closed my eyes for a few *minutes*. I didn't mean to but then I woke up as the announcement said this was the last station.'

'This is so typically you! You said you'd stay awake if I slept. You promised!'

'I'm the one who got us this far! Who booked the train? Who stopped you bringing your entire flat with you? And anyway . . . look!' She brandished her phone at Libby and startled the pigeon who fluttered away to a safe distance. 'Google Maps says we're only half an hour away!'

Libby took the phone and peered at the screen, 'Half an hour away *by car*, Dawn. I didn't pack a car in my rucksack – you said to keep it light!'

'Well, you fell asleep too! It's not all my fault!' There was a moment of silence that emboldened the pigeon to begin to stalk them once more.

Of course Dawn would act like this. She would never think to stay awake whilst Libby slept, would never consider that they would then miss their stop because that was not how things worked for Dawn – she was a sun, and the earth moved itself around her. If she wanted a nap but also wanted to get off a train at the correct platform well, then the universe would work that out for her. She didn't have to worry. Or rather, *Libby* would work that out for her.

They headed through the platform exit and came out at the top of a short, deserted village: grey stone terraced houses with slate roofs and a sullen Sunday air, wedged in on either side by rock-strewn hills. A solitary shop sat glumly in the middle of the street. The sky above was heavy with cloud, holding in a sticky heat. Used as she was to the city air laced with the metallic tang of exhaust fumes, Libby at least enjoyed the feeling of breathing something cleaner.

Dawn nudged her. 'Okay, let's find a taxi, or a bus, or a fricking donkey if we have to.'

Libby couldn't help but smile. They shouldered their rucksacks and began walking.

Chapter 8

The shop was open, but it didn't look pleased about it.

One large, smudged window still held the Easter display: pastel bunting, papier-mâché eggs and a cuddly bunny wearing a disappointed look and a frayed waistcoat. One of its ears drooped.

'This is it?' Dawn looked around as if another row of shops would pop up in front of them like a children's toy, complete with cheery red-cheeked shopkeepers and colourful awnings. 'This place has one shop – that's all?'

The street was merely a flick of tarmac, pavement and terraced houses, a gouge in the hillside that led to an angular war memorial at its end and a road burrowing into the steep rise of land. It felt like those hills were the coils of a massive snake choking this place, squeezing itself around the dwellings as if they were its next meal to be suffocated.

The 'Come on in! We're Open!' sign had faded in the sun and the bell above the door gave a half-hearted tinkle before something clunked as Libby pushed on it and the door stopped fast.

'Bloody thing. Don't shove on it – you'll break the hinges.' A rasping voice came out of the gloom. 'Joe! Joe! Bloody door's stuck again.'

'I think I can—' Libby began.

An old woman's face appeared around the edge of the door, wrinkled soft skin, a generous application of purple lipstick and blusher at least an inch below where her actual cheeks were. 'Did you not hear me? Jesus! Stop shoving. I'm not made of doors, y'know. Do you need to come in?'

Libby paused, the ferocity of the question making her suddenly unsure. 'Umm . . . yes?'

'Well, you're going to have to squeeze through. Here.' A bony hand fastened itself on Libby's shoulders and yanked at her. There was some manoeuvring as they discovered the massive rucksack would have to be left outside and then Libby was through, quickly followed by Dawn.

'My bag . . .' Libby weakly began, eyeing the rucksacks she could see abandoned on the step.

'Ah, no one'll steal it here. Nobody in their right mind would want those things.'

The woman backed off and considered them with a tilt of her head. She wore a bright yellow shop apron over a clashing pink jumper and velour jogging bottoms. On her feet were a pair of fluffy slippers with big, lashed eyes on them. After what seemed like much longer than an excruciating minute, she sighed. 'Oh. You're one of *them*.' Her voice was loaded with disappointment.

Libby felt herself flush. 'Them?'

'The festival. You're one of *those*.' She gave an extra dismissive emphasis to the word 'those'. 'Joe! Get out here! We've got two of those festival lot in the shop!' She crossed her arms.

Now Libby's eyes had grown accustomed to the dim interior, she could see a few rows of metal shelving, which managed to hold a huge amount of things that she was almost sure people didn't buy nowadays: unappetising tins of meat and soup, plain, dry biscuits mixed with the kind of household items perhaps a housewife in the 1950s might have coveted. Swamp-like, the linoleum floor had begun to bubble.

'Look.' Dawn hardly raised her head, engrossed in her phone from the back of which Dolly Parton gave a benevolent smile in a cover bedazzled with rhinestones. 'Uber doesn't seem to work here and we just want to leave, so can you give us the number of a taxi, or something?'

The woman's arms remained crossed. She frowned.

'Uh . . . and this, please,' Libby added, grabbing a multipack of tissues, hoping that buying something would sweeten the deal.

'Interesting choice.' A man about their age came out from behind a beaded curtain at the back of the shop with a pair of big headphones slung around his neck.

Libby realised she was not, in fact, holding a bumper pack of tissues but a bumper pack of incontinence pads. The man raised an eyebrow with a smirk. She felt her entire body break out in an anxious sweat, tried a smile, gave up on it, and shoved the incontinence pads back on the shelf, picking up a pack of tissues instead.

If this had been an action film, the man would have instantly been cast in the part of the suave villain with his longish dark hair, fine-featured face, high cheekbones and slim nose. Wardrobe hadn't quite got the memo, however, as he was wearing a Garfield T-shirt, and they had gone overboard with the sheer number of keys they had given him to wear on the thick silver and leather loop hanging from his belt.

The woman stalked over and straightened the items that Libby had touched. 'Joe, you deal with them. Bloody festival. And if they touch anything else, they pay for it.'

Libby saw the glare forming on Dawn's face, a familiar expression. Once, when they had both been eleven years old on the school bus and easy pickings for the older bullies, the favourite thing for those tormentors to do had been to yank on an unsuspecting girl's ponytail, hard enough for the scalp to throb afterwards. Libby's solution? Change her hairstyle to something that couldn't be grabbed. Dawn's solution? Wear a ponytail again, get it yanked again, then turn around and punch the boy who did it, right in his face, nearly breaking his nose. She was suspended for a few days afterwards, of course. But for the rest of her school life she wore her ponytail completely unmolested.

Before the shopkeeper suffered the same fate, Libby cut in, standing almost in front of her friend. 'Hi, Joe. I'm Libby.'

'Hi. This is Edna, my nan.'

'Mrs Kirk to you,' the woman corrected in a firm voice as she patted the incontinence pads back into shape.

'We seem to have got off at the wrong station.'

'Not wrong,' Mrs Kirk muttered taking up her position behind the till, slippers scuffing on the floor.

'Nan,' Joe said, a warning note in his voice.

'Well, it's not, is it? It's the right bloody station. The Blakes screwed us.'

'Nan.'

Libby came forward and laid her tissues on the counter, along with a pack of mints and a lolly on a stick. 'What do you mean, Mrs Kirk?'

The older woman eyed the prospective purchases for a pointed amount of time and, eventually Libby got the hint. She slid across an extra chocolate bar, her cocoa bribe.

Mrs Kirk nodded in approval. 'Grey Sisters was the only station when that whole circus started up. This place, we could've bene-fited from the people, y'know? Become something. A proper row of shops, some tat, the odd coffee place – you young'uns love coffee; meself, I prefer a nice cuppa. The Blakes, they knew what they were doing when they used that old trunk line and created their own Solstice station. Said they were doing it so we wouldn't get annoyed by the crowds but that's balderdash. They cut us off on purpose.'

Joe raised his eyes and sat on a ledge behind the counter, grabbing a tube of sweets.

'But why would they do that?' Libby asked.

'No freebies, my lad.' Mrs Kirk reached out, palm up, to her grandson who sighed, fished in his jeans pocket and put a pound coin in her hand.

'I apologise for my nan. Seems she's taken to conspiracy theories in her old age. Most people just play bridge or something.'

'I'm not old, you cheeky little sod. In my prime, I am. And anyway, what do you know? You were only in nappies then.' She rang up Libby's purchase on the till as she continued. 'Now the council have even helped the buggers out by adding that bypass. Wouldn't be surprised if the Blakes bunged them a backhander for that. Like I said, we're cut off. Left us to rot.' Mrs Kirk pushed the items towards Libby and pressed her lips together as she smoothed her apron.

'Look, you'll get no taxis here on a Sunday,' Joe said as he jumped down from his perch behind his grandmother and emptied the rest of the sweets straight into his mouth, his next words muffled by chocolate. 'I'll give you a lift if you like.'

'You could be an axe murderer.' Dawn gave him a cool stare, finally abandoning the idea her phone could help them in this situation. She pocketed it.

'Oh no, that's far too much effort. It could give me tennis elbow.' Joe crumpled the empty tube and then took aim at the bin by the door whilst Mrs Kirk busied herself looking in a drawer under the till.

'Axe murder elbow,' Libby muttered with a smile.

'Yeah, that's it.' He smiled back. She blushed on top of the blushing she had already been doing and feared her face might explode. 'Occupational hazard.'

'Here.' Mrs Kirk offered her a bag with her purchases already in it. 'Bag's no extra charge. I'm in a good mood. Now bugger off.'

It was only when they were back on the street that Libby searched though the bag for the chocolate bar and found something else that Mrs Kirk had slipped in. It was a rather dog-eared piece of A4 paper with holes in its corners where it had once been pinned somewhere. Home-made, the black-and-white photo was of a thin young woman with limp hair who viewed the camera with the youthful kind of hope that only ends in disaster. At the top of the page were handwritten words in felt-tip pen capitals:

MISSING: TESS SANDERSON.

Chapter 9

Skeletons greeted them.

'You're in a band?' Dawn asked, climbing into the van. It was the first time she had sounded vaguely interested since they had entered the shop. After a nudge from Libby, however, she had at least thanked Joe when accepting his offer of a lift.

'Lead singer . . . and driver,' Joe said. 'We all have to multi-task . . .'

Painted on the side of the van were flames coloured like the northern lights and in their illumination a group of skeletons danced, or maybe writhed in agony. It was hard to tell the expression on a skeletal face. Above the picture were the words: 'Savage Night'.

Libby gazed at the beautiful flames, coloured like an electric sea. 'The painting's really good by the way.'

'Thanks, it came with the van . . .'

'The name too?' Dawn joked but Joe remained serious.

'Yeah . . . well, it's expensive to get a respray.'

Halfway into their journey the three of them were crammed in the front cab, the rucksacks placed in the back with the speakers, music equipment and pallets of tinned goods. It wasn't just the band that multi-tasked, but the van too, doubling up to do deliveries for the shop. Joe changed gear and the van clunkily protested.

Flicking his glance to the bag his nan had handed Libby before they left the shop, Joe asked, 'She's given you one of the posters, hasn't she?'

Libby smoothed the paper on her knee – a knee that was very close to Joe's. Though the windows were open there wasn't even a hint of any breeze and, despite it being afternoon, the sun hadn't managed to break through clouds that were a clammy palm pressed over the earth.

'Who's Tess?' Libby stared at the black-and-white girl.

'You have to understand, the village, the bad feeling – it's bound to happen when something big like Solstice takes off.' Joe spoke to the road, not turning to her. He was a careful driver, indicating in plenty of time, taking corners at a glacial speed, not quite the reckless rocker Libby had expected. 'Nan's right, I was too young to really understand it but . . . rumours like these, my nan still handing out these damn posters – it doesn't help.'

'Tess went missing at the festival?'

'Yeah. But it was years ago—'

'Oh my God!' Dawn leant forward and gripped Libby's leg, her fingers digging into bare flesh and the hem of her cargo shorts. 'Boring! I don't know about you but I came here to get away from being bored. Joe, let's hear what kind of stuff your band plays and for God's sake, let's stop talking about a girl we don't even bloody know! Because—' here she gripped Libby's face, squishing her cheeks '—we are on our way to the festival of the freaking summer. SOLSTICE!' She leant out of the window and howled the word at the passing cars.

And then there was The Gate.

Joe dropped them at the end of a road choked with wellie-wearing people lugging rucksacks and wheeling trolleys that held tents and camping chairs.

Before they could even see The Gate, however, they had to get through The Queue.

They slowed to a geriatric shuffle. As they inched towards the entrance, every so often they had to get out of the way of the Sun Bus, the shuttle service that took people from the train station to the festival, two identical coaches with massive suns painted on them, the rays stretching around to the back windows.

'The bus from the *correct* train station . . .' Libby nudged Dawn.

'Zip it, Lib-Lob.'

They queued.

Then they queued some more.

Then they continued to queue.

Still no sun broke through those grey clouds above them. To Libby, wiping sweat from her neck, it felt as if the mountains she could see in the distance were insulating the heat, the bowl of the valley simmering away in its muggy dampness.

'I need to pee.' Dawn dragged her rucksack on the dirt path. Both of them had given up trying to carry them on their shoulders. 'The queue is so bloody long! It feels like we haven't moved. Some people have camped overnight to get to the front – we should have done that.'

'We should have brought more stuff,' Libby said, ignoring Dawn's lament that there hadn't been an extra night of camping and looking longingly at the box of water bottles balanced at the top of the pile of belongings wheeled in front of them. A serious woman stood in charge of it, the leader of a fearsome foursome in their thirties, dressed in hiking gear, with the air of people who knew what they were doing.

'Cool pictures though,' Dawn said, pointing to the fences that ringed the festival site, sheets and sheets of corrugated iron lining the whole perimeter, each panel handed over to local artists to make their own. Currently they queued in the shadow of a giant painted tree woman, the branches her hair, around her the Grey Sisters, not stone any longer, but dancing wraith-like women.

The gate itself was also a work of art. It was made of two tall slabs of wood with big brass panels, polished to a shine that made her eyes water even in this cloud-smudged light. On one door was a sun, its face smiling, the mouth a huge wide curve that put Libby in mind of the Cheshire Cat from *Alice in Wonderland*, its rays shining from it in deep etchings. On the other door was a moon, expression much more sombre, eyes half-lidded and wearing clouds like hair. Both were heavy, solid things engraved by hand, taking months to complete. Through them, Libby caught a glance of green fields, the heads of the people in the crowd in front of her the flowers growing out of the soil. She hoisted her rucksack onto her shoulders.

Queue.

Queue.

Queue.

Then the gate was behind them. In front were trestle tables covered by awnings and manned by officials, processing the revellers and directing them onwards. Beyond that the fields opened up, flanked either side by the two stages, both of them currently empty. A woman put a fabric band the colour of sunset around Libby's wrist and they took their first steps into the festival.

Libby had not expected to be met by screaming.

Well, she had. Screams of people singing along to bands, whoops of laughter, of yelling, she had expected all of that.

This was a banshee shriek.

It came from the security tower diagonally across from them, near one of the main stages. Possibly, at first, the structure had started out plain – black-painted steel criss-cross scaffolding rising high to an airport-control-style glazed room at the top, a curved spiral of steps winding its way through its middle. But then, year on year, a bit more colour had been added, a few more flounces and flourishes until it looked as it did now: a helter-skelter that could perhaps also be launched into space. Huge, long strips of material in bright yellows, reds and purples hung from the top, covering the metal supports, and a conical circus tent peak in the same colours crowned it all.

Around the glazed room was a metal balcony and on the balcony was a woman, long silvered hair streaming, feet bare.

'Is that . . . Ma Blake?' Dawn asked, standing at Libby's side.

'Is this some kind of performance?' Libby added.

In photos, Ma Blake was slow to smile, dressed conservatively in long sleeves and skirts, sensibly booted, observant, reserved – a muted background for Abel's spotlight shine. But here she was high on a balcony in what looked like a voluminous night gown flapping at her skinny ankles, her mouth stretched wide, a horror film ghoul sprung to life.

Then her screaming stopped.

People began to cluster under the tower, pointing and muttering amongst themselves, many still wheeling their trolleys filled with camping equipment, or lugging rucksacks, as they had only just entered the site. Some began filming on their mobile phones, though when Libby checked hers she found she had no signal, so it was unlikely that this would be posted on social media any time soon. Their ticket had informed them the festival was meant to be a screen-free experience and so the mobile signal was deliberately non-existent. The organisers would probably be relieved that none of this footage would be seen for days.

Speculation swirled under the tower.

'Can't be Ma . . .'

'Not been seen at the festival for years . . .'

'I heard she's been ill . . .'

'. . . gone mad . . .'

Above them and a few feet away from Ma stood another woman, one arm held out beseechingly towards her, the other holding a walkie-talkie to her mouth. The safety rail around the balcony was slatted black metal and the spectators watched with expressions of shock and horror as Ma began to climb over the rail, surprisingly sure-footed. The walkie-talkie woman lurched towards her and Ma, one leg over the rail, wobbled as she jerked backwards.

There was a collective gasp from the people below.

Libby remembered that when banshees howl, it is a warning that someone will soon die.

'I don't think this is meant to be entertainment . . .' Dawn said.

Two golf carts sped through the crowd, one man a flash of gold hair and a white shirt hardly even letting the vehicle stop before he dashed out and through a flap in the bottom of the tower.

High above them, Ma clutched onto the balcony, a leg on either side, the woman with her paralysed by fear or indecision. Libby was too far away to see Ma's face clearly. She didn't know if she was speaking, or crying, or if she was tight-lipped and silent. Dawn slipped her hand into hers.

'I can't look,' she said, her eyes fixed on the balcony anyway.

'Somebody will get her now – she'll be fine.' Libby kept her voice firm.

At that moment Ma simply . . . tilted a little, throwing herself off-balance and Libby braced herself for the fall, for the crack of bone and the wet, ripe splitting of soft flesh. But that did not happen. Instead three men barrelled through the doorway at the top of the tower, roughly pushing past the woman with the walkie-talkie and launched themselves at Ma, rugby-tackling her off her perch and onto the balcony floor.

The tense thread that had held together the massed people below suddenly sagged as loud music blared and a man with a megaphone made his way through the gathering. 'This way to the camping grounds, people, this way!'

'See? She's okay – they're taking her in.' Libby pointed to the balcony.

Someone had thrown a blanket over Ma. It covered her head and most of her body so what walked into the security tower flanked by guards was almost a duvet-cover ghost.

'That woman must have some major issues . . .' Dawn said.

Megaphone man continued, 'This way, people! Nothing to see here now. This way!'

The music got louder and the crowd, now their focus had been hurried out of sight, lost interest, trailing off to set up their tents, though some stuck around as if there might be an encore to the macabre show they had just witnessed.

Solstice had begun.,

Chapter 10

'Perfect.' Dawn stood back and surveyed their work, hands on her hips.

It had taken them over half an hour to lug their rucksacks from the gate to one of the two camping fields and by the time they got there Libby was sweaty, tired and sore and so thirsty she would have sacrificed Dawn for a bottle of water. She tried a smile and felt the skin tear on her lips as they stuck to her teeth.

The problem quickly became clear: they were under-prepared. Camping at Solstice was going to be one of two extremes – the result of military-style planning and execution where the whole expedition was plotted to every minute detail or . . . well this. A bit of plastic badly fixed to a poorly chosen patch of soil.

'Did you not practise putting it up before we left?' Libby watched as one end of the tent sagged. They had spent at least an hour wrestling with it, but it was a great metal spider that kept wanting to crawl away.

'Did you even realise we'd need a tent?' Dawn fired back, wiping her dirty hands on the front of her denim shorts.

'Fair enough. Well, at least it's big and we've even got ourselves a porch here. It'll be grand.' Libby had never said that phrase before: 'It'll be grand'; she had no idea where it had come from. Dehydration was making her delirious.

Libby had thought the tent would have been one of those ones that simply popped up in a second with a quick shake, not knowing that Dawn was going to bring something from a 1960s Girl Scouts trip. She should have known it wouldn't be straightforward, not when it came to Dawn.

The rest of the tents in the field stretched around them like bubble wrap, plastic domes undulating in cheerful colours. The festival was bisected by a river. On one side lay the two stages: a Sun Stage topped by a metal sun for all the daytime music and a Moon Stage with its own metal moon for the evening performances. In the middle was 'Sustain', the place where stallholders sold food and drinks. There were two camping fields on either side of the site and a big archway made of twigs leading into the trees, on it glowing letters like cinema lights spelling out WYRD WOOD. Beyond that was the river and the Blake farmhouse with its white-painted walls and black slate roof, the tips of the oak tree only just visible due to the screen fencing for Sanctum blocking any view of the Grey Sisters. The woody warm scent of bonfires hung in the air.

They were a modern-day medieval encampment with their bright colours and the sound of material flapping in the wind, only waiting for a signal of trumpets to announce the coming of their king. Libby knew who that was: Abel Blake, probably at some quiet vantage point watching the whole thing unfurl across his land like an intricately stitched heraldic banner.

'Do you think she's okay now – Ma Blake? She seemed pretty distressed.' Libby retied her hair into a rough ponytail, strands of it sticking to her clammy neck.

'She was probably high or something. Who cares? She's rich – she'll end up in a fancy rehab place. She'll be fine.'

Dawn led the way into the heart of the festival and Libby, as she had always done throughout their friendship, happily followed.

* * *

42

If Solstice had been a battlefield, then Sustain was the strip of No-Man's Land in the middle. Between the opposing stages there was a wide path with food trucks and stalls on either side, each one individually decorated and personalised with hand-painted signs and cloth bunting, the golden glow of fairy lights beginning to shine in the dimming light of the afternoon.

So far, Dawn and Libby had taken full advantage of their free food and drink allowance. Between them they had eaten a burger, a portion of thick-cut chips, a strangely coloured noodle dish with some kind of purple vegetable in it, a delicately spiced samosa and had each drunk some of the local beer. Above them awnings in all kinds of materials and patterns blocked out most of the sky and kept in the comfortable fug of melted grease and charred meat. A lot of the conversations they had walked past had centred on Ma Blake nearly jumping from the security tower earlier that day.

'I'm stuffed.' Dawn swilled the last of the beer in her bottle. The awnings above them blocked out the sky but not the heat; in fact they seemed to wrap it up and push it down hard onto the people wandering below.

Libby wiped sweat from her neck as she spoke. 'We should make a plan, y'know, of the bands we want to see, what we want to do—'

'Sanctum.' Dawn didn't even let her finish.

Libby scrunched up the paper bag that had held her samosa. 'No one knows how you get passes to that. I don't think we'd get in.'

'But we won these tickets, right? We've got a VIP tour of the whole place tomorrow – surely we can charm an invite then? We've got to get in there, Libs – it's like, life-changing . . .'

'Life-changing? It's a . . . bonfire next to some old stones. It's just a party.'

'No, no, no. I've read stuff about it. It's *not* just a party, it's like a therapy session and a cleanse and life coaching all in one. People have been really moved by it.'

Libby gulped the rest of her beer, knowing she would need the effects of some alcohol before she attempted her next task.

'Yeah, well – we'll see. I need to use the loo,' she announced, with the solemn tone of a funeral director imparting an update on a loved one's ceremony.

'Oh God. You're going to hate it.'

'I know.'

'Here.' Dawn sombrely handed over a roll of toilet paper from the smaller bag she carried with her. They had left any possessions they didn't mind being stolen back at their tent, with a hopeful padlock securing the zip. 'Just don't breathe in and make it quick.'

How bad could they be? Libby had read the horror stories online, however, so she already knew the answer to that question as she began the long walk over to one of the banks of Portaloos that were situated as far from the main stages as they could possibly be.

They lived down to her expectations.

First there had been a queue, which had allowed Libby ample opportunity to enjoy the smell coming from the plastic cubicles waiting for her. Oddly sweet, oddly cloying, definitely rank, it was the kind of scent that settled into the fine hairs of the nose and clogged in the back of the throat. Libby considered holding on and walking the thirty-minute slog back up to the camping ground where there was a toilet block and a long drop, the compost loo rumoured to be slightly – *only ever so slightly* – more bearable.

Her bladder made it known that it would not be co-operating with that idea.

She sighed and shuffled nearer, hoping she had enough strength in her thigh muscles for the workout they were about to get helping her hover above the seat whilst having a wee. Actually touching anything in there was a prospect she didn't want to consider.

Then she was next. She had hardly got in, however, when a sudden loud bang on the roof made her freeze. Libby had been prepared for many things when using a festival toilet but not the roof caving in on her.

'What the hell?'

There was a desperate scrabbling and a muffled voice as the whole plastic structure . . . rocked . . . just a little. Libby braced herself by instinctively putting her hands out to the walls and immediately wished she hadn't as her palm encountered something suspiciously slimy.

That was it. It was bad enough being in one of these things when they were upright – if it was about to topple over then it could do so without her inside. Stumbling out, fishing in her bag for a wet wipe to clean her hand, Libby raised her head to see, with some surprise, that she had an audience. But it wasn't for her.

It was for the young man clinging to the top of the toilet.

All she could get a glimpse of was the back of a scuffed army jacket as the person heaved themselves over and then a red-cheeked face stared down at Libby.

'What're you doing?' Libby asked, gaping, as someone elbowed past her to get to the Portaloo.

Behind them was the fence, and Libby guessed the man must have somehow scaled that and then jumped from the top onto the toilet, though how he thought he was going to get down from there was a mystery.

A cloud of dust and the sound of a small motorised engine heralded the arrival of two golf cart buggies, the same ones that had screeched to Ma's rescue a few hours ago. The drivers, serious men dressed in black security T-shirts, got out and stood under the man now sat with his legs dangling from the top of the toilet.

'Down! Now!'

The man on his perch wobbled a little and pushed his thick-framed glasses higher on his nose. One of the guards frowned and reached for his radio as the other man slammed his palm against the side of the toilet, making the interloper sway. 'Get the fuck down.'

Another golf cart drew up. From inside came a smooth, confident voice: 'Gents, we're going to politely help this chap down, and then I'm sure he'll be willing to pay for a ticket like everyone else here—'

Abel Blake. Even without the thrill of recognition that went through the crowd, Libby would have known him anywhere. He was tall, his knees pressed up against the front of the buggy, dressed in jeans, sunglasses and a smart cream shirt. His hair might have been greying a little now at the temples but his jawline was still sharp and the smile had kept its Hollywood superstar shine.

Abel's companion was shadow next to sunlight with his dark clothes and buzzcut stubble as hair. He was a vibrating wire pulled tight, a fidgeting energy coming from him as if he was holding himself back from leaping out of the cart and dragging the interloper down from the fence himself.

She had seen a video clip from the channel 'The True Crime Twins' on Joe's phone as he had driven them to the festival earlier that day. It had some very interesting theories on the younger Blake brother. Rumours swirled about Silas Blake like cheap Eighties music video smoke, rumours that seemed to fit the grim-faced man sitting in the golf cart, with a look on his face that could crack the Grey Sisters themselves.

Silas Blake. The man who had murdered his girlfriend.

Chapter 11

(YouTube video entitled 'The Dark Side of Solstice' created by YouTubers The True Crime Twins, a channel dedicated to true crime stories, subscribed to by more than one million viewers).

On the screen are identical twin sisters, both in their twenties, both dressed in baggy pastel-coloured sweatshirts, their make-up perfect, their filler-injected lips pillowy and glossed. Both of them have long dark hair but where one has a streak dyed purple, the other has a stripe of blonde.

'Hi, folks, and welcome to our latest vid!' Purple Streak begins, smiling in a way that won't crack her carefully blended mask of make-up.

'Hi, folks.' Blonde Stripe smiles too.

'I'm Melanie and this is my twin sister Abigail and together we are . . .' Melanie pauses and glances towards her sister so they say the next words in unison:

'The True Crime Twins!'

'And do we have a chilling true crime story for you, people! This one centres around a festival we know many of you LOVE, right? Solstice, that magical place deep in the Welsh countryside – more than a festival, more than some old standing stones in

47

a field, more than a ticket no one can ever get their hands on no matter how much you click that refresh button. Solstice. A celebration of sunshine . . .'

'. . . Well, we're here to talk about its dark side. And boy, does it have one.' Abigail twists her long dark hair around one finger as she speaks.

'Oh yes.'

Behind them pictures of the festival flash up: green fields, glitter on sweaty, sunburnt skin, bands mid-action, brass suns shining, blue sky and perfect fluffy white clouds.

'Gotta say at this point due to us getting sued six ways to Sunday if we don't – all of what we are about to say is personal opinion and has no basis in any proven fact. Okay? Okay.' Melanie points up and the montage freezes on a familiar face: blond tousled hair, strong jawline, tanned skin and that wide smile.

Abigail takes up the story. 'So, we all know Abel Blake, right? The, like, king of Solstice, came up with the idea, runs it, is a total boss and made sure Solstice was one of the first big festivals to get in on the whole green ethos: recycling, cutting back on plastic, all that. God-like, yeah?'

Behind the twins the picture changes. A different face, jawline softer, shaved head, skin paler, smile nowhere to be seen.

Melanie continues, 'But Abel has a younger brother called Silas. And, I mean, it can't be fun being Abel Blake's brother, can it?'

'Umm . . . gotta disagree, sis! It'd be tons of fun. Your brother's like the coolest person on the planet—'

'Exactly! That's a lot to live up to, right? Anyway, Abel is fit, we can all agree, even though he's gotta be in his forties, and well, if we're honest – Silas just . . . isn't . . .'

'He's giving me evil librarian nerd vibes . . .'

Melanie smiles in that careful way. 'Yeah! Like he'd lecture you on some weird old book and then eat your liver . . .'

The twins scrunch up their faces in disgust, remember that their make-up masks might crease or flake and so smooth out their expression once again. As they get into the meat of their video, the two of them slip and slide into each other's sentences, Melanie beginning.

'So, the gossip. Okay, back when the whole thing started in the early 2000s there were some pretty dark rumours flying round the village nearest the Blake farmhouse—'

'—that Silas had a mean streak to him—'

'—Yeah. Bit wild, partying too hard even before the festival, bit of drugs, bit of being a total dick to his girlfriends. We all know the kind, right?'

'And then there's Tess Sanderson.'

'Oh yes, Tess Sanderson.'

The twins gave each other a knowing glance.

'Local girl in the village called Grey Sisters. Twenty-one years old. Also got her own demons, falls in with Silas, and get this . . . *disappears* in the weeks before Midsummer's Eve, which was the night before the very first festival.'

'Never seen again.'

'Her mum had skipped town by this time so there's no family left to fight her corner or keep looking for her. She just vanishes.'

'Thing is, she's not seen going into the festival from the security camera at the gate – not the gate there is now; this was like a basic thing. Back then the festival was just one day and night, Midsummer's Day. So, the camera doesn't show her walking in . . . and there's no footage of her walking out. None at all. But there is *some* footage . . .'

'Oh yeah.'

Behind them a new photo appears, a young couple wearing big smiles and peace beads.

'So there's a video made by this couple when they were helping set up the festival on Midsummer's Eve. Here's a still from it. See where they are? There was no Sanctum in that first year so these two are actually over the bridge by the standing stones, not far from the Blake farmhouse. But it isn't them we're interested in.'

'Nope.'

On cue, the picture behind them zooms in to a blurry figure in the background, then, through digital effects, it is sharpened a bit, the colours made brighter, the clothes a little easier to recognise.

'See that person in the background, looks like she's arm in arm with someone else?'

'And here's a pic of Tess.'

The two stills are shown side by side.

'Same clothes, same style of trainers, same hair, hell, same damn face turned to the camera even though she's kinda huddled over a bit . . .'

'Tess Sanderson.'

'She was at Solstice. She was there at the standing stones, only a day before the festival . . . *and then she was never seen again.*'

'And let's remember who her boyfriend at the time was, shall we, people? The person with her in the photo?'

'Yup. Silas . . . fricking . . . Blake . . .'

Chapter 12

Libby knew where she was heading next.

The cinema bulbs were a beacon spelling out her destination on an archway made of woven twigs: WYRD WOOD.

As night fell and gave a gauzy haze to the sky, the spaces between the trees came alive. Speakers hidden in the branches allowed an atmospheric music to wind its way from trunk to trunk as circus performers swallowed fire or swung from thick red silk that gleamed in the light from old-fashioned Narnia-style street lamps placed at intervals. Others stomped on stilts, dressed in garish colours, or cartwheeled and tumbled whilst magicians held small groups in awe with their sleight of hand, card tricks and quick-fingered illusions.

The wood was packed with people, faces tilted to gaze at the lights, or turned to the latest performer, stopping to marvel, to taste, to smile. At different points during their walk through the woods Libby and Dawn came upon street food trucks selling jewel-coloured cocktails and small, sweet pastries. Libby didn't really drink much and, when she did, she had never gone in for spirits or liqueurs. But these were so pretty . . . and free. The alcohol quickly went to her head. It made her body feel lighter but her brain heavy, which was a good thing; it slowed down her pesky thoughts and blurred the edges from memories of a sickroom that were parasites lodged tight in her mind: curtains closed, a dying figure on a bed, the harsh rasp of her mother's last words . . .

Dawn swallowed a thimbleful of ruby liquid as a group of people in beautifully feathered masks danced by, the women in wide hoop skirts and gold-edged lace, the men in frock coats. One of them whisked Libby into the routine and she happily swirled, marvelling at how her feet followed his lead despite her having zero dance skills. The trees and the lights and the fire-breathing people, the gymnasts, the giants on stilts, red silk ribbons and drinks made of precious stones all whirled past her in a golden light as night pooled under the trees.

As she was spun away and the masked dancer moved on, she tumbled into Dawn who laughed and they continued the dance together, much like they used to do at school, the two of them making up routines to the latest pop song.

'I . . . am . . . wasted . . .' Dawn said with glee as they both collapsed onto some cushions on the ground.

There it was, Libby thought, there it was on Dawn's face – that smile she wanted, the one that had no hesitant twitch at the corner, as if it would have to be pulled back at any moment. She gave it a go.

'Jeez, Libs – are you having a stroke?' Dawn struggled to sit up but her limbs had become floppy rag doll bits of cloth. Libby tucked her legs neatly out of the way of anybody walking past.

'How do you do it?' She leant forward to Dawn, an eager acolyte to a drunken spiritual guru.

'Hmm? What?' The guru in question idly traced the faded sequin pattern on the cushion next to her.

'You're so happy all the time . . .'

'Look, I know what you're getting at.' Dawn stopped tracing and grasped one of her friend's hands. 'These past two years, caring for your mum like you have, I mean, I'd have been fucking miserable.'

'Am I?'

'What?'

'Miserable?'

'No! God! You're a bloody saint.'

But that hadn't really answered Libby's question, she thought as Dawn slumped back again, and anyway she'd seen pictures of saints in stained-glass windows and frozen as statues. They always looked so sad. Pale, and ill and unspeakably miserable.

'I'm not . . .' The next words were wasps in her mouth; she had to free them. 'I'm not like her, am I?'

At this Dawn did not try to sit up again but she fixed Libby with a fierce stare. 'Your mum was Queen among bitches. I don't know how she was ever nice enough to anyone to get laid and get pregnant with you. You, my beautiful, gorgeous friend, are nothing like her.'

Dawn sank further back into the cushions as if they would swallow her, drag her down into leaf mulch and thick tree roots. But it wasn't Dawn's voice that Libby heard, it was her mother's, back before it had become a dry rasp, when Libby had finished her GCSEs and had got a summer job. With her first wages, after she had given her mother her rent and board, she had bought some make-up of her own, nothing elaborate like the YouTube tutorials she had watched, women buffing layer upon layer of cream and powder onto their faces as if they were plastering a wall. No, all she had picked were a pinkish-red lipstick, a mascara and a blusher, domed and perfect in its little pot.

Her mother had drawers full of such stuff and Libby had seen her in the morning, her fingers fluttering over her face in an incantation that Libby had no idea how to copy but had given it her best shot anyway. Her mother had taken one look at her afterwards and had raised her eyebrows. 'I wouldn't bother, if I were you.' Of course, there are two ways in which to say that sentence. In one, a mother could suggest that their daughter was pretty enough already and did not need the make-up. But Ann Corrigan was not that kind of mother. Libby had rubbed everything off with tissue in the bathroom minutes later, the new mascara making her tears sting.

Dawn herself had not escaped Libby's mother's opinion. Some friends might have backed off at the thought of being around a person who was caring for a family member as their body essentially shut up shop. But not Dawn. She had come round two or three evenings a week with takeaways, pushed Libby out of the bedroom so she could have a long bath, and had settled in to read a fantasy novel to Mrs Corrigan, who hated fantasy novels and told her so at every occasion – a fact that seemed to always slip Dawn's mischievous mind. Mrs Corrigan's increasingly vicious comments always slipped over Dawn's head like just-cooked eggs sliding off a frying pan.

The soft glow in the clearing nearby illuminated a gypsy wagon painted in black, blue and silver to suggest a night sky, a constellation of stars across its side, black fringing hiding the door and gleaming polished metal trims on its wooden wheels. Two trees bent their branches over it, like protective arms. On a board by the steps flowing cursive spelled out the words: *Madame Mystic, Fortune Teller*. A queue of four people waited outside.

Libby wasn't sure where the feeling came from, but she really wanted to get her fortune told. Possibly it was down to the alcohol she had consumed, or maybe it was the fact she needed a bit of reassurance that her future would be bright, no matter how grim and dim her recent past stuck in a sickroom had been.

Dawn took one look at it, caught Libby's hopeful expression and frowned. 'Nope, not for me. You go. I'll wait here.'

Finally, it was her turn. The door opened at last and a young woman, looking as if her predicted future had not been quite as rosy as she would have wished, pushed past her and down the stairs. Libby waited to be called in.

The call did not come.

'Umm . . . hello?' She raised her voice, putting her foot on the next step, her palm on the glossy polished wood of the handrail. Up close she could see the care that had gone into painting those stars and the moon above the door. It had a kindly cratered face, a smaller sister to the one on the massive festival gates.

'Come in,' said a curiously toneless woman's voice, neither imperative nor welcoming.

So Libby did.

Chapter 13

Brushing aside the silky black fringing in front of the door, Libby had perhaps expected more of that kind of thing: delicate scarves draped over lamps, embroidered tapestries, the slow lazy trail of incense smoke making the room smell of patchouli or sandalwood. And in the centre a crystal ball, a figure hunched over it, head covered by a veil.

That was not what greeted her.

'Five pounds.' A middle-aged woman held out a hand from where she was perched on the sofa built against one side of the wagon. Her head was completely veil-free and she wore a fluffy jumper and sensible polyester trousers. No scarves, no tapestries, no smoke, no crystal ball, the whole place was clean and neat, decorated in beige and white like the inside of a budget hotel room.

Libby had got so used to floating through the festival without thinking about money due to their free food and drinks wristbands that she had to fumble for her purse.

'I've got one of those machine doodas,' the woman said though she made no move to hand it over. Low lighting came from a plain lamp in the one corner and some fake tealights lining the windowsill. 'I don't give change, either. No refunds.' This information was given in the same bored tone that she had used to tell Libby to come in. Her big wire-rimmed glasses hung around her neck on a cheap-looking beaded chain and stuffed down the side of the sofa was a dog-eared puzzle book.

Libby passed over five pounds. There was a small stool next to the sofa but the woman gave no indication that she should sit in it so she stayed standing awkwardly where she was. 'And you are . . . Madame Mystic?'

The woman shot her a look, 'Yeah, that's me.' Catching Libby's expression she continued, 'Not all of us go in for the, y'know . . .' She waved her hands over an imaginary crystal ball and made a face. 'Stereotypical, that is.'

'Sorry. Yes. Sure – hello.'

Madame Mystic sighed. 'It's the wagon, innit? Gives the wrong impression.'

'I—'

'I told Dave down at the garage not to go nuts on it but he thinks he's bleeding Van Gogh.'

'I like the wagon.'

'Yeah well, that moon face reminds me of an ex and the silver paint is flaking off.'

There was silence then and Libby glanced at a clock on the wall shaped like a cat, its tail flicking the rhythm of the passing seconds, its gaze fixed on her as if she were an unwary bird. Madame Mystic shifted position so she sat closer and then she stared into Libby's face.

Libby stared back.

Seconds were flicked away by a cat tail.

'I—'

'—Shh. I'm concentra—'

And then Madame Mystic slackened a little, a balloon losing air, her sentence left unfinished as her jaw lolled, though her eyes remained gimlet-hard.

The words, when they came, pushed themselves from her mouth like maggots out of a carcass. 'You're . . . jagged. You don't fit.'

57

Above them the cat tail flick, flick, flicked.

'I don't understand . . .?'

Madame Mystic frowned. 'I tell what I see. You're . . . yes, jagged. Your aura is . . . broken.'

'What?' Libby backed away a pace.

Flick. Flick. Flick.

It was an act, Libby told herself. A very good one, but an act all the same. It was the way this woman made a living, by scaring gullible customers with her thousand-yard stare and stupidly creepy proclamations. *You don't fit.* That wasn't even telling her future. She should ask for her money back.

With a shrug, Madam Mystic straightened her shoulders and blinked, her voice clear once more, that strange slackness now gone. 'Aura doesn't lie. And yours—'

'Is jagged, yeah, I got that, thanks!' Libby moved then, away from the woman and her flick, flick, flicking cat clock, out of the door, swiping aside the stupid fringing and down the steps.

You're jagged. You don't fit.

Libby couldn't stop these words from slithering around her brain because, no matter what she told herself, well, they were true, weren't they? She didn't fit. Not here amongst the festival-goers with their proper, ready smiles, not anywhere really, as her mother used to point out, all too eagerly. She was too plain, too clumsy, too unfashionable, too serious, too silly, whatever it was, she was always too much of it. This place, with its dancing and music and pretty lights and thousands and thousands of achingly fashionable people – this was not for her.

She turned back to where she had left Dawn . . . except Dawn was not there.

There were the cushions, there was the Dawn-shaped dent where she had made herself a nest, but there was no Dawn.

The wood now had a dream-like quality to it with its masked dancers, its circus performers and the thin, reedy music seeming to come from the very trees themselves. Moths fluttered against the

58

lights, straining to toast themselves on hot filaments. She should have felt cold. In June no matter how warm the days, the nights could chill with a suddenness that nipped at unwary bare toes and fingers, but tonight the thick soup-like heat remained, despite the darkness. Everywhere she turned there were people and, where before those figures packed together had been respectfully marvelling at the delights set out for them, now there was a rowdy, ragged edge to their laughs, their shouts and their staggering.

'Dawn!' she shouted above the music that had definitely got louder since she had been with Madame Mystic. There was a beat to it; it had a thrumming heart that suggested a kind of urgency and made her own blood thump in response.

On her own, the wood became wilder, those street lamps not giving light but casting shadows, the performers twisting and jumping and breathing fire, not a marvel but a threat. She should never have left Dawn alone, knowing how drunk she had been. This was exactly the kind of stupid stunt Dawn pulled, her attention that of a toddler, immediately gripped by any new thing that floated past her eyes, ready to wander off at any given second and never stopping to think of boring stuff like safety and consequences and her bloody friend left waiting for her.

Libby didn't need to search her memory for all the other times Dawn had done something like this. In crowds she had always been slippery, a fish darting off into the depths. In break times at school, in shopping centres, one time a year ago in a packed Christmas market where she had been gone for nearly an hour, Libby getting more and more frantic, ringing and ringing her, for her to calmly return with two cuddly Christmas gonks and a flat phone battery, completely oblivious to the worry she had caused.

'Dawn!'

No response and so Libby began to move aimlessly, keeping the cushions as her fulcrum and spiralling out from it, trying to catch a glimpse of blue and pink hair. Behind her was the fortune teller's wagon with trees bent over it, whispering their secrets.

The masked dancing troupe whirled past her once more and one of them tried to swoop her back into the dance, one hand on her wrist, the other on her waist. Now, however, she did not admire how her feet understood the steps, now she flailed and tried to wriggle free.

'No, please . . .'

As she spun she could see flashes of the glade, pools of light and shadow and figures in both, faces she did not know, none of them Dawn. With a wrench she yanked her arms free of the masked man who hardly even noticed as he danced on, whilst she wobbled, slightly unbalanced from the twirling.

'Libster!' Dawn appeared, veering over to her, following some kind of crooked path only her drunk gaze could see.

Libby felt her shoulders lower, not able to keep the frustration out of her voice, 'Oh my God, you scared me! Why'd you move? I thought you'd left me on my own!'

'Huh? I went to get another one of those cute little mini drinks, that's all. I was hardly gone . . .'

Libby was about to continue the admonishment but she stopped herself and took a breath. Instead, she slung her arm around her friend's back and under her armpit so she could haul her in the direction of the glowing arch that marked their exit, all the while still thinking of her fortune:

You're jagged. You don't fit.

Maybe she didn't. But she could fix that. Not fitting just meant you had to change shape somehow and that was what Libby was going to do over the next couple of days, here at the festival. She was going to relax and work on that smile and not worry about things so much. It could be done.

She would be a whole new person by the time the festival ended.

Chapter 14

That night, trying to sleep next to Dawn in their flimsy tent, Libby found the hours stretching like warm dough.

She was used to that.

What Libby had discovered was that when a person cared for someone seriously ill, the concept of day and night really only became important if there was a hospital appointment or medicines to pick up. Pain had been king of the sickroom. Time had been marked by the hours her mother had spent floating on a drug-stuffed chemical pillow, and then those hours when that pillow sagged and jagged metal slices of agony tore through. Even now, Libby found herself waking up at odd times with a jolt, her body tensed for a cry that would no longer come.

Dawn snored softly. The night was a sponge, sucking up the day's heat and now clammily breathing it over everyone. Libby threw off her sleeping bag to sit up and feel some slightly cooler air on her legs, moving slowly so as not to wake her friend. Not that much would, she thought, as she looked over at Dawn who was in a deep sleep, one arm flung out in wild abandon, still dressed in the clothes she had worn all day.

There was only a thin groundsheet between them and the grass, and Libby could feel the damp seeping up. Dew. Perhaps if she opened the tent flap some fresher air would drift in. It wasn't quiet outside. From around the tent came the sound of people laughing, the odd snatch of music, a burst of singing, though muted somewhat in deference to the late hour. She glanced at her phone, the clock telling her it was nearing three in the morning, and, as soon as it heard that a few hours had passed, her bladder made it known that she was going to have to get up anyway and face her worst nightmare: a festival toilet in the dark.

Something scratched at the tent.

Libby jolted away instinctively, thinking it a rat or some kind of animal. It had come from low to the ground, just outside the thin canvas wall, near Libby's hip. This was the countryside after all, teeming with stuff that liked to crawl over a person whilst they slept. She fumbled for her torch, but a new thought stayed her hand. Perhaps a light would attract it, whatever it was. Maybe, if she did not move and did not draw attention to herself, it would crawl away. She sat in the dark.

There it was again. A short scritching sound, followed by a longer, more drawn-out scratch across the material of the tent.

Just an animal. Except there was something . . . measured about it, something lazy and deliberate, something very not animal-like at all.

Scritch-scraaaaatch.

She switched on the torch, noting the way the light trembled in her shaking hand. That was when she saw it: the bulging in of the tent, a point appearing like a finger trying to break through and then slowly tracing a path along the material. It put her in mind of schoolchildren running sticks along fences, but this was not a fence, this was their tent, where they were trying to sleep.

The bulging stopped as if the person outside was deciding what to do next.

Scritch-scraaaaatch.

And then Libby had to haul herself backwards as a terrible scraping sound started, the tent bellying in again as if two hands began to grate against the canvas like a dog burying a bone. Frenzied and out of control. Just as quickly as it began, it stopped.

'Dawn,' she whispered, giving her friend a nudge.

Dawn didn't even stop snoring.

Gripping the torch in one hand Libby fumbled with the padlock she had secured when they had stumbled in from the Wyrd Wood earlier. She had to get out; she couldn't simply cower in the tent and let the scritch, scritch, scratching etch its way into her brain. Unzipping quickly, she crawled out into the night holding her torch in front of her, ready to strike at whatever rat, badger, mole or person lay in wait.

There was nothing there.

The campsite slumbered in its way, disturbed by those distant raucous laughs and yells, a few lights dotted in amongst the tents like a join-the-dots picture Libby had yet to complete. The tents were pitched quite close together, each one with just enough room around it for people to walk past without tripping over tent pegs, though Libby imagined that getting an unwary foot through the side of your tent was not uncommon in festivals like these. In fact, she reassured herself, this was what the noise had probably been. Some clumsy, overstimulated reveller, not taking enough care on their way to their own sleeping spot.

Or it had been an animal.

Nothing to worry about.

Libby walked around their tent, peering into the light thrown by the torch as, off to one side, a chorus of whooping noises came from the dark. It sounded like wild creatures, Libby thought, like being in a zoo at night, except there were no enclosures, no fencing to keep everyone safe.

The scratching sound did not have to be sinister. But then she thought of the fortune teller's words – 'You're jagged, you don't *fit*' – and her gaze fell on a piece of white paper speared under one of their tent pegs.

Four words. Thick black marker pen, the capital letters bold and confident.

YOU NEED TO LEAVE.

Chapter 15

Libby woke the next morning with sleep crusted in the corners of her eyes, a dry throat, the beginnings of a pounding hangover headache, gritty sweat at her hairline and a note clutched in her hand.

YOU NEED TO LEAVE.

She had tried to wake Dawn in the night, to show her the paper, but the girl could have slept through Armageddon and the best she got was a half-open eye before she fell asleep again.

Just as she was about to shake Dawn, a voice could be heard outside their tent, 'Hello? Libby Corrigan and Dawn . . . Hoxton? Hello?'

Dawn woke in a tangle of hair and clothes, pushing herself into a seated position. 'Wha . . .?'

'I need to show you something—' Libby began but was interrupted by the voice from outside again.

'Umm . . . hello? Dawn and Libby? I'm here to take you on your tour . . .'

'The tour!' Dawn sprang up, realised that was impossible and got stuck in a strange crouching position as she crab-walked to the zip.

'Wait! Dawn, I—'

'Look, we can shower and get breakfast later, Libs – this is the VIP tour. Get moving!' And with that she slid the zip down and let in bright sunshine and a peering face.

'Sorry to wake you up but we're on a bit of a schedule. My name's Sal and I'll be your guide for the morning.' Sal wore a yellow staff T-shirt rolled up high to the shoulder and had a green Mohican hairstyle that, despite the already mounting heat this morning, was not wilting even a little.

Libby stepped out into sunlight and strange snatches of music as the campsite got on with its morning around her. Quickly stuffing the note into the pocket of her shorts she took a surreptitious sniff at her armpits. Not her most fragrant. She longed for a shower, for hot water to sluice away the sticky film that had settled on her skin but Sal had already moved ahead and Dawn was following, pushing her hair out of her face and tying it up into a messy bun. The pink strands left on her neck stuck there with sweat.

For a moment Libby paused. She should call Dawn back, show her the note and explain about those sounds during the night . . .

. . . scritch-scraaaatch . . .

YOU NEED TO LEAVE.

When she thought of those words, she heard them in her mother's tone of voice. There was even a shadowy corner of her subconscious that half-believed it had been a spectral finger scratching at their tent, her mother's ghost come to express her disappointment with her only child even after death. She could imagine the look on the apparition's face, the mix of disgust and confusion that Libby had dared to come somewhere like this, had ventured out to have what for Libby's mother was always a swear word – *fun*. If anyone had the sheer will to come back from the dead then it was Ann Corrigan, especially if it was to bring her daughter down a peg or two.

'Dawn – wait! Stop!' Libby dragged on her friend's arm, her other hand bringing out the note ready to show her, but Dawn wriggled out of her grip.

'No time, Libs – come on!'

She lolloped over to Sal, and Libby could see her total joy at going on this tour. She couldn't tarnish that for her. Mentally, she gave herself a good shake. The note was simply some stupid person trying to ruin people's enjoyment: there didn't have to be anything more disturbing to it than that. In fact, she was probably over-reacting, the last vestiges of alcohol in her blood making her paranoid. It could wait until after the tour; in fact, she could show it to Sal once the VIP thing was finished, hand it over to someone in authority who would know what to do with it. Also, she told herself sternly, wasn't she meant to be enjoying herself too?

She jammed her concerns down with the note, tried unsuccessfully to tame her fringe, pulled on her boots and insisted they at least have the time to brush their teeth and go to the toilet before their tour began.

'So, here's the Moon Stage.'

There were five of them, the free ticket winners, sat in one golf cart and all looking slightly dishevelled and queasy from an overenthusiastic use of their free food and drink wristbands last night. Libby had missed the names of the three young women with them and instead gave them the nicknames Dancer, Prancer and Vixen. They all looked Instagram-ready, dressed in little crochet tops, wearing fairy wings and an orchestra of jangling bangles. In front of them shone a huge metal moon, fixed over a stage that would be empty until the festival officially kicked off with the lighting of the huge beacon on the hill above the farmhouse, signalling the start of the night's gigs.

Libby's hangover worked busily, insistently pounding her skull, making her temples sore and, despite the bottle of water she had drunk, stripping all moisture from her throat. As they had settled into their space on the golf cart, Libby had finally remembered why her face felt so tight. Back at the campsite before bed, Mia, a friendly tent neighbour, had flourished a box of face paints and Libby had made an instant, and now highly regrettable, decision. She rubbed at her cheek with her finger and bits of purple flaked off.

'Oh God. What am I?' Libby nudged Dawn and gestured to her face.

'Umm . . .' Dawn narrowed her eyes and tilted her head to better consider her answer. 'I think a butterfly. Or a really colourful tiger?' She had a sequinned heart glued around one eye.

Libby rubbed some more at her face. 'How did you find us?' she asked Sal as she hopped into the driver's seat.

'Ah, your wristbands – they've got a tracker in them. We've got surprises planned for the winning ticket holders during the festival and we need to be able to find you.'

That sounded both exciting and rather creepy at the same time.

'So, the Moon Stage is for the evening bands,' Sal continued as they trundled past people lugging speakers, unravelling wires and checking lights, and she nodded at a man in a black security uniform who opened a big sliding gate for their cart. 'But behind this stage is the guts of the place, where all the staff work pretty much every hour of the festival to bring you the best experience we can.' They passed a succession of trailers and freighter-crate-style offices, some with a little space outside filled with camping chairs and the remains of beer cans and glasses on folding tables. 'Not as glamorous as you think, eh? But talking of experiences, here's our first stop and a little gift for you.'

'Merch!' Dawn grinned.

'Exclusive merch – just for you winners. So we'll know who's selling it if it all ends up on a resale site later . . .' There was a smattering of laughter.

This golf cart did not hold the entirety of the free ticket winners, Sal had told Libby. Apparently a few free tickets had been scattered across the country in clubs, cafés, bars and pubs, ready for people to win. This golf cart was just one of many doing the tour that day, Sal had explained, the Blake family ethos being to try and allow all types of people access to the festival whether they could afford a ticket or not.

'Freebies!' Dawn leapt down from the cart, which had stopped next to a covered table waiting for them.

There was the obligatory hoodie, though Sal assured them that the print was a strictly limited number of fifty, a perfume or aftershave made locally from flowers grown in the wildflower meadow on the farm, Abel Blake's autobiography called 'The Rising Sun' (signed by the man himself) and, much to Libby's delight, new designer flip-flops decorated with artwork exclusive to the festival. The temptation was too strong; she was desperate to yank off her heavy hiking boots and let her beleaguered feet enjoy the cushioned soles and some fresh air. An available plastic chair next to another tent with its flap firmly closed looked an inviting spot to change her footwear. As she sat Libby overheard a low conversation coming from inside.

'Another three bloody fence jumpers already today.'

'They nearly had the fence down yesterday over on the Sun side, I heard.'

'Not surprised. That fence is a mess now – needs replacing.'

'Yeah well, it can get in line. Lots of things need an upgrade around here, including this damn computer. Ugh! It's frozen again!'

'Okay?' Sal threw a shadow across Libby's feet and she stood quickly, blushing at being caught listening, so busy eavesdropping she hadn't even unlaced her boots. Giving her a tight smile, Sal ushered her onto the golf cart once more where Dancer, Prancer and Vixen were already wilting like glittery flowers drying out under a heat lamp.

Next was the Sun Stage.

'This is more bloody like it!' Dawn jumped down from the cart.

They had been driven through another gate and Libby had expected the same sad collection of freight containers and trailers but this was the area reserved for the bands and singers who would be performing and so the trailers were big and clean, the outside space fun, bright and stocked with food and drink. The sofas were draped with throws and cushions, there were cute tables shaped like red-topped mushrooms dotted about, and there was a free bar at one end, made out of an old but shining Airstream camper van.

Once Sal had shown them around, she gathered the five of them near the bar and handed out new wristbands, these ones bright green. 'This is the end of our tour, but you can hang out here for as long as you like – just pop these on. They're valid for today only.'

'What?' Dawn gaped. 'We can . . . we can . . . just stay . . .?'

It was unclear whether it was due to that particular piece of news, the heat, or the partying from the night before but at that moment one of the women behind Libby simply crumpled like old paper left out in the rain. Her friends tried to support her as her knees gave out, her face ashen-grey, her fairy wings twisted out of shape as they helped her slump to the ground.

'First-aider!' Sal yelled.

Libby moved without really thinking. Muscle memory. She had gone over this in her head, watched the videos, remembered the mnemonics that would help save a person's life – her mother's life if she was alone in the sickroom with her and she suddenly choked, or passed out. Her hands were deft but gentle. She manoeuvred Dancer, Prancer or Vixen – whichever one she was – into the recovery position, shifting her hip over and into the correct place. So intent was she on her unexpected patient that she did not notice the man appear at her side, his footsteps quiet, shod in expensive leather shoes.

'Well done, very calm.' The man stood over her, a black shadow against the sun. Libby brushed the hair from the woman's face and let the first-aider take over, shading her eyes to try and see who had spoken. 'I'm wondering, as a thank you for stepping in, if you'd like to have some brunch over at the farmhouse?'

Golden hair. White linen shirt. Strong jawline. The founding father of Solstice – Abel Blake.

Chapter 16

Ma Blake, Twenty Years Ago

There it was again, the knocking. Ma crouched behind a kitchen chair, holding on to the slippery-skinned carcass of the rabbit she had been preparing for tea.

Ma didn't know who it was because she hadn't had time to glance out of the window before diving for cover into this hiding spot, but it didn't matter. They all wanted the same thing. Money. And they could go on wanting it – there was none left.

More knocking.

Ma cursed having a front door that opened straight into the kitchen with windows on either side that could be so easily peered through. It could be Dez, the guy they had bought that second-hand farm thresher from a month ago, promising him that he would get his cash, as soon as they got to the bank. Of course, they hadn't gone to the bank. The bank would come to them soon enough anyway. It would come to reclaim everything, the whole lot: house, fields, livestock, standing stones and the damn thresher.

They had failed.

No. *She* had failed.

This was all her husband George's fault and she couldn't even complain to him because he was cold under earth, had been for the past five years. Not that the farm had been a spectacular earner before then. These places were tied up in razor-wire red tape. The farm's throat was well and truly sliced and all that was left to do was watch it bleed into the grass.

Another type of blood dripped onto the flagstones from the skinned rabbit. Sighing, she carefully placed it on the kitchen counter above her head, its floppy veined body slithering out of her hands.

More knocking.

She wondered how long she would have to wait. Yesterday she had crouched behind this table leg for twenty whole minutes whilst the vet had prowled outside. In the end he had stuck a bill under their door like that would spur them into action. Ma had speared it on the nail where all the other unpaid bills lay dying.

George had had dreams. He had been idealistic and bright-eyed when they had bought this place as newly-weds over twenty years ago, spending his evenings with her walking amongst those standing stones, the Grey Sisters as they were locally known. Sacred land, they had called it. Blessed. Of late, Ma was more inclined to think it cursed. She was a countryside girl, had grown up with all the myths and stories and she knew the tales of this place – how those stones had once been witches, how they had killed a man and then turned to rock to save themselves and, on Midsummer's Eve, they shrugged off their heavy disguise and danced again in the moonlight.

Unless they started paying rent, those sisters, she had no more use for them.

Once again, Ma glanced at the earthenware bottle high on a shelf on the dresser. In their first week living on the farm, all those years ago, they had found it, tucked into a narrow ledge in the big fireplace, squat and grey with a slim neck upon which a stern, bearded face was etched.

73

'A counter-spell for witch's magic.' She had looked at George's puzzled face and smiled. 'This might be really old.' She had given it a gentle shake and had heard a rattle.

'What's in it?'

'Oh, all sorts of horrid stuff, probably. Hair clippings, sharp things like rusted nails and pins, even some of the homeowner's urine . . .' She had held the bottle out to George who had pushed it away. 'Had to be brewed in silence and then stoppered up to protect against the witch's magic. Powerful stuff.'

'Get shot of the thing.'

But Ma hadn't. It had stayed on the high shelf of the dresser ever since and held a strange fascination for Ma, so much so that she would find herself standing in spots in the kitchen where its solemn bearded face could not balefully glare at her. In the end she had turned it around.

Objects like that, they had power. The land too. The quiet breathing earth under the full dark stars – if you lived in the silence and screech of the countryside for long enough you realised that the stories handed down, the folklore, the little superstitions . . . well, they were things you shouldn't ignore. Ma had made sure to pass those tales on to her children when they had been small. Silas had yawned and turned to play with his toys, but Abel had always listened, his cherubic face upturned to her like an obedient flower.

There was one more round of knocking and then a tremulous voice: 'Mrs Blake?'

Ma sighed. She knew that voice. Getting up from her kneeling position she smoothed at her hair, tucking any stray wisps back into its bun as she walked to the door and opened it a sliver.

'Tess.'

No inviting question, no greeting. Tess was another thing in which she had no interest. The person waiting on her doorstep was pale-faced, wearing a baggy sweatshirt dress and a big coat over the top. Dark shadows ringed her eyes and she looked as if she could do with a good meal.

'Is Silas here?' Tess tried to keep the anguish out of her tone but Ma heard that frantic edge anyway. Desperation was a family trait. Both Tess and her mother slid into it, letting its gloopy quicksand close over their heads. Everyone in the village knew this. The last she'd heard, the mother had disappeared again, following after one of her men like a mangy dog. And now here was Tess, doing the exact same thing.

'No.'

Ma went to close the door, but Tess put her palm flat against it, more for show than anything else as Ma doubted she had any real strength. She coughed, a deep rattle that sounded as if something vital in her had shaken loose.

'Will you tell him to call me?'

Ma nodded and Tess opened her mouth to say something else, but the door closed in her face. Standing for a second, staring at the thick wood planks, Ma took a breath. She would not be telling Silas anything. Everyone knew, everyone could smell that desperation on the girl. She was on a path to destruction, via drink or drugs or whatever she was shoving into her system, and maybe Silas had set her on that path, maybe not . . . but he would not be following her down it. Not if Ma had any say.

That was when it happened. Moving too quickly, she stepped in some of the rabbit blood that had dripped on the floor, her heel skidding out, her hands flailing for purchase and finding it in the solid ledge of the huge dresser standing against one wall.

The dresser with the witch's bottle on it.

Helpless to do anything to stop it, Ma could only watch as the bottle teetered and then toppled, catching the edge of a shelf before smashing onto the tiled floor below.

The pieces of salt-glazed pottery lay broken on the floor along with the tangled, gritty mess that had been inside. She bent to see clearer the desiccated concoction, certain she spotted a shard of yellowed tooth amongst the coarse hair, before quickly scooping up the stuff as best she could and piling the large shards together with the mess on top.

Her fingers gritty with old tooth enamel and who knew what else, Ma stopped at the bin, unable to bring herself to throw the broken bottle away. Instead, she placed the remains of it back on the shelf, half of the bearded face glaring at her from one cracked eye.

She climbed the stairs and paused on the landing. Faded flowery wallpaper, scuffed skirting boards, threadbare carpet – there was not a part of the house that did not require paint, or patching, or ripping up and starting again. The floorboards creaked under her step as she neared the bedroom door with the padlock on it.

This was all for Silas's own good. If he would not at least try – if he would insist on spending strange hours with his slacker friends getting high in fields and lay-bys – well then, he would need to be shown. And that is what she had done. Silas needed to clean up his act; he could not rely on his brother all the time to step in for him, to shoulder the farm work and the worry. Silas needed a lesson.

She couldn't help but hear again the sound of pottery cracking against the floor as she unlocked the door and found the bed empty, the nailed window broken open and almost ripped from its frame. Silas had escaped. She ran to her own room but she knew as she moved that breaking the bottle had set some terrible bad luck in motion. Below her in the kitchen she imagined the bearded face on the bottle howling a splintered warning at her as she grabbed the suitcase she kept under her bed, which held the last of her ready cash.

It was empty.

Chapter 17

Ma Blake, Twenty Years Ago

The village was a place Ma hardly ever went.

On either side of it the mountains rose, ridges of flesh around this scar of road, war memorial and some terraced houses, their windows white-rimmed eyes in dark stone. She had no need to come here. They did what shopping they needed over at the big supermarket a half hour's drive away in the other direction and this village called Grey Sisters, named after the stones, well, it had never given them a warm welcome. The rumour had always been that they had not paid a fair price for their farm, that George had squeezed the deal as hard as the cholesterol squeezed the arterial veins in the farmer he'd bought it from, choked veins that killed the man a few months later when his heart gave out.

Not true of course. It hadn't been George who had haggled; it had been her.

'Ma Blake,' the voice called from the shop doorway.

Edna Kirk. Ma clenched her jaw. The woman ran the local shop but, if truth were told, she thought she ran the whole damn village. Ma turned to her and considered the grimy shop window. If she spent a bit more time cleaning up the place and less time watching her neighbours from its big glass front, she might make a lot more money.

'Edna. How are you?'

'I saw your boy.'

That sentence set Ma's heart thumping. Silas. He was why she had rushed to the truck, leaving the skinned rabbit on the worktop, her hands shaking as she locked the farmhouse door. He was why she had driven here, barely concentrating on the road – him, and the money he had stolen from her.

She wasn't quite sure how much had been stuffed into that suitcase under the bed. It wasn't enough to save the farm – there was no way she could have squirreled away that much over the years – but it was enough for a few months' rent somewhere small and cheap, to give her and her boys breathing space to work out what to do next. Cash. No bank trace. Nothing for those bloodsuckers to see. She wasn't a fool.

And now it was probably being snorted up her son's nose as she stood here with bloody Edna Kirk.

'Where?'

'How's the farm, Clara?'

Ma gave a rueful smile. Edna did it on purpose. No one used her first name anymore. She had arrived at the farm as Ma Blake, liking the sound of it, the matriarchal air it gave her despite the fact she had been only in her twenties at that time. Ma Blake sounded like the head of a family, it sounded like the person who went by that name would have power and authority. Clara . . . well, Clara was gone. She still had no idea how Edna had even found it out.

'Farm's fine.'

'Because I was hearing . . . let's see, there's Dez for a start. He seems to be owed some—'

'Farm's fine, Edna. Where did you see Silas?'

Edna leant against the doorframe. The woman was about ten years older than Ma, in her late fifties, to Ma's forty-one, but she dressed like a child at a holiday camp, always in brightly coloured tracksuits, or shorts in the summer, silly plastic clips in her dyed hair, the kind of cheap shoes that would fall apart after a week working on the farm. Ma's own boots were made of sturdy leather with thick soles, cleaned every Sunday, though no longer polished because that was a waste of time.

'Headed on over to the old Stuart place. Usual crew.'

Ma didn't even say goodbye. Instead she made herself walk, not run, back to the truck; Edna would not witness her panic so she could gossip about that to anyone unlucky enough to visit her shop that day.

The Stuart house was a bit further out, now derelict and falling into a soft death just like the village itself. It was a well-known fact that Edna only kept the shop going because of a dead husband and a hefty mining accident pay-out that funded the building. The young people, so few in number, moved away as soon as they were of age and left the old to hang grimly on, but the Reaper was shuffling nearer each day. And, of course, where you got a corpse, you found maggots feeding on its flesh. In this village most of those had burrowed their way into the Stuart house. It was down a dirt path in a dell where trees choked out the sky and where sun hardly ever warmed the soil, not a family home anymore but a squat – a desperate last resort for the homeless and hopeless, problems that were no longer city issues but had pushed their way into the countryside like deeply rooted ivy.

She stopped the truck at the rusted gate and walked the rest, imagining how she would drag her youngest out of that den, by his heels if she had to; how she would nail even more boards over his damn window and take everything from his room that could be used to jimmy them open.

That was when she saw them.

Two figures, one supporting the other. In an instant she was taken back to so many views of them just that way, through their childhood, the two of them together, holding hands, running with each other, one helping the other up, as she had taught them to do. *You always take care of your brother.*

'It's okay, Ma – I've got him,' Abel said as she ran to them. His arm was slung around Silas's shoulders, and her younger son's head lolled at an awkward angle. 'He's out of it.' She looked down at Silas's feet, dirty and bare, the skin purplish with the cold. She had taken his shoes from him when she had locked him in the room, thinking that would stop him leaving. She had been wrong.

'I don't know what to do with him.' She supported his weight on the other side and, between them, they half walked, half dragged him back towards the gate. Abel looked at her, her golden older son, tall, broad-shouldered, with an open, handsome face and a ready smile. How could she have produced two such different boys, she had often thought to herself? More importantly, what had she done wrong with Silas?

'We'll get him through this. I'll keep him busy,' Abel said as he shouldered most of his brother's weight.

'Wait – the money!' Ma stopped.

'What money?'

'He took it, my savings from under my bed. Surely he couldn't have spent it all?' She began to pat at Silas's pockets in a frantic way until Abel stayed her hand.

'Silas doesn't have your money,' he said softly.

The world closed in around Ma. She knew it as soon as she had raced out of the farmhouse and into the truck only an hour or so ago. That was it. The money had been a ragged safety net, full of holes and far too small, but it had been something at least. Now there was nothing. She thought of the face on the broken witch's bottle, howling like she wanted to right now.

She must have started to sink to her knees because suddenly Abel gripped her arm, and she struggled to understand his next words: 'Ma, it wasn't Silas who took it. It was me.'

'But . . . why?'

'I've got an idea that will save the farm.'

Chapter 18

Libby was pretty sure that Dawn was about to explode.

'Oh my God.' She gripped Libby's arm, her eyes huge, her whisper taking on a manic edge. 'Oh my God!'

'I know!' Libby squeezed her hand.

Abel Blake. *The* Abel Blake, superstar founding father of Solstice, had invited *them* to brunch. The same Abel Blake who was at that moment making small talk as a member of security drove their golf cart away from the Sun Stage and towards the river that created a natural division between the farmhouse and the festival land.

Libby had no clue what he had just said but he swivelled slightly in his seat up front and gave her a grin that caught and stunned her with its dazzle. She smiled back and pulled at her T-shirt. Dawn was still wearing her slip dress in tie-dye swirls of colour from the night before which, along with the glitter striped over her cheeks, the sequin heart around her eye and her pink and blue hair, made her look like a dishevelled fairy with a hangover. On the other hand, with her painted face, Libby looked more like an overstimulated child at the end of a birthday party.

To get to the farmhouse the cart had to drive through Wyrd Wood but this was a very different place to the one Libby and

Dawn had been in just last night. The atmosphere of it relied upon lights and smoke and music and upon the shadows of night to make its glow shine brightest. This clear morning was unforgiving, a harsh mirror lamp illuminating all the flaws, lines and wrinkles in the wood's face. A sleeping quiet settled in, the performers gone to get some rest before the evening's entertainment, and – when they passed it – the fortune teller's shepherd's cart was locked, its neat little curtains firmly drawn.

The woman's words came back to her: '*You're jagged. You don't fit.*'

But Libby wasn't going to let them cloud this morning, nor was she going to think about the stupid note nailed outside their tent telling them they should leave. They were on their way to brunch with Abel Blake himself and then they were going to have a sun-filled day of fun and music and as much food as they could eat. And a shower. Libby flapped a bit of air under her T-shirt in the hope it could cool her down. She really needed that shower.

The golf cart came to a stop next to a fast-flowing river, deep and swift, a natural security perimeter to the farmhouse and the standing stones.

There was no bridge.

There had been one. Libby had seen pictures of it when researching the festival: a rickety thing made of rough wooden planks but that had been demolished years ago. Abel got out of the golf cart and the girls followed him as he went to stand on the riverbank.

'Here we are. We'll leave the cart and walk across. Hope you're hungry because brunch is a serious business in the Blake household.'

'Walk?' Libby looked at the river and the opposite bank. Did this man think he was Jesus – able to walk on water? Dawn nudged her and raised an eyebrow.

'Ah, I love this bit!' Abel ran down a set of stone steps cut into the bank and then he simply carried on moving, setting one foot out in front of him. By rights it should have plunged straight into the river.

Except it didn't.

Instead, a circular stepping stone rose out of the water to meet him.

Ahead of him, more of the large flat stones emerged from the river, making a path to the other side. The water was too deep, and the current too strong, for anyone to get across without them. Abel turned and waved a small remote control, grinning like a schoolboy. 'My idea! Good, aren't they?'

Dawn jumped onto them, leaping from one to the next, and Libby followed. She could see the appeal of this kind of bridge, especially now the festival had got so popular, a crossing that could disappear as quickly as it rose, leaving the farmhouse and the standing stones inaccessible from the fields beyond.

They climbed the steps on the other side. Ahead of them on their right was the house, limewashed white with a black slate roof. The deep front porch ran the entire length of its front, interspersed with cast-iron pillars, the effect much as if the house itself was muzzled, an animal liable to bite. But Libby turned to the left.

'You know the stories about them, yes?' Abel came to her side, shading his eyes against the sun. Preparations for Sanctum were underway, but through an archway in the screens the circle of stones could be seen with the oak tree in their centre.

'No,' Libby said. The five stones were crooked and grey, patched with moss, and there was a stillness here, a waiting peace that seemed loaded somehow. Listening. There was even a welcome breeze, a cool trailing of air along Libby's collarbone, a hushed shushing accompanying it.

'They used to be witches. Five of them. The Grey Sisters. Local stories tell that they came together to kill a man called Eurig Swain before he condemned them to burn. Lured him out to the oak tree with a promise of a confession if he came alone. So he did. After all, they were only women, right? What danger would he be in?' Abel gave a wry smile. 'Those stories, they never say how he was killed. Ma would tell them to me when I was little and I always wondered – how did it actually happen? Did they ambush him? Stab him? Knock him out? After it was done, they strung him up from a branch of the tree and then turned themselves to stone, making this a special spot. A place where the sisters can grant wishes. Do you believe in that kind of thing?'

Libby gave a sad smile. 'It's another way of praying, isn't it? My mother prayed, at the end. It didn't stop her from dying.'

There was quiet for a few moments.

'I'm sorry for your loss.'

Libby didn't respond to that because she suspected it would make Abel uncomfortable to hear that she wasn't sorry about her mother's death – not at all. Quickly she added in her head that, of course, she would never have wished for such a painful way to go, the cancer gnawing at her mother like a predator would on the bones of its prey, but having her gone . . . where there should have been an emptiness, a loss, there was instead a feeling of refilling, of her own octopus sense of self stretching out into spaces no longer barb-wired by her mother's caustic opinions.

'So . . . what would you ask for, from the Grey Sisters?' There was something in Abel's frank and questioning gaze that made her think perhaps he would not be too shocked by her lack of daughterly grief.

'I don't think I would – that kind of thing never ends well for anybody in the stories, does it?'

He laughed then, head tipped back, leaning fully into the emotion, a king at the feast bestowing upon a guest the full weight of his approval. Libby felt like she had passed a test of some sort. For a second she wondered how it would feel, to be part of a family like the Blakes, the kind who had brunch together in a glorious festival they had created themselves. Ma clearly had some issues right now but the love she had for her boys shone through everything she had done, especially her steadfast support

84

of Abel's dream to turn their farm into this wonderland. If Libby had gone to her own mother with such an idea, it would have been flicked away like an insect at a picnic, as all her thoughts and opinions had been.

Dawn had already headed towards the house, and the two of them followed her to the front porch where a wooden table had been set with pastries, cereals, platters of cheese, meat and fruit and jugs of coffee, milk and orange juice. There were six chairs set around it.

And on one of them was Silas.

Chapter 19

Libby and Dawn climbed the steps and into the muzzled mouth of the farmhouse porch.

Silas did not smile and he did not say anything. His sunglasses were reflective so Libby could only see a blue-tinged version of herself when she looked at him, a tiny person in a curved world.

'Ah, it seems we have company.' Abel climbed the porch steps and stood opposite his brother. 'Silas – I thought you had an early start?'

'I did. Now I'm back for breakfast.'

The brothers' words were merely the tips of pond plants, the knotty and tangled roots of what they were actually saying to each other submerged way beneath. Libby recognised the tone. It was the one her mother had liked to use when sharpening innocent sentences into a blade. If Abel was television-movie-actor smooth, all blond and tanned, dressed in his signature white linen shirt and jeans; Silas's shaved head, dark clothes and fidgety, wiry frame made him more like backstage crew.

'Bit early for groupies, isn't it?' Silas muttered as Abel rushed his own words over him.

'Very funny. No, this young lady . . .' here Abel put a hand on Libby's shoulder '. . . performed emergency first aid just now so

I thought, as a thank you, she and her friend—' He paused for the name.

'Dawn—' Dawn obliged, already seated and reaching for a croissant.

'—Dawn should come for brunch.'

'Did you?' Silas leant back in his chair. 'Don't we have first-aiders for that kind of thing?'

'Well, as you can see, my brother is not a morning person. Sit, sit. Help yourself.' Abel almost pushed Libby into a waiting chair as Dawn piled her plate high with pastries and ignored anything even remotely nutritious.

Next to her, Libby fiddled with a spoon and glanced at Silas. She was still wearing that stupid face paint, making her a strange butterfly/possibly lion hybrid creature, hiding her own features completely with its now smudged colours. He probably thought them both idiots.

'Where's Ma?' Silas tapped his fingers on the arm of his wooden garden chair. Libby had noted it before, his fidgety energy, even when most of him was still, there was always movement some-where: a foot, a hand, a crossed knee bobbing.

'Ah, much as she would have loved to meet our guests here, she's not feeling very well. She won't be coming down, but I took a breakfast tray up to her before I left this morning.'

Because of the sunglasses Libby couldn't tell if Silas was looking at her or not. A prickling up the back of her spine made her wonder if he was secretly studying her out of the side of his gaze. She shifted in her chair, the backs of her thighs sticking to the wicker seat pad.

'I'll make sure to check on her later.' There was a challenge in Silas's statement as if he believed Ma was faking her illness, or that Abel himself was lying about it.

Libby stuttered out her question: 'Is . . . is Ma okay? I mean, we saw her—'

'—Yes, most of the festival caught that little scene,' Abel cut over her, irritation in his tone. 'No, she's not been feeling herself for a while now, you see, and the medication often does strange things to her. Rest assured she is being well cared for. Anyway . . .' Abel reached for the coffee jug and changed the subject. 'How have you been enjoying yourselves so far?'

'Bloody brilliant!' Dawn tore strips of croissant into long buttery curls, which she then dunked in her own coffee. Abel watched her with fascinated shock. 'We got totally wasted last night.'

Libby opened her mouth to correct her, almost hearing her mother sigh in her head at such an unladylike response. But then she pressed her lips together and smiled instead; after all, it was true: they *had* happily got completely wasted.

Ahead of them was a view of the oak tree in the clutch of the Grey Sisters, that stone-fingered hand breaking up through the soil. Deep-green hills were a misty backdrop. It was shaded on the porch but Libby could already feel the heat building, no clouds today, no respite from the full force of the sun and there was the scent of fire smoke as if the very air had been scorched by the heat, baked on too high a temperature.

Silas moved from tapping his fingers to tapping on his phone. 'So wasted that one of you turned into a . . . psychedelic lion?' he said as Libby felt her cheeks burn, glad at least that no one could see that under the paint. She rubbed at her nose and bits of orange flaked off, tiny embers that set nothing alight.

Abel cut in. 'Tell me about yourselves.'

Dawn did, managing to almost demolish the food on her plate at the same time as explaining about the final year of the chemistry degree she was heading into and her hope to get placed in a research lab at the end of the course.

'And you?' Abel turned to Libby. 'Are you at university too?'

That had never been an option for Libby. Her mother had been diagnosed with stage-four cancer not long before Libby's A-level results had come out and then all plans for degrees and the like had got shelved as the two of them had adjusted to a whole new life that was on a rapid countdown to death. 'I work at a library part-time so I could look after my mother . . .'

'Ah, yes, your sad loss.' Abel sipped espresso from a tiny white porcelain cup.

Silas spoke over him. 'And what's your name again?'

This was the first time Silas had stopped swiping at his phone screen and Libby found him turned directly towards her. The question was abrupt, a job interviewer tired of the preliminary niceties.

'Libby Corrigan.'

He removed his sunglasses and studied her for a second, his expression eagle-sharp and intense, burning bright in his stern, angular face.

Dawn, puzzled, looked from Libby to Silas before sighing and asking, 'So, Sanctum. Spill. What's it like?'

Abel took a sip of coffee and Silas sat back once more, flicking his sunglasses over his eyes. Abel answered, 'I can't tell you what goes on in Sanctum, Dawn, otherwise I'd have to kill you.' Then he gave a short snuff of delight at his own joke.

'I've always wanted to go . . .' Dawn, not to be put off, deliberately left that sentence hanging but neither Blake brother picked it up. Silas stood, taking a napkin and a sugary swirl of bun, before stuffing his phone in his back pocket.

'Trouble at the Sun side fence, Abel. And that new security firm you employed this year are worse than useless. You really do get what you pay for.'

'Hmm. Well, I'm sure you can handle it.'

Silas was about to say more but there was the sound of wood scraping above their heads and a tremulous voice called, 'Abel? Is that you I can hear?'

Abel sprang out of his seat and rushed out from under the front porch roof so he could look up at a window above their heads. 'Ma! What are you doing up? You should be resting. Go back to bed.'

'I'll go—' Silas moved to the farmhouse door.

'No, you've got work to do. I'll check on her.' Abel pushed past him and nearly disappeared into the house without even a goodbye to the two women before turning to them. 'I'm so sorry but—'

'I think that's our cue to leave, yeah, Dawn?' Libby tapped Dawn's hand and made a motion with her head, the universal sign for *'Let's get out of here'*. Dawn nodded and grabbed three croissants, a Danish pastry and a flapjack for the road. 'Thank you so much for brunch.'

Silas had already stalked off, heading towards the river, and the girls started to run so they could catch up with him, knowing they would be stuck on the wrong side of the water if he got across before them and those stepping stones disappeared back into the depths.

'Wait for us!'

Silas stopped. When they got nearer, he finally turned to them, throwing his words out like shrapnel, and, like shrapnel, they scattered, hard to catch.

At the sound of these words, Libby stopped in her tracks.

'What did he say?' Dawn frowned.

They had hardly escaped the shadow of the muzzled mouth of the porch when something made Libby turn back to the farmhouse one last time. An electric finger dragged itself across the back of her neck, making her raise her gaze to a high window from where they had just heard that querulous voice, the glass glinting in the sun. And behind that glass, a still face, blurred by a net curtain, watching them.

Ma Blake.

'What did he say, Libs?' Dawn asked again, tugging her towards the steps before Silas got across and lowered them once more.

Libby stared up at Ma's face in the window. *You need to leave.* That was what he had said.

The same words that had been on the note spiked on their tent peg.

Chapter 20

Libby scrubbed at her face until her skin tingled. She was done being a butterfly, or a colourful tiger or whatever she was, the dry paint pulling tighter and tighter at her temples until she thought her skin would split like a blister.

She had got it wrong. Silas's words had been hard to hear, twisted by the wind. In reality he had said something else, something innocent. Or . . . it had been a coincidence. There were only so many words in the English language, Libby told herself, and only so many combinations of them. It was a coincidence that Silas had said the exact sentence that had been written on the note: YOU NEED TO LEAVE.

Had Silas left them that note? Had it been him creeping about in the dark, leaving cryptic yet disturbing messages? But why? What possible interest could he have in Dawn and herself, and what possible reason could he have for wanting them to leave?

The water troughs lined this edge of the field, places to fill reusable bottles, or to have a quick stand-up wash. The woman next to her, dressed in a bikini and flip-flops, lathered under her arms whilst her friend poured water over her and Libby wished she had her toiletries too. Her toothbrush was a bone-achingly long walk away back at the campsite.

'You finished?' Dawn nudged her. Silently, Libby unfolded the note she had kept in her pocket: YOU NEED TO LEAVE. After hearing the same words from Silas, it felt like the right time for Libby to show Dawn this piece of paper and get someone else's opinion . . . and maybe some reassurance, anything to stop her mind whirring over it.

'What's that?' Dawn sat cross-legged next her and began to unlace her boots.

Libby passed it over. 'There was this odd scratching at our tent last night and when I went out to look at what was making the noise I found this stuck to one of our tent pegs.'

Dawn frowned and took the piece of paper. 'That's weird.'

'And Silas? Back there just before we left. He said the exact same thing to us as he walked away. Well . . . I'm pretty certain he did . . .'

Around them the glorious, sweaty, furiously busy whirl and toil of the festival swarmed. Libby wondered if the constant thud of music from the speakers would permanently shift important organs inside her, so she would never again feel comfortable unless she could feel a subterranean rhythm. She rested a cold bottle of water on the back of her neck and wiped sweat from her forehead as the sun showed no sign of wavering in its intensity.

Dawn rubbed at the paper. 'Do you see that? It's like, printed, I think. It looks like handwriting but it's not.'

Libby leant over to take a closer look. 'Do you think we should report it?'

She remembered the scritch-scratch on the tent material, the way it had seemed like a lazy finger being dragged across the thin sheet that was their only night-time privacy.

'Ah, it's just a weirdo. Or a stunt, trying to advertise something, especially if it's been printed. Forget about it. And I didn't hear what Silas said but I'm guessing it was probably to tell us to hurry the fuck up or he'd leave us behind.' She ripped the piece of paper into quarters and stuck them in her shorts pocket. 'Stop overthinking everything.' She nudged Libby, teasing her.

It was a relief, like a patch of shadow in blazing sunlight, to feel the cool sense of Dawn's reasoning. And it was true – she did overthink things, proved by her inability to pack light. Overthinking had been an essential survival tool for living with her mother, with the various ways she could infuriate, disappoint, or wound her – every action carefully weighed with all of its possible outcomes, always choosing the one that would cause the least angst. With Dawn she made a good team in that respect: between her overthinking things and Dawn not thinking at all half the time, they often ended up doing just the right amount of thought.

'Come on then, what do you want to do next?'

'Hyperventilate here for a while . . .'

'Not an option.' Dawn stood and put her hands on her hips. Libby knew that look – she was about to become the vapour trail to Dawn's set-course aeroplane.

The received wisdom for a festival like Solstice was that a person shouldn't try to experience everything on offer, that they shouldn't pack their day so full it left them stressed and too exhausted to fully enjoy anything. Dawn took that received wisdom and stomped all over it in her hiking boots as she took them both from Sun Stage to Wyrd Wood, to pop-up comedy tent, to Sustain and back again. Backflips, booming vocals, belly laughs and burgers – in the end Libby flopped onto the grass just a few yards shy of the wood and refused to move one more step.

'My feet are killing me.' She fumbled in her little cross-body bag, which she had taken care to fill with festival essentials the day before: lip balm, bank card, phone (though there was no coverage), sunscreen, tissues and plasters. She remembered how carefully she had considered different styles of boot, having been warned by Dawn that she would need sensible footwear, something to trek around in and cope with mud. Totally useless now in this searing heat. Her feet felt raw inside their heavy leather prisons. Dawn pulled off one boot, unpeeled her sock and let her rather red toes waggle in a non-existent breeze.

Libby tugged at her own laces. 'I'm done with these boots; they're torture in this heat. Time for my new flip-flops. My feet feel like they're on fire.' This had been her plan earlier at the VIP tent, but she had got so caught up in eavesdropping on the staff and then performing first aid, she hadn't got a chance.

'Oh yes!' Dawn waggled the tote bag full of merch that they had been given earlier. '*Exclusive limited-edition* flip-flops, I'll have you know . . .'

They both rummaged in their bags. Libby's toes emerged from their socks red and angry like a row of overfed backbenchers in a parliament debate and she happily rubbed her feet before slipping them into their new cool, cushioned footwear.

'Right! Let's get into Sanctum. I'm on a mission, Libbles.'

'Oh my God, just give it up.'

'Nope, not gonna happen. I'm getting us in . . . somehow . . .'

Libby smiled and stuffed her socks back into her dust-covered boots. Her toes would get just as grimy within half an hour but she would readily exchange that for the feel of air on her skin. No one could escape the dry dirt kicked up from the arid ground, clouds of it swarming in the wake of any buggies or carts as if the vehicles were haunted by shapeless dust demons.

For a while they both sat and watched the festival. There didn't seem to be a typical Solstice attendee. There were lots of women of around their age, dressed in whatever Instagram had told them was the 'correct' festival wear this year, mostly cowboy boots and floaty scraps of tops paired with shorts or mini-skirts. Older couples could be seen too, dressed more for hikes and camping, wearing sun hats and making sure they rehydrated between beers. But there were also quite a few groups of young men, bare-chested and tribal in their roaring yells. Libby watched the group closest to them, some lounging on the grass, the others

standing around. One young man with a bleach[...]
wore a pair of shorts in neon colours, twitching [...]
need, to do something, anything: start a fight, k[...]
another, steal a drink, run a race. The ragged, [...]
coming off him made Libby want to scoot back o[...]
get a bit of distance between them.

'Is it me or does it seem extra packed in here?' She turned to
Dawn and kept her voice low.

Dawn leant back on her elbows. 'A bit maybe.'

Because there were lots of those groups of men, Libby saw.
It was as if a whole set of wrong invitations had gone out to a
nearby sports bar, or skate park, because surely this wasn't the main
audience for Solstice with its beacons welcoming in the sun, its
circus performers and Wyrd Wood and sun and moon talismans?

There was a commotion over to Libby's left and the crowd
began to part, two security staff in black T-shirts and walkie-talkies
crackling at their hips carving a path through the sweat-soaked
people. Between them they had a firm grip on a smiling young
man with spiked hair and tattoos on both arms like a shoulder-
to-wrist net, who gurned at everyone as he was dragged past.

'This is a violation of my human rights!' he yelled, looking far
too pleased for someone feeling violated.

The security staff said nothing but kept barrelling through.

'I had a wristband! It fell off!' Mr Violated told the crowd
with a grin.

'Mate, we saw you. That fence has to be repaired now. You're
lucky we're not billing you.'

The punch, when it came, was viciously sudden. The man
with the bleached buzz cut had been standing as normal, arms
at his sides, until the security guard came within his reach and
then he swung, his whole body moving with it, barrelling into
the guard and setting off something within the men around
him. It took only seconds for more to pile in, kicking, spitting,
shouting, a writhing mass of arms and legs, the intense flare of

. violence something that made Libby back away, dragging awn with her.

Help came quickly enough. Order was restored and blood in the dust was the only sign of the savagery that had just taken place.

Libby took another look around at the stages, the flags limp in the still air, the rag-tag awnings of the food trucks and the people moving, moving, moving through it all. These fields in the bowl of the mountains around them, they were a soup overheated by the heavy sun, its flame turned far too high.

Ready to boil over.

Chapter 21

Libby's days had always been neatly guillotined.

Her job in the library had required her to be up at seven in the morning, in at nine, with a break at eleven, lunch at one, and the end of the day promptly arriving at five. When not at work and instead caring for her mother, there had then been the medication hooks upon which their days had been hung, those fixed points that could not be loosened.

At the festival, time slipped and slid.

It was around seven in the evening and Libby was drunk, not so much on alcohol, but on a day where she had been able to do exactly as she wanted. There had been no chores, no chastising, nothing to do except relax and listen to music as the festival began to fill with even more people ready for the beacon on the hill to be lit and the party to officially start. The two of them were sat amongst the crowd in front of the Moon Stage where the first of the music would start as soon as the sun went down.

'I love you.' Dawn clutched her hand and pushed her flower tiara up from where it rested rakishly on one ear. She had gone full festival now: there was not an inch of her that hadn't been henna tattooed, glittered, or adorned with beads or flowers.

'I think you might have sunstroke.' Libby smiled and dipped

her head so Dawn could put the flower tiara on her hair. That bob of her head was about all she could manage in the way of moving. During a heatwave a tall dinner candle could flop, simply bend over on itself so its wick ended up touching the tabletop in a strange, exhausted yoga contortion. She was that warm, weary, slumped lump of wax.

Dawn shoved her face into Libby's. 'No, like I *really* love you . . . y'know, like you're family. You *are* family! I love you more than my actual sister . . .'

As more people swelled into the space in front of the Moon Stage, Libby could feel a tinge of expectation in the air, that undercurrent of excitement making everyone's voices a bit louder, their senses a little more heightened. She dragged Dawn to her feet so they didn't get trampled on and they stood together arm in arm. They were not a field *full* of people, Libby thought, half-drunk on sun and free cocktails and a dizzying sense of liberty. No. They were a field *of* them, each person a blade of grass. The wind could make that long grass dip and bend and she could imagine the same here, how one breeze-like emotion would sweep over the people-meadow and flatten them all in the same way. It wasn't a terrifying thought. She wanted to share this experience with all of these humans because their relaxed, blissful joy would join with hers and increase it to an almost unbearable point. The sky above them began to take on the watery blue of the end of the day.

'Hey! Hey!' Dawn suddenly began to yell behind her.

Libby frowned, interrupted mid-idyllic vision of a field of ecstatic swaying long grass people. 'Who are you shouting at?'

'Hey! Over here – it's Joe!' Dawn waggled Libby's arm.

It took Libby a few moments to work out who Joe was, their brief time in the local village almost forgotten, but then he came shouldering his way through the crowd with a knowing grin aimed straight at Libby.

'I can see. Hi, Joe.' She smiled and took a sip from her water bottle, trying to act like Dawn would in this situation, not the Dawn right now, she amended herself hurriedly, because that Dawn was currently trying to get the rest of Joe's band to form a conga line.

'You remember Libby, right? Libby is my bestest friend. I love her. I love her and not like a sister because my sister is a total cow. She's better than my sister.' Dawn happily swung Libby's arm back and forth as she spoke, her words only a breath away from slurring. Libby decided that it was time they both switched to soft drinks. 'I can't believe your nan let you come here. She hates Solstice.'

'Well, I'm in a band and bands generally play at festivals . . .'

'Get out! Your band is playing here? Whoa! What was it called again? Wait, I know, I know . . . it began with an S . . . Sandy Nights?'

'*Savage* Night.'

'Yeah, that was it . . . Savage Garden.'

Dawn nodded happily and turned her attention to the rest of the band behind him, leaving Libby and Joe together.

Libby cast around in the dusty corners of her mind where the file 'Flirty Conversation Starters' was stored, flipping it open to find only moths and dry dead things. 'Congrats, for playing here – it's a big deal . . .' This was all she could manage. For him, she discovered, she wanted to be wittier. She liked the way it felt to have his attention on her.

'Thanks. Obviously, after that little conversation I might have to change my band name . . .'

'Well, play your cards right and Sandy Nights might still be available.' Libby was pleased to see that she made Joe smile and he gave a low chuckle. 'You on tonight?'

'No!' He laughed again. 'We've got the graveyard slot tomorrow at midday. No one will be listening then, will they?'

'I will.' She wasn't quite sure why she had said that. But he was standing very close to her and looking at her in an earnest way that made her feel more light-headed than the alcohol she had drunk.

She wanted to keep his eyes on her and perhaps she could do this if she made him laugh again, if she could somehow make those eyes skip over the fact she was plain and boring, clumpy, frumpy and without charm. Completely unlike her mother.

The crowd tightened in around them, pushing Joe even closer and a thrill of adrenaline fizzed through her. From huge speakers came a thrum of sound and that low twanging noise was something that coursed through the crowd too, a note of anticipation, the beginning of the show. The diaphanous grey of twilight was about to fall even as the air held on to the heat of the afternoon in a tight, sweaty grip.

It was time for fire to signal the start of Solstice.

With Dawn's head on her shoulder, Libby watched as, high up on the hill behind the farmhouse, a huge flame burst into life, the festival beacon that would burn for the next few days, a symbol of Solstice, a celebration of the sun, of long days and short nights, of summer and plenty and warmth.

'I know she said something to you,' Dawn whispered in her ear.

'Hmm?'

'At the end, your mum. She must have done because she always liked having the last word,' Dawn lifted her head and took Libby's face in her hands. 'Don't believe her, okay? Whatever she said, she's wrong.'

Libby's throat swelled and she blinked back tears. Once again there was the rattling rasp of her mother's voice, the feverish hot hand dragging her down, closer to the bed, so she could whisper into her ear. But the music roared into life; lights began to sweep over the crowd and the simmering anticipation boiled over as the people around them rushed towards the Moon Stage taking Libby with them, dazzled and disorientated. People's hands reached for the air, there was a fine spray of drinks thrown and open mouths stretched wide in a way Libby knew was singing but under these lights it looked different, more primal. Anxiety made her stiffen as she was buffeted and moved, just one blade of grass in the meadow, no will of her own and so she closed her eyes for a moment, to try and calm her heartbeat, to take a breath and stand her ground.

Dawn moved in front of her, one hand still holding Libby's so when she opened her eyes she kept her gaze on her, making Dawn the focal point, the anchor in this overwhelming scene of too many people crushed too closely together. Dawn turned back to her and said something, but it was far too loud to catch the whole sentence, though the word 'Sanctum' had definitely been in it.

Later, Libby replayed that moment, twisting it this way and that like a Rubik's Cube, trying to find the combination of actions that would provide a different outcome. But in the end, it was simple. The music roared, as did everyone around her and there was nothing Libby could do to stop Dawn's fingers from slipping out of her grasp as the throat of the crowd swallowed her friend whole.

Chapter 22

There was no need to panic.

Colour swam over her, a deep beat thudded through the ground and there were people everywhere. Dawn could not be far. She had done this before, disappearing off for a few moments, causing needles of fear to drive straight through Libby's brain.

There was no need to panic.

The back of every head she saw was not the one she wanted. Every shout, every arm raised, every twist and jerk of bodies dancing was not the one body she desperately wanted to see. A bright white beam flashed in her face and made the world a series of chaotic freeze frames, each frame slightly different, each bit of blackness in between a pit where anything could happen.

Stepping backwards she bumped into Joe who bent and peered at her. 'You okay?'

'Dawn? Do you see her?'

And then the music came to a crashing end and cheering broke out as a familiar figure walked on stage. Above him glowed the metal moon on top of the stage, its sad smile and sleepy eyes watching over everyone. Abel strode confidently to the centre and raised his hands.

'Thank you. Thank you. Thanks . . .' He waited until there was as much quiet as he was going to get. 'Welcome to my home. Look, I'm going to keep it short because we have some truly amazing music for you tonight but I just want to take this opportunity to tell you how much this all has meant to me over the years. It was actually twenty years ago that we held our first Solstice.' More cheering. 'The festival saved us. This land, this farm – we wouldn't have been able to keep it going if it hadn't been for the festival, for people like you coming here and supporting us and allowing us to do this year on year, for giving me the best job in the world.' As Abel spoke, Libby's attention wandered, scanning the crowd for Dawn.

'Ma would have loved to have been by my side tonight, to see all of your beautiful faces but, as many of you witnessed yourselves yesterday, Ma is not at her best right now . . . We have a very good doctor who is working with her and we hope to have her fighting fit once more and standing here on this stage with me. Her rightful place.'

Abel raised his arms in a Christ-like pose. 'So here we are again, ready to celebrate all things Solstice! May the sun always shine on you! Love you all, goodnight!'

He walked offstage and the first deep chords of a song began, sparking a surge of energy that made the crowd move not like grass in a field at all, because that wasn't aggressive enough. This was stamping and sharp elbows and hands pushing at her and she needed to get out of there, needed some high ground to seek out her impetuous, foolhardy friend.

Shoving her way through, she headed to the back of the huge mass of people where pockets of space began to appear near the stalls that made up Sustain, the long strip of land that provided the boundary between the Sun and Moon Stages. There was a hand on her shoulder.

'Hey – you all right?' Joe had followed her out and seeing him at her side made the roar of noise around her quieten a little.

'I've lost Dawn. Did you see where she went?'

'No, but I wouldn't worry, She's probably still in there, it's turned into a bit of a mosh pit. Happens all the time in places like these – you lose each other. She'll turn up, I'm sure.'

From where they stood, Libby couldn't see much past the bodies of the people loitering at the back of the crowd. The stage itself was raised high, screens behind it flashing up pictures that went with the music, the lights swivelling and sweeping and the band, one that Libby didn't know, strutted, strummed and shook sweat from their hair.

She checked her phone. There was no signal so no text or call from Dawn. She attempted to ring her despite knowing it was useless, the call not even connecting. Her curt text wouldn't even send:

Where are you? I'm at Sustain. CALL ME!!

Dawn would have made fun of her lack of text speak, her use of full words and punctuation, the librarian in her respectful of the sentences, reluctant to reduce them to merely letters left hanging with no safety net.

'Damn it.'

'Did you have a meeting place agreed between you, y'know, for if you got lost?'

Libby's blank expression gave him the answer and her next words came out in an anxious rush: 'No, no, we didn't because we're idiots – I've got to find her . . .'

She jostled her way back into the crowd, not looking back for Joe. As she elbowed and shoved a path through, she was pushed in return, each jab feeling a little more aggressive. Why couldn't Dawn just stick with her? Why did she always have to leap off at any given moment like a startled bloody meerkat? Libby used her hip and shoulder to force her way past a huge guy in a straw fedora and jeans that really needed a belt, stopping to glance around. What she needed was some height, a vantage point.

'Need a boost?' Joe's voice came from behind. He had followed her back in, and that simple decision, to keep her company, made the fear in her throat lose its grip just a little.

She nodded and he crouched so she could sit on his shoulders. There was no time to consider the sense of mounting a strange, possibly drunk man and wrapping her legs around his neck because he had already hoisted her and she put a steadying hand on his hair.

'Thank you!' she called down to him, glad she was wearing shorts.

From this height the crowd spread out below her. Other women like her were sat on people's shoulders, one waving a flag and screaming the words of the song at full tilt back to the singer on the stage.

No Dawn.

Not that she would have been able to spot her, even from this raised position. Darkness had now fallen and in the lights faces blinked in and out of view, each one with its own kind of wild abandon, neck tendons taut, mouths wide, a flash of teeth, arms waving, wrists adorned with glowing neon bracelets.

Libby wanted to scream, not Dawn's name, because no one would hear that above the noise of the thrashing, thumping music but just scream anyway at her careless friend for leaving her alone, for going off God knows where, probably still in search of passes for Sanctum. She was surrounded by more people than she had ever seen in her entire life and the one person who mattered most was nowhere to be found.

Her scream was lost amid the others.

An hour later, Joe walked Libby to her tent.

A black sky hung above and below were the bright lights of the Moon Stage, the soundtrack to it all a distant rumbling of bass beat punctuated by yells. The campsite was as quiet as it would ever be, most people still listening to music. Libby tapped out another text to Dawn, even though she knew her phone wouldn't be able to send it:

Back at tent. Where are you?

'I'm sure she'll turn up soon, y'know.' Joe stopped and nudged the tent pole peg with his foot in an idle way. Libby thought of that note that had been speared there only this morning. YOU NEED TO LEAVE. She wondered whether they should have taken it to security. Dawn had ripped it up though, hours ago, so there wasn't much point trying to do anything now. They would just think she was high, or drunk.

'If you're worried about being on your own, I could stay with you . . .' Joe immediately corrected himself. 'I mean, not stay with you, like in the tent. God, no! I just mean, umm . . .'

'I know what you mean . . . I think?'

Libby laughed but it was an awkward thing, dying away too suddenly. Her mother's voice in her head was caustic, telling her that this man and the way he looked at her, really focused in as if she was interesting, as if she was worthy of attention, his charm a headier thing than those jewel-coloured cocktails they had drunk last night, *this man was not for the likes of her*. The mantra of her faults played once again like a radio jingle in her head: she was too plain, too dull, too boring.

'Anyway, so I'll – I mean, I've got to – good luck with tomorrow,' and with those coherent sentences, she almost dived into the tent, sitting completely still until she was sure he had gone, embarrassment making her sweat as much as the trapped, stuffy heat.

She spent a wakeful night, tensing at every sound in anticipation that it would be Dawn's face appearing through the tent flap, her brain whirring through all the things she could have done differently, all the ways in which she could have stopped Dawn from running off. The ground was hard, the air stifling, and the shouts and singing were a hellish chorus.

Dawn would be back by morning, she told herself.

So when she woke late into a sunlight harsh enough to have already made the tent an oven, beads of moisture clinging to the inside, she took a moment to keep her head turned to the wall, convinced she could hear Dawn breathing. But when she rolled over, she found herself alone.

Chapter 23

Ma Blake, Twenty Years Ago

Ma stared at the dead thing on her doorstep.

A rat. Big, fat, with a pale tail the thickness of her index finger, blood and froth seeping from its mouth. It could have been a gift from one of the farm cats but there was something about the careful placing of it, dead centre, the way the tail had been laid out straight. That and the fact it was the fifth dead rat on their doorstep that month.

This was a message.

It was three months since Abel had told her he had taken her money and now there was a week to go before the festival. Abel's idea to save the farm. He had told her about other events like the one he was planning, had shown her clips of masses of people all crowded together, singing to bands in a sunset glow and she had seen the food vans and the alcohol in their hands and the tents they had brought with them and she knew all of that could be profit. The money she had scrimped together over the years had disappeared into a stage, already set up beyond the river and into paying those bands.

She had essentially footed the bill for a massive outdoors party.

That day when Abel had told her that it had been him who had taken the money, she had been as stunned as a bird flying into a window. This was Abel, the boy who had never caused her a moment's grief since he had been born, her mop-top sunshine head. He had stolen from her.

'But I'm not *stealing* it, Ma. I'm *investing* it. In our future,' he had said.

Ma stared at the dead rat. They had never been popular with the villagers. Interlopers. Wouldn't matter how long they'd been living there or whether they now remained on the farm for the rest of their days, they'd not been born there, or in the village. They would always be outsiders. Partly her fault. She had never mastered the art of smiling at people when she didn't feel like it, apparently something women in particular were meant to do if they wanted an easy life.

But it was never too late to start.

Be more Abel. That had to be her mantra. The festival needed the village, if not onside because that might be a stretch too far, then at least grudgingly accepting of it, otherwise it would open a rift that would never be healed. She had to be more like her sunny eldest boy. Charisma: that was what she needed. People either had it or they didn't. It wasn't simply being handsome, it was something else, something in his smile, in the way his attention settled on a person like gold dust, making them feel better about themselves. In medieval times he could have led an army to war and in a way this was a war, a fight for their survival. He had yelled his battle cry and they had come, his troops, his friends, the people who had always wanted to be his friends, the women who wanted much more than friendship. He had made them a battalion and they had created the festival, voluntarily.

Before getting out the shovel to move the dead rat, she eyed the sky with a frown. For a farmer's wife, the long-range weather forecast was a constant companion but one that didn't always get its predictions quite right. Posters had been put up, local bands had agreed to come, the site had been cleared, the stage erected, the various forms had been filled in, sent off, rubber-stamped for approval. Tickets had even been bought, lots of them, apparently. But that sky. That sky was a troubled mind, worried by cloud and heavy with rain about to fall, the colour of the spanner it would throw into the works if Midsummer's Eve turned out to be stormy.

It was the colour of that broken witch's bottle on the shelf of her dresser, its toothy innards piled on top.

Tipping the rat into a plastic bag, she threw the bundle into the bin before the dogs could get at it. With that chore done there was no excuse to put it off any longer: the charm offensive. She grabbed her purse and some of the festival posters and stepped outside, planning how she would smile and nod and make the smallest of small talk before reassuring everyone in the village that the festival would not disrupt their fossilised lives. No, not everyone. She only needed to reassure one person: Edna Kirk. The rest would then fall in line like the obedient dominoes they were.

Sometimes of late she thought she heard a murmuring – quiet female voices, low and conspiratorial, carried on the wind from the standing stones. The Grey Sisters. She flicked a glance towards them before heading to the truck. It had started happening after the witch's bottle smashed and she couldn't help but think those stones were grumbling at the accident.

The village huddled into the main road, turned in on itself with the backs of the houses facing the mountains that loomed over them. Inward-looking, Ma thought, same as the people who lived there. She parked the truck and practised her smile in the rear-view mirror, trying to make it look natural and not as if the corners of her mouth were being tugged by an unseen hand.

The first one she saw was stuck to a lamppost. SAY NO TO SOLSTICE! Big red letters pasted over one of the original festival posters. Further along, in someone's window there was a cartoon drawing of hills and fields with a familiar ring of standing stones and the words: OUR VILLAGE SAYS NO TO SOLSTICE! And, of course, there was a whole row of them lining the bottom of the window of Edna Kirk's convenience store, possibly the first time she had changed the display since Christmas, a painting of cutesy big-eyed mice, rabbits and voles and a speech bubble coming from them: SOLSTICE – DON'T SPOIL OUR HOME!

What about her home? Ma thought as she pulled open the shop door with more force than was necessary. Where was her cutesy big-eyed poster – her family thrown out on the street, no roof over their heads, no money? She yanked open the shop door and reached over to rip away one of the A4 sheets of paper from the window. 'What's this?'

Edna Kirk turned from where she had been chatting to two other women at the till. She wore a lilac tracksuit and plastic studded clogs, her lipstick Barbie pink and feathering into the lines around her mouth. One of the women, tall and thin, dressed in shades of beige, had been telling an elaborate story but paused at Ma's intrusion, her arm raised in a frozen gesture like a classical sculpture wearing cheap velour.

'You can see what it is,' Edna said, folding her arms across the teddy bear blowing kisses on her sweatshirt.

'But . . . We've heard nothing of this. I don't understand.'

'Oh, you have, I can guarantee. We've put in complaints but your boy Abel seems to have friends in the local council.'

Complaints? Ma didn't know about any complaints. But, she realised, that had probably been deliberate. Abel must have kept it from her. After all, it would be like him, to want to protect her. If that was the case, however, what other things was he keeping from her? What else did she not know?

'What concern is it of yours, anyway? The festival's on our own land,' Ma said.

'So it might be but to get to that damn land they'll have to go through here, *our* village, *our* countryside. Hordes of them, traipsing through and leaving their litter . . . antisocial little buggers they'll be too.'

'But, they might buy things in the village and—'

'And then the noise – have you thought of that? We don't want the din of that godawful music keeping us up all night.'

'It's only one night, Edna. One day, one night.'

'Bloody disaster, it'll be!'

There was a pause. Ma knew she shouldn't say the next words fighting to break loose from her, that she should remember she had come here to reassure, to assuage, not to create fresh animosity, that she had promised to be more Abel. But she wasn't her kind-hearted son. She was Ma Blake.

'No. You know what is a bloody disaster?' Ma's real thoughts spilled from her, the whole mess of them sour like that stuff she had found in the witch's bottle. 'It's a disaster that we can't make a living on our own land, the land we've shed blood, sweat and tears for. It's a disaster that we're going to be kicked out of our home unless we make some money fast and so that's what we're doing. And if you disagree with that . . . if you wish to lodge a complaint, well, you can lodge that complaint right up my arse because you know what? *When* this festival succeeds, which it will, when, year on year, we have thousands and thousands of people flocking here and the money is pouring in, I will make sure that none of it – not one single penny, Edna Kirk – makes it into the pockets of anyone in this damn village.'

And with that she left them, their gaping mouths slack, as she marched onto the street, ripping down every poster she passed on the way back to the truck. There was a whole sheaf of them as she got into the driver's seat and it was only after she drove half an hour to the nearest shopping outlet to buy superglue and the rest of the things on her shopping list, that she quickly flicked through them.

To the one that was different from all the rest.

A blurred, badly printed photo of a familiar face and the words underneath:

MISSING: TESS SANDERSON.

The sky held a quiet waiting darkness as she drove back to the farm, her hands shaking despite her fierce grip on the wheel. She could feel the storm brewing as an itch in her gums, and it wasn't long before she was proved right. Above her thunder rumbled, ushering in the first hard pattering of rain.

Chapter 24

The security tower was a colourful circus rocket.

Libby nearly ran towards it, having spent only a few minutes making herself look and smell vaguely presentable. She had brushed her teeth, splashed some soap and water on the important bits she could decently do so in public at the water trough and had braved the compost toilet at the back of the campsite. It was always quieter because it was further to walk and so therefore slightly fresher than the Portaloos, if by fresh you meant a smell that did not immediately drive a fist into your throat and make you want to gag. Then she had put on her boots, even though her hot, blistered feet protested, because she needed to be able to move fast and her flip-flops, though cool, would likely trip her up. More than anything she needed to be sure-footed.

All the while one thought raced around and around in her head: Dawn had not come back.

If last night she had managed to keep her worry at bay with all of those sensible, rational excuses as to where Dawn could be and why she had not returned, now in this sticky new day, they peeled away like flakes of sunburnt skin. Dawn had been gone all night. Libby had stayed awake long into the early hours, tensed for the sound of her returning and so, when she had finally fallen asleep at around four in the morning, she had slumbered so heavily it had been gone noon when she woke.

It was time to get security involved.

As she rushed past the Sun Stage she saw an audience begin to form, still waking up, or coming down, sunglasses on, a sheen of sweat on limbs, clutching reusable cups of coffee, some half-heartedly swaying whilst others sat or lounged on the grass. Until they stepped on stage, Libby had forgotten that it was Joe's band due to play. There they were, dressed in black, and Libby expected a screech of guitars, an angsty sing-shout from Joe, the drums about to punch into her temples. But the music that played out was softer, more thoughtful, the guitar riffs gently teased out, not tortured, perhaps a deliberate decision on their part as a nod to the time slot, and the delicate heads of those in the crowd. There was a crowd too, despite Joe's fears, and Libby pushed herself closer to the front.

It was Joe himself who was the focus of people's attention. He had that lazy, easy magnetism of a performer who could make each person watching feel as if he was singing just for them with only a flick of his glance, a nod of his head, a careless smile. That stage presence wasn't something that could be learned. The glow of stage lights and the gaze of an audience did something to certain people. It fired them, like an oven setting clay, sharpening the features, hardening the whole thing to a gloss.

Then he saw her and that flick of a glance, that head-nod, the careless smile was all for her, and the feeling of being in his gaze, it was a case of sunstroke all of its own. But there was no time to stand and watch and she carried on, trying not to break into a run, hoping Joe would understand.

The colourful security tower with its circus peak and strips of bright material was near the Sun Stage, placed so it had a good view of either side of the river from festival to farmhouse and high enough to see over the tips of the Wyrd Wood trees. Libby remembered seeing the distressed figure of Ma screaming from

115

the top of it, how it had brought to mind a banshee, those ghosts that wailed a warning of death.

The man standing at the bottom wore dark clothes and a darker scowl as he put out a hand to stop her. 'Not allowed up there,' he said, looking over her head.

'I'm reporting a missing person? My friend.'

'Your friend's probably sleeping it off in a cowpat somewhere.' But he then shrugged and stepped aside a fraction, yanking at the edge of the material so a few of the poppers fixing it to the base came free. 'Five minutes – we're busy.'

Libby had to stop halfway up the spiral stairs because the circling of the steps made her head swim, only the echoing of her own footsteps keeping her company. At the top she expected a hubbub of serious concentration, a team of people monitoring screens and speaking into crackling walkie-talkies, benevolent eyes in the sky watching over the people below and keeping them safe.

Instead she found a man sitting at a desk, facing away from her with his feet on the table, wearing headphones and eating a sandwich. She waited a few seconds for him to turn around, watching the way his shoulders bopped to a beat she couldn't hear. He gave a yelp when she tapped him on the arm.

'Jesus! Who let you up here?' Some of the tomato from his sandwich dropped onto the arm of his swivel chair as he stretched out one side of his headphones, not bothering to take them off completely.

'Umm . . . the guy at the bottom? I need to report a missing person.'

In a bored voice the man asked, 'And how long have they been . . . missing?' The emphasis on 'missing' suggested he spent a lot of time around festivalgoers and thought this idea entirely unlikely.

'Since last night.'

'One night?' He eyed the fallen tomato.

'But we can't use our phones here so I can't call her and she would never be out all night and she'd definitely come back for breakfast. Dawn Hoxton, that's her name. She has blue and pink hair and she was wearing—'

'Nope. Don't need to know. That's not a missing person. That's just someone at a festival. People disappear all the time, get separated in a crowd and it sorts itself out—'

'But—'

'Look.' He made a show of tapping on the keyboard in front of him. 'I'll log it, okay? Dawn Hoxton.' He tapped some more. There were breadcrumbs crusted at the side of his mouth.

'You'll log it?'

'Yep. See? Logged. Come back tonight if she's still not turned up.' And with that he turned his back on her once more, swiping the bit of tomato from the arm of his chair and eating it.

Glancing down at her wrist gave Libby an idea. 'Wait!'

She heard the man sigh as he didn't turn around but gave a lazy wave of his hand, dismissing her. 'Come back tonight.'

'No, we have these – these wristbands. We won tickets here and so they gave us these so they could track us and hand out gifts and VIP treats during the festival. Sal! That was the woman who did our tour yesterday – she told us!'

'So?'

'So, there's a tracker in the wristband. It will tell you where Dawn is!'

For a moment Libby had the hope that the man would finally do something useful, that his chair would move and he would spring into action at last, but that was quickly dashed with his next words: 'Can't do that here. Different department. You'll have to ask Sal about that.' He pushed his headphones back on properly.

'So . . .' Libby didn't bother to mask the irritation in her voice. 'Where's Sal?'

But she didn't get an answer to that question because suddenly a clatter of footsteps could be heard on the staircase below and soon a head appeared at the top of the stairs, one hand clutching the rail, the other holding a strange squat ceramic bottle with a howling face on it. The woman's grey hair was long and wild and her face, a very familiar one to every person at the festival, was wide-eyed with fear.

Ma Blake.

Chapter 25

Newspaper feature article:

Whatever Happened to Ma Blake?

Written by our features editor, Orla Meeks

Everyone knows the story of Solstice. It has been the UK's most sought-after music festival ticket for twenty years. Everyone knows how Abel Blake and his mother organised a last-ditch, desperate attempt to raise some funds for their farm and so the first ever Solstice took place, more successful than they could ever have hoped. So successful, in fact, that they gave up on the farming and grew the event instead, year on year, until it became the behemoth that it is now.

Everyone knows Ma Blake, how much she loves her son and the festival in equal measure. It can be seen in every interview she has ever done, and at every festival.

Everyone knows that she was the one who began the mysterious Sanctum, the festival within a festival, an event people are randomly picked to join, a place, apparently, for spiritual and emotional growth, for healing, for retrospection . . . or simply a pretty spot in the middle of standing stones to drink more alcohol. Who knows? What happens there is a closely guarded secret.

So why has Ma not been seen for over two years?

As respected music journalist Tim Norton explains, 'If Abel is the golden son of Solstice, then its mother is, without a doubt, Ma. In the early years she fronted the festival as much as her son, a regular presence out in the audience, overseeing the campsite, the catering, even greeting people as they came in through those huge sun and moon double doors. Bands have stories of her bringing them biscuits and cake before their shows, insisting they drink tea and put their beer bottles away, brushing any suspicious-looking cigarettes into the bin. And those who had been unfortunate enough to end up in the first-aid tent told of Ma bustling about with ice packs, drinks of water and lollies on sticks. So it makes it even harder to understand why, without any real explanation, she has suddenly disappeared from view.'

Ma Blake's last festival sighting was over two years ago. Photos from that time show her smiling and acting as normal: lighting the festival beacon, helping pick up litter, giving out free sunscreen and water to the people in the crowds, dressed in her customary long skirts and neat top, her hair sternly tied back in its signature bun.

When asked about his mother, Abel has never really explained her absence from a festival she helped set up and clearly loved with all of her heart. 'She's just taking some time for herself' is the most any interviewer has ever got from him.

Tim Norton continues, 'So what has happened to Ma Blake? Rumours abound. Does she simply want to step back and let the festival carry on without her or – and this is the theory doing the rounds on the internet – has she become very ill and so cannot leave the house anymore?'

But there is a more important question, one that Abel himself should carefully consider. As stories rise about the festival overstretching its budget and cutting corners, Abel and the whole Solstice team must be questioning, without Ma Blake, what kind of festival will Solstice become?

Chapter 26

'No.'

Ma Blake stopped at the top of the stairs and stared at Libby, holding the strange ceramic bottle close to her chest.

'No,' she said again.

The woman before Libby was a version of Ma Blake that had been dragged through some very unfriendly bushes. The hair that would previously have been neatly smoothed back into a tight bun was now loose and tangled, white streaks among the grey and brown. The long skirt, where before it would have been ironed, was creased and stained, and where once she would have greeted any festivalgoer with a serene smile, now her expression was one of panic. Her movements had an odd jerky quality to them, a broken marionette doll forced to perform.

'Mrs Bla—' The man stood up quickly, his chair sliding out from under him, another piece of tomato slithering free of his sandwich.

But Ma cut him off, not even glancing his way, her eyes fixed on Libby as she dashed towards her. 'No, no, no, no, no, no . . .' She grabbed her hand and Libby could feel the heat of her palm, her fingers digging in as she pulled her close, staring at her as if searching for something in her face. 'You. You leave. Now!'

Then she started dragging her towards the stairs. Both her voice and grip were strong and Libby began to protest as they reached the first step.

'I'm not leaving, I—'

'Oh yes you are.'

'Wait!' Libby clutched at the handrail and braced herself to slow Ma's momentum, making the older woman almost swing around to face her. 'I haven't done anything wrong and I'm looking for my friend. I'm not leaving!' She tried to wrench herself free of Ma's grip but only succeeded in making her wrist sore.

Ma's face crumpled. 'We don't have time for this,' she said, in a voice that now trembled. Libby could see that her fingernails were bitten to the quick, the skin red and sore.

The man at the desk finally put down his sandwich and took his opportunity to gain some sort of control over the situation. 'Mrs Blake, would you like me to call Abel?'

'No!' The power roared back into her tone and she tugged at Libby again, who dug her feet into the ground and refused to budge.

The security guard's voice called from the bottom of the tower: 'Everything okay up there, Mrs Blake?'

Ma hauled Libby down the steps. 'This young woman has to leave! Help me escort her off the site!'

'Wait!' Libby could feel herself being pitched forward by Ma's strength, no matter how hard she tried to stand her ground. The sound of heavy footsteps clanged up the staircase towards them and Libby knew that as soon as the security guard arrived, any struggle from her would be useless. 'I don't understand!'

Suddenly, Ma let her fierce grip lessen a little. 'I know,' she said with a deep sadness in her voice. 'I know you don't understand any of this and that's how it should be. That's why you need to go.' Her face was so close to Libby's that she could see the lines creased into her flesh and smell the earthy, herbal scent on her breath. Her eyes in that moment were calm and almost kind.

'I've got every right to be here.' Libby hated her voice for being too small and childlike. 'I won tickets.'

Ma shrugged as the security guard from below reached the top of the stairs, frowning and stern, muscles bulging the arms of his tight T-shirt. Faced with the prospect of being man-handled down the stairs or going with some level of dignity, Libby chose the latter. Ma didn't loosen her grip and took the steps far too quickly, making the soles of Libby's boots slip on the metal treads.

Turning to the security guard, Libby tried to explain, 'You can't just kick me out – this is insane! I haven't done anything wrong!'

But Ma Blake pushed her through the flap of bright yellow material that hung from the tower and then marched her onwards, past the Sun Stage where Joe's band had ended their set and there was now a lone singer dressed in layers of floaty chiffon, wailing something about love, or loss, or both. Ma Blake had decided that Libby needed to leave and so, Libby thought, as they neared the awning-covered path that made up Sustain, maybe she *had* done something wrong.

More likely, maybe *Dawn* had done something wrong.

'Get Sal to bring her stuff,' Ma told the security guard hovering near them, and he nodded and veered off.

'Has this got something to do with my friend?'

Libby hadn't seen Dawn since last night and she had been pretty drunk then, so her getting into some sort of trouble was a scenario that Libby could easily imagine. Dawn never shied away from voicing her opinion, or getting in the middle of something that didn't need her input at all. Libby had lost count of the number of times she had tugged at her friend's sleeve, a warning touch that Dawn knew meant: 'Keep your nose out'. Not that she ever took much heed of it.

'I don't know anything about your friend. When she turns up, she'll be going the same way as you. Out.'

Through Sustain they went, past the food trucks, gleaming silver things on wheels and wooden huts with cloth bunting, past sizzling grills and the smell of roasted meat mixed in with the spicy aroma of noodle bowls and street food, a dappled shade caused by the patchwork material of each individual awning. People stopped and took a closer look at them as Ma drove a path through the crowd, and Libby could see the surprise on their faces, the whispering surrounding them like radioactive crackle on a Geiger counter.

'Is that Ma Blake again?'

'I thought she'd had a nervous breakdown—'

'—Well, it definitely looks like she's had one—'

'No, she got ill, I heard . . .'

Ma Blake. Ma Blake. Ma Blake. Her name again and again and again. Not that she seemed to hear it, her face one of fixed determination, lips pressed tightly together, one hand on Libby, the other clutching that small ceramic bottle that was stoppered by a wooden cork.

Stewards and staff parted for her, their expressions of shock and confusion quickly smoothed into something more business-like. The huge brass gates came nearer, polished to a flashing glare, the faces etched on them both grinning, the sun with a manic joy, the moon with a sulky sadness. Happiness and despair were in constant opposition in this gateway and there was no room for a calm, even keel.

'Open them!' Ma called with an authority born of years.

They parted and she pushed Libby through. Too stunned to do much else, Libby staggered to a halt at the spot where she had waited only a day or so before. Ma paused for a moment and considered the earthenware bottle in her hand with the odd bearded face carved into it, mouth open in a howl.

'You should have one of these,' she muttered to herself. 'I should have thought of it. This one's no good for you. No good. I should have made you one.'

But the doors were already closing and Libby had no more time to ask what Ma meant or what she should do now. With some laboured screeching and a clang, the sun and moon met each other once again and Libby was shut out of the festival.

Chapter 27

Ma Blake, Twenty Years Ago

In the end, Ma took the project outside.

It was the smell. She had done her preparation, using one of her well-thumbed books about local myths and folklore that had originally been her mother's.

There was work to do.

It was all laid out on a camping table on the front porch. Superglue. Nails. Pins. Some of the old hair and tooth shards. Her own hair, pulled from her head, the needle pain making her wince. The pieces of the broken earthenware. This festival needed more than her, more than a charm offensive, she thought, watching the rain fall as a sheet beyond the porch steps. It needed luck. A talisman, just like the one she had broken back at the house.

Afternoon was a glum and gloomy affair, the light sullen and dim. Ma hadn't long returned from her poor attempt to win over the village, the one that had ended in cross words with Edna Kirk.

First, she fixed the bottle. There was a Japanese process called Kintsugi where a person mended something in such a way so as not to hide the scars but to make them beautiful. Ma had not achieved that – her superglue patching was Frankenstein at

127

best, but it held, the bearded face now whole once more, if not happy about it.

Boiling the foul mix of stuff needed to go inside the bottle created a hideous smell, an invasive thing that caught on the inside of her nose and seemed to seep into her clothes. Some witches' bottles supposedly had witches trapped inside, but her mother had told her that most of them were made by the victims of people who thought they had been cursed in some way, a protective object to ward off the evil. Therefore, the sharp pins and nails were meant to cause pain to the witch but the hair and the nail clippings – they had to be from the person creating the spell, so the whole thing bound itself to them.

The urine too.

Not her finest moment, collecting her own urine to pour into the pan, but nothing she hadn't done in the past to provide a sample for a doctor, she told herself. Crouching over the camping stove on the front porch to stir the gently heating foul mix, she watched the rain continue to pelt and paused for thought, suddenly realising how feral she must look, huddled over this witch's brew.

What was she doing?

But that was a rational question, the kind that was asked in a calm, measured voice, and it had no place here. There was nothing rational about this: it was a scratch for the prickle down the back of her spine, some kind of ancestral shiver passed down through the generations.

She was doing what women and men had probably been doing for centuries: using an old magic, the kind that could not be rationalised, the kind that needed blood and belief and stories as ancient as the hills that she could see around her.

Basically, she was desperate.

That witch's bottle needed fixing and then maybe, just maybe, their luck would turn. Because this wasn't all to do with a piece of earthenware crockery; no, it was to do with that Missing poster with the picture of Tess on it. She couldn't get it out of her head. After all, she had wanted the girl gone, out of Silas's life, but she hadn't meant for it to happen like this. She hadn't meant for the girl to disappear.

When had been the last time she had seen her? Months ago, probably. They had managed to keep her away from Silas, understanding, as he could not, that she was no good for him, that they were no good together. There were people who brought out the worst in each other, who dragged at each other like a riptide pulling at a drowning swimmer. Ma, Abel and Silas, along with a group of other willing volunteers, had been setting up the stage when she had seen, across the river, Tess heading towards the farmhouse. Ma had squared her shoulders, ready to send the girl packing, but before she could move she had seen Abel striding over the bridge towards her. Glancing behind, she had noted that Silas had his back to the whole thing, fixing a metal support under the stage and oblivious to their visitor. She had angled herself to block his view if he did decide to look her way.

Ma had watched as Abel reached Tess. She saw the two of them, Tess flailing her arms as if she was shouting, Abel with his hands at his hips, two little toy figures in a play countryside landscape. Eventually, Abel had led Tess away, along a path that led to the main road, out of sight of anyone in the field, and Ma had breathed again.

Back on the front porch now, Ma hunched over the stove. So this witch's bottle – it wasn't just for herself and the farm, it was also for Tess, that she would be found, possibly drug-addled and a mess, but alive with not a speck of harm on her.

Silas would never need to be involved.

'Ma?'

It was as if she'd summoned him. Silas rounded the side of the farmhouse and immediately put his sleeve over his mouth, muffling his words. 'What're you doing?'

'Making a poultice, like your grandmother used to.'

'For what? Jesus, that smells like hell.'

'For my shoulder. It's seized up again.'

Silas studied her as she continued to stir. He was right. If hell were ever to produce a signature perfume, like some of those posh hotels she had read about, this would be it: the scent of rancid desperation and lost hope. She willed him to leave, because, before it cooled into too much of a cement sludge, she would need to ooze the concoction into its bottle and she didn't want to do that with him around.

Once again a whispering floated to her, low mutterings full of hissed words she could not catch, and she shook her head a little. It was just a trick of the wind, she told herself. She could see the standing stones from the front porch, and the skin on her neck prickled.

For a moment it looked as if Silas was about to say something but she carefully avoided his eye, concentrating instead on the camp stove and the saucepan she would probably have to throw away because she couldn't ever imagine being able to scour out the smell. In the end he sighed and turned to the front door, letting it slam behind him. With a shaking hand she let the sludge slop into the bottle and then stoppered it.

By the time she had packed away the little stove and got everything back into the kitchen he was nowhere to be found. With care, she placed the bottle, not on the dresser shelf, but back on its original spot on the ledge inside their massive fireplace.

There. Done. She waited for a sense of calm to wash over her.

'What's this?' Silas's voice came from the hallway and Ma jumped, nearly hitting her head against the sooty bricks as she backed out of the huge fireplace.

There was an excuse already on her lips as she turned to face him but he wasn't talking about the witch's bottle at all and didn't care that she was clambering about underneath their chimney. No, what he cared about was gripped in his hand: a piece of paper, A4-sized with thick capitals on it, one she had ripped from a lamppost that morning after her argument with Edna Kirk. One that, in her rush to fix the bottle, she had left under all the other posters on the hall table. Silas held it up for her to see:

MISSING: TESS SANDERSON.

'Tess's missing? When were you going to tell me?' His voice trembled on her name.

'I only just found out, I—' But he didn't let her finish, striding across the room and pushing past her. 'Where are you going?' she asked, grabbing his arm.

He didn't answer, instead he shook away her hand, hardly breaking his momentum as he opened the door. Ma ran after him, cursing the fact she had left those posters on the hall table. She would have told him – of course she would – but maybe she would have done so after the festival and by that time Tess would have stumbled back out of whatever drug-induced hole she had ended up in this time.

'Silas!' she shouted as he took the porch steps at a run and headed for the path away from the river, towards the farm's main gate. 'SILAS!' She heard a razor edge cutting a crack into her yell as she stood in the doorway and watched him leave, felt the anger rush into her. 'Don't come back!' she shouted into a spitting rain that had just begun, drops stinging her face. 'I won't have you back this time if you start on the drugs again. I'm done! Do you hear me? SILAS! Don't come back!'

Despite her words she willed him to stop, to turn, to listen to her for once in his damn life. But she held firm to the doorframe; this time she would not go running after him. This time there were other things that had to come first, like the farm and the festival and her other son, the one who was actually trying to help save their home. There was a point where she had to watch Silas go and let him make his own mistakes.

Maybe that bottle on the ledge in the fireplace would guard him too.

Now that the howling ceramic face had been mended and the farm's protection restored, Ma expected the rain to stop, for the bad weather that was forecast to clear in time for the festival. If anything, the water started to fall even heavier, almost like one of those beaded door curtains Edna Kirk had in her shop. The farm, the festival, the village, the rain, Silas, Tess, all of it dropping on her like a storm, and she could only stand and try not to get swept away in the mudslide.

Finally, she closed the door.

Chapter 28

The festival gates were firmly shut.

Libby had expected to cry. The shock of being thrown out, of not having Dawn with her, she thought that would trigger sobs, great big childish heaves of frustration, but that wasn't what happened. Instead, where the cries should have come she felt a heat build under her breastbone, as if her heart itself was enraged on her behalf, pumping so hard she felt she could scale a wall, kick an enemy in the head, win a race.

A hand patted her back. 'Here, love – don't upset yourself. Gate-crashing, were you? Pay no mind, it's only a festival . . .' Libby guessed this was one of the stewards who manned the entrance. She had seen their open-mouthed faces as Ma had thrown her out, the neon yellow of their high-vis jackets.

She couldn't give a response. Possibly the same hand placed her rucksack at her feet as she sat on the ground and put her head between her knees. That was the advice, wasn't it? The brace position and that was what she felt she needed – to brace herself against what had just happened, how quickly her day had twisted and shuddered and spat her out here. Alone.

When her mother had died, as her body had been cooling on the bed and Libby had sat next to her, there had been a time, before she called an ambulance when she had simply . . . not moved, trying to take it all in. In death, her mother had looked different, her face even more sunken, the mouth relaxed, the skin taking on a waxy tinge. Perhaps this other person had always been lying in wait, someone with lips more ready to smile, with eyes more ready to look kindly on her only daughter. The woman who had taken up much of Libby's life, who had pretty much *been* her life, was now an absence, a shell of flesh now stilled and silent. No more careless, cutting comments, no more bending to the iron will of a woman much more skilled than her at getting her own way, no more tiptoeing around the edges of a life that was centred around a person who couldn't see anything past their own likes, dislikes, wants and needs.

Libby had been an apple and her mother the worm tucked tight within, but now that worm had been plucked out and there was only a hole into which the fruit collapsed, soft and rotten. There had been so little time to sit with this new reality of hers, to understand what her apple world would look like with just her at its core. The whirlwind of Dawn and the festival had swept her up and away.

Dawn.

Libby took a gasp of air, breath hitching in her throat.

Dawn was still in there.

A kind, slightly sunburnt female face swam into view, white stripes of sunblock on her cheeks like a cricketer. 'You all right, love? Now, I can see you're upset but you've got to move along. Go home. You'll feel better about it all after a night in your own bed.'

Libby considered trying again – telling this woman that she shouldn't have been thrown out, that she hadn't done anything wrong, that her friend was missing and she couldn't leave without her. But then she pressed her lips together, picked up her rucksack and checked her phone and purse were in there. To her relief they were. Her phone still had no signal and so there was no point trying to ring Dawn or send another text.

Why would Ma Blake kick her out of the festival? Usually, Libby would be the first to admit if she had done anything wrong – after all, she was her mother's daughter. She knew that most things she did were irritating; her mother had told her that often enough. But, despite racking her brain to try and think of something, she couldn't come up with any reason for her to be so unceremoniously evicted. Unbidden, the words on that note speared to their tent on the first night came back to her:

YOU NEED TO LEAVE.

Had that been something to do with Ma? They hadn't heeded that warning and so, first opportunity she had, the woman had thrown her out herself. But why? There was absolutely no reason for it.

YOU NEED TO LEAVE.

The same words Silas had said to her as he had walked away from the farmhouse after brunch. Or at least, she was almost certain that was what he had said, his words snatched and flung by the wind. And he had been decidedly unfriendly towards them . . .

Libby, aware that the steward was still watching her, started walking away from the gates and along the wide path that would eventually take her to the main road. But she wasn't looking ahead to that road. No, instead she was looking at those fence panels, ones that could be climbed. After all, she had seen it happen, that young man perched on the top of her Portaloo on the first day at the festival.

If he had done it, maybe she could too.

But hopefully not land on a toilet.

Of course, he had been immediately caught and tossed back out again but, well, she was going to think a bit like Dawn and not focus on those pesky negatives. Every sheet metal panel she passed was brightly painted, countryside scenes in vivid greens, animals like rabbits and badgers, a whole constellation of suns and moons, some with faces, some without and the standing stones, those Grey Sisters in both rock form and as women with

135

tangled hair dancing under the stars. Festival posters had been pasted onto the panels, and Libby skimmed her gaze over them as she walked until a familiar eye, half covered by another poster, brought her to a halt. She peeled back the covering paper.

MISSING: TESS SANDERSON.

The woman who had disappeared only a few days before the first festival. Libby remembered Edna Kirk from the village shop putting a piece of paper exactly like this in her shopping bag, one printed with the same direct stare of the black-and-white woman, her features slightly blurred by the photocopier. Libby gazed at her and imagined Dawn as another face like this, printed poorly on A4, one more missing person almost forgotten about.

YOU NEED TO LEAVE.

Silas.

He had been Tess's boyfriend back then, Libby knew because she had watched The True Crime Twins YouTube video on her disappearance after Edna had given her the poster.

A thought crept into Libby's mind, rat-like and twitching its whiskers: Did Silas have something to do with Dawn disappearing?

No. She picked up the rat-thought by its tail and threw it out of her mind. Conjecture. She was trying to make meaning out of nothing, like the human brain was programmed to do, always creating patterns in things where no pattern really existed.

Overthinking. That was what she was doing, what she always did. This was all a big mistake. Ma Blake had gone mad and thrown her out with no reason and now she was going to get back in because Dawn was still in there, being Dawn and getting into trouble, most likely. Libby kept walking. The path began to softly curve and soon enough she had moved out of sight of the stewards. Beyond the fence she could hear the music and cheering, a swell of sound and a thudding like a heartbeat as if an enormous beast lay just beyond this fence, only tethered by tent pegs and liable to come out roaring, bunting flying behind it like streamers.

Totally helpless. Totally useless. That's what she was right now. She could imagine all the silly, reckless things Dawn could have got up to and the longer Libby was away from her, the more time she had to do something even more stupid. She had to get back into the festival as soon as possible. Of course, there was the option of phoning the police but the reaction of the man in the security tower made her question that the police would even take her seriously. At events like these, people disappeared for a while, under the influence of drink or drugs and, if any drugs were involved on Dawn's part, Libby didn't want to get her in trouble.

She looked at the band on her wrist and remembered Sal explaining how she had found them in their tent yesterday morning. In that band coloured like a summer cocktail there was a tracker. Libby did not need anyone knowing where she was from now on. She tugged at the wooden bead that secured the band on her wrist, which seemed to only make it tighter and so she yanked the material over her hand, leaving red marks on her skin, flinging it from her as hard as she could, into the trees at the other side of the road.

She had expected more security. Apart from the staff at the gate, the rest of the fence was unguarded and Libby remembered the snatches of conversation in the staff area behind the Moon Stage when she had been on the VIP tour:

'Another three bloody fence jumpers already today.'

'They nearly had the fence down yesterday over on the Sun side, I heard.'

'Not surprised. That fence is a mess now – needs replacing.'

'Yeah well, it can get in line – lots of things need an upgrade around here, including this damn computer – ugh! It's frozen again!'

It sounded like there wasn't quite enough money to go round for this year's festival. Everything was on a tight budget and the seams were starting to fray. However, the fence panels she saw looked pretty firm to her, and – dishearteningly – smooth. No handholds, no footholds, nothing to grab, too high to jump and clamber. The man who had climbed it must have used a rope ladder or grappling hook or something Libby did not have. Despite this she gave it a go, kind of scrabbling at it uselessly as if she were a gecko that had lost the stickiness of its toe pads.

Sweaty and frustrated she stood and considered the fence, hands on hips. There had to be another way in.

Then came the sound of tyres on the road and, smiling, she realised there was.

It was driving right towards her.

Chapter 29

It was a mistake.

The car driving towards her did not offer a way back into the festival site, she realised as soon as it neared her, a red city run-around with plastic eyelashes over the headlights. When it stopped next to her she spotted a familiar face through the driver's window.

'Get in.' Sal's tone was a demand, not a request, though Libby did briefly think about running away. 'I've got strict instructions from Ma Blake to put you on a train.' There was a pause as Libby glanced around at the empty road, the heat of the day building around her, making her limbs weak and hollow. Sal read her mind. 'Don't be stupid. Get in the car, otherwise Ma will just send a team to get you. Easier this way.'

The fence was too high to climb, it was too hot to run, and Libby couldn't think of anything else to do. She was not Dawn. She was this: a sweating, scared young woman out of ideas. She got in the car. Sal handed her a bottle of iced water, deliciously cool condensation clinging to the plastic.

'I—'

'—Nope, don't want to know. I'm not paid enough for this crap.' Sal frowned at the road. 'And I've got stuff to do, not ferry

139

you around.' Libby hugged her rucksack to her chest and watched the hedgerows whizz by. 'Shit!' Sal glanced at her watch, a chunky thing that flashed messages at her. Swerving, she shoved the nose of the car into a lay-by, slammed her hazard lights on and tapped at her phone.

'What did I do?'

'Don't know, don't care. When a Blake tells me to jump I just ask how high.'

Libby watched a small, speckled bird hop about at the bottom of the hedge outside her window, bobbing its head to peck at what looked like dirt to her. But one woman's dirt was another small, speckled bird's feast. As the idea popped into her head, she turned to Sal, furiously tapping on her phone.

'Sal?'

'Hmm?' Sal didn't look up from the screen. 'Shit!' Her fingers flew over the message before she pressed send and sighed. 'My last year, I swear. It's a bloody circus, that festival.' She darted another glance at her watch.

'Sal? Look, you're busy, you don't have time for this. Just drop me at the village station, not the Solstice one. It's closer and I can make my own way back home from there.'

Sal went quiet for a few seconds, chewing her lip. Libby hardly dared move, afraid this moment would hop away from her like that tiny bird outside her window.

'Where's your friend?' Sal trained her harried gaze on Libby for the first time. 'You had a mate with you. Where's she gone?'

'I don't know. She didn't come back last night and I was trying to find her when Ma kicked me out. For no reason.' Libby had given up trying to make people understand that she had done nothing to warrant being manhandled out of the festival. There were only so many times she could explain.

'They didn't help you try and find her?'

'No.'

Sal considered her, head tilted a little and Libby couldn't keep still. She put down the water bottle to fiddle with a strap on her rucksack, clicking and unclicking its fastening. The phone beeped away to itself like a demented chick until Sal took a deep breath and swiped it silent.

'That doesn't sound like normal procedure to me.'

Libby wanted to scream her agreement but she doubted that letting out such a sound would convince the other woman to help.

Sal sighed. 'Look I can't go against Ma's orders. She's Ma Blake. But you say you want to be dropped at the village? So that's what I'll do. Saves me time and Lord knows I need about an extra day today to fit in everything I've got to do. Sooner I get rid of this stupid loan car, the better too. It's got bloody eyelashes, you seen 'em? Foolishness.' Quiet fell and Libby could hardly believe the way this conversation was going, expecting any minute another car to screech up to them, one with Ma Blake at the wheel, ready to haul her away and onto a train.

Sal continued, 'What you get up to in the village is your own business, none of mine. And I'll get a call put out for your friend, use the little wristband tracker to find out where she is. Frankly that should have been done straight away.'

Libby nearly snapped off the rucksack clip. 'Thanks! The village, yeah, the village is perfect. Thank you!'

Sal turned off the hazard lights ready to pull back onto the road. 'I'm sure your friend's just fine and this is all a misunderstanding but like I said: what you do in the village is none of my concern.' Sal put a heavy emphasis on these words but kept her gaze straight out in front of her. 'Clear? No trying to get back to the festival. Stay out of trouble.'

So eager was she to nod agreement that Libby nearly pulled a muscle in her neck. But of course she wasn't going to stay out of trouble. That wasn't what Dawn would have done in her situation and she was now, very firmly, channelling her inner Dawn. Her inner Dawn told her to get out of the car when it stopped on the only road in the village, thank Sal again, heave her rucksack onto her shoulder and march to the nearest place she could think of where she could find someone to help get her back through those gates and into Solstice.

Edna Kirk's shop.

The dusty Easter front window display had been dismantled, one forlorn cotton wool bunny tail left abandoned at the bottom, a half-hearted swipe of white doing a terrible job at obscuring the view into the shop. Only days before Edna Kirk had been eyeing Libby sternly from behind the counter, the shelves full, even if the produce had looked like it had originally been bought in during the Second World War.

When Libby pushed on the door, it did not budge.

She knocked on the glass and peered in. This had been her pathetic plan: a hope that Edna would be able to help, maybe drive her back to the festival, or ring Joe to come and get her.

No response.

Time was ticking, a hellish clock at her shoulder tick-tocking the minutes away since she had last seen Dawn. Minutes that had become hours in which Dawn could have got into all sorts of trouble and yet here she was, now stuck in this Village of the Damned. Anxiety choked her throat.

There was nothing else for it. She was going to have to walk all the way back to Solstice. In boots that had blistered her feet.

Caught up in her thoughts and reaching for her phone to check if it now worked as she was out of the festival, she stepped back, off the kerb and into the road, not even looking if anything was coming her way. A sudden loud beeping jolted her into awareness.

A van stopped a few feet away from her, decorated with flames coloured like the northern lights, a group of whirling skeletons having some kind of party in the glow, 'Savage Night' spelled out above them.

'Jesus! I could've run you over!' Joe jumped down from the vehicle, which had stopped only a foot or so away from where Libby stood in the middle of the road. 'What are you even doing out here?'

A new idea immediately fizzed into Libby's head like a sour sweet. 'Please tell me you're taking that van into the festival.'

Joe pretended to be Libby. 'Hi, Joe. Yes, I'm an idiot, I ran out into the bloody road and nearly got myself killed and now I don't even acknowledge the person who did not in fact crush my skull into the tarmac with his huge bloody van—'

'Sorry.' Libby took a breath, tried to remember how to behave like a normal person. 'Hi, Joe. I got kicked out of the festival but Dawn's still in there so I need to get back in and I could hide in your van I think—'

'You got—? What? Why'd they kick you out?'

'I don't know! Ma Blake herself just looked at me and then dragged me away.'

'You pissed off Ma Blake?'

'No! No, I didn't!' Libby took another breath because the last one clearly hadn't worked. 'I swear, I've done nothing wrong. I just want to find Dawn.' Behind Joe, Libby could see those skeletons dancing away on the back of the van. 'So, are you heading back in?'

'Well, yeah, I will be. Got to pick up our equipment but I'm stopping here for a bit to grab some boxes for my nan. You can wait a few minutes, right?'

No, no, no, no, no – no more minutes. Libby itched to be in the passenger seat but instead she watched Joe slam the van door shut and walk towards the shop, fiddling with a set of keys before finding the right one far too slowly. He was moving in treacle, not air, and of course the door stuck as he opened it because the whole universe was against her ever getting back to the festival.

The sunlight was a heavy weight pushing onto the top of Libby's head like one of those flower presses she'd had as a child, the ones where the screws tightened and the ceramic tiles jammed down harder and harder turning each petal to a dry sigh of itself.

'Nan! Nan – you in?' Joe shouldered the door and sent it screeching wide.

'You be careful with that door, my lad. This isn't our property now and I'm not paying for anything new before I leave.' Edna Kirk flapped aside a string curtain and shuffled into the shop in her furry slippers, strands of the curtain sticking to her hair and stretching out behind in a glittering octopus hug. 'Oh. She's back. What—?'

Libby rattled off the by-now well-learned answer to the question Edna hadn't even finished, 'Got kicked out of the festival. Not my fault. Need to get back in and find my friend.'

'Ah yes, the one who was with you. The mouthy one?'

Libby didn't have the energy to correct her and anyway, Dawn would have happily agreed to being mouthy because that just a meaner way of saying confident, and confidence was something that Dawn proudly claimed.

But suddenly her eyes stung. There was no sobbing, just a huge sense of being choked, that the room itself had become very small and her head had bloated to the size of those blimps she saw in films, huge and ready to pop.

'Do you need to sit down?' Joe was at her side, looking around for something to use as a seat and finally he kicked over a box for her, which she sank onto gratefully, blimp-sized head so huge it had to be supported by her hands. It was a lot. No wonder her head was a hot air balloon, it had had to take in the last few days in all of its mad sunburned chaos: smoke, people, smiles, music, warnings, stares, dark wood, midday glare and a grey headache-coloured absence where Dawn should have been.

There was the sound of shuffling and then two pink furry feet came into Libby's view of the floor. A hand clamped onto her shoulder, strong from years of shop work. 'Girl needs a cup of tea.' Edna's voice.

'I don't think we've got time—' Libby began, sitting up straight with effort and looking at Joe. 'I have a plan.'

He heaved a box into the back. 'Hit me.'

'You say you're picking up some of your equipment – get me through the gates in your van and then I sneak back in.'

'Umm . . . okay?' Joe's tone did not convey conviction.

'What?'

'Well, I thought that maybe your plan would have . . . a bit more detail to it?' He caught her expression. 'But it's probably sensible to keep things simple,' he quickly amended. 'Right! Let's get you in!'

This was going to work, Libby thought as she climbed into the front passenger seat, Edna leaning against the doorway of her shop. This was definitely going to work.

That was when, with impeccable timing, the van's engine gave a long, clanking, grating cough and then sputtered into silence, smoke coming from the bonnet.

Edna sniffed. 'Looks like you'll be having that cup of tea after all . . .'

Chapter 30

Time had never moved so slowly.

'Watching won't fix it faster,' Edna said, bringing in a tray with tea and sandwiches as Libby reluctantly let the net curtain drop. They were in Edna's flat above the shop and below them Joe was neck-deep in the van's engine.

An hour had passed. It was now three in the afternoon. Libby had already discarded the idea of simply walking back to the festival because that wouldn't get her in. For that she needed the damn van. Her hiding space.

The flat was in even more disarray than downstairs. Bubble wrap and newspaper lay scattered on any available chair, table or sideboard. Figurines, their little porcelain faces set in delicate smiles, had been half-packed and then abandoned so it looked as if they were stuck drowning in a plastic bubble sea. The kitchen drawers were all open and most of their contents had been upended onto the counters. Edna had swiped a load of wooden spoons and stainless-steel ladles out of the way to reach the besieged kettle.

'Sit, sit, sit.' Edna waved an imperious hand and Libby made for a chair. 'Not there. Gloria will have your eyes out.' There was a hiss from high on top of a grandfather clock and a baleful ball of black fur gazed at her, no movement except for the occasional twitch of a tail. It reminded Libby of the cat clock in the fortune teller's wagon, its tail flicking away the time as she had been told *'You don't fit'*. Maybe Ma Blake had sensed that straight away, that Libby's free ticket had been a mistake, bestowed upon someone far too boring and plain, and so out she had to go.

'You're selling up?' Libby asked.

'Sure am.'

'Someone wants to run the shop here?'

'Don't know. Don't care. Good luck to 'em.' Edna stirred the spoon in her tea rather more viciously than needed, the chinking sound a warning that Libby needed to change tack or she'd get thrown out before she could finish her drink.

Gloria took this opportunity to launch herself from her perch and land quietly on the arm of Libby's chair just as Edna handed her a mug. Hot liquid sloshed on her leg.

She had a feeling that Edna was waiting for her to start talking, standing there with a watchful gaze in her sequined loungewear, surrounded by a chaotic carpet of her own belongings.

'You gave me that missing poster.' Libby patted at the spilled tea with her hand.

Edna smiled a tiny bit, as if she were a teacher and Libby had finally given her an answer of which she could approve. 'I did.'

'What do you think happened to her – to Tess?'

'Well.' Edna perched on the arm of a chair and considered Libby. 'I don't think we'll ever find out now. But the Blakes were mixed up in it somehow, that I'm sure of.'

A small warm sensation on her leg made her glance down at Gloria's little pink tongue lapping up the spilled liquid from her knee. The cat paused, flicked an ear and continued.

'My friend, Dawn . . . before I got kicked out, she wandered off and I'm worried about her . . .'

'Ah, now then – your friend is fine. Probably sleeping it off somewhere.'

'Yeah but . . . some odd things happened – before . . . there was this note stuck to our tent telling us we should leave—'

'Wait – what?'

'A note. Dawn said it looked as if they'd been printed off. She thought it was—'

'Oh.' Edna sank into the seat from her perch on its arm, in a defeated, floppy way. 'I didn't think there were any of those left.'

Now it was Libby's turn to be confused, 'What?'

Edna rather sheepishly studied her mug whilst Gloria glared at Libby's leg as if more tea would magically appear on it through sheer force of will. 'That note you saw. That was me . . . well, us. Some people here at the village. We did all sorts of things over the years, you see, to try and . . . oh, I don't know . . . throw a spanner in the works, that kind of thing. We had those notes printed out and then got people we knew on the staff to leave them around the tents. To spook people, I guess, but it was a stupid idea, really. We had a lot of stupid ideas back then.'

A paw tapped Libby's leg. 'Oh,' she said.

'Yeah, sorry about that. Didn't think anyone was still doing it.'

'Well, they are.'

An awkward pause sidled into the conversation. Gloria batted Libby's leg once again and gave her knee a hopeful lick. The note was nothing, it was just as Dawn had said, a silly prank meant to scare people and Libby had been taken in, like the gullible little idiot she always was.

Edna fixed Libby with a stare. 'But whatever you do, when you go back, don't trust the Blakes. Make a fuss until you find your friend. Scream, yell, shout. Do whatever it takes. That place. It's a curse.'

Libby took her last swig of tea and offered the dregs to Gloria who gazed at the mug with imperial disdain and then turned her head away. Edna came closer and took Libby's chin in her hand, angling her face up so she could see it better, searching for something Libby could not work out.

'It's none of my business,' Edna finally said, letting go and retreating to her chair once more, brushing sheets of newspaper onto the floor from the table next to her. When she sat she picked at the sequins on her purple velour tracksuit before leaning forward with an urgency. 'Tess was a nice girl. You should know that. Kind. Fell in with a bad crowd. Her mother never looked out for her and she had it tough but she was a sweet girl, really. A silly, sweet girl.'

There was nothing to say to that because it wasn't the point, was it? It didn't matter how nice, how sweet, how kind Tess had been. Nice, sweet and kind don't stop bad things happening to a person. In fact, those things make a person a target because all of that good nature, it makes someone weak, makes them vulnerable. Libby had to be smarter than that – she had to go against every instinct of hers to cringe away, to do what Ma Blake told her and stay away, to be good, to be sweet, to be kind. Because none of that was going to get her back into the festival.

There was that silence again, the way Edna seemed to simply stop at points in the conversation and slump into a thinking pose before jumping back to life. She fiddled with a china figurine in a swirling ball gown, the feet and hands both badly chipped.

Shifting in her chair, Libby was suddenly tired of Edna and her dramatic pronouncements, her dusty ornaments and her baleful cat. She just wanted to get back into Solstice, find her infuriating, thoughtless friend who was probably asleep somewhere after failing to get Sanctum passes and then both of them could leave. She'd had enough of the Blake family, of the heat and the dust and bubbling sense of everything boiling over.

Four o'clock. Finally convinced that he could not fix it himself, Joe called out a car repair service. Edna made more tea.

Five o'clock. Now two men stood in front of the van, Joe and the repairman, both intermittently diving into the engine and standing with their hands on their hips, hoping inspiration would strike. Libby checked her phone, seeing that the texts she had tapped out to Dawn last night had now sent but there was no reply and no answer when she called her. Edna turned on the television and began watching *Murder, She Wrote*. Libby thought she might explode as Jessica Fletcher genteelly unmasked a murderer.

Six o'clock. Edna had fallen asleep. Libby made the decision to get a taxi back to the gate only to discover that no local taxis ran after five in the evening. She considered exploding again. The two men stood for a little bit longer with their hands on their hips until . . .

. . . seven o'clock. Success. An engine purring into life.

Chapter 31

Libby nearly leapt into the front cab, but Joe stopped her. 'Sorry about the wait.'

'Couldn't be helped,' Libby said, turning to climb in, biting back any words that were more impatient. After all, Joe was doing her a favour. 'Let's go.'

'Hang on. You'll have to change your clothes at least.'

Libby looked down at her shorts and T-shirt. It was a new top on this morning and she was fairly certain it didn't smell, though the stand-up sluicing and baby wipe washes she had resorted to over the last few days probably weren't up to the job. 'Why?'

'If you don't want to be spotted. There's a band tee in the back and some caps.'

Libby marvelled at how her day was going as she got changed without flashing her bra too much, back turned to Joe who sat resolutely facing the front in the cab seat, studying his windscreen as if it was a fascinating precious artefact. She had managed to lose a friend, had got thrown out of a festival, tried to climb a fence and now was half naked in the back of a man's van. Her new T-shirt had the words 'Savage Night' printed on it in a big gothic-style font. On one side of the van was a bench, covered roughly in some cushions, a crate of beer stuffed underneath it, next to another box of cleaning products and a few cloths. Someone liked to keep a high standard of hygiene. In one corner were Edna's boxes, leaving just enough empty space for the band's equipment.

'Why that name?' she asked as she pulled the material over her head.

'Hmm? No, honestly, it came with the van, like I said before.'

'No!'

'Yeah – we really can't afford a respray, so we stuck with the name. Might change it. Think it sounds like an aftershave now, if I'm honest . . .'

'I like it.' Libby clambered through into the cab from the back of the van, a cap in hand, glad of something to hide her sweaty, greasy hair. Blushing she added, 'I saw a bit of your set, y'know, despite . . . everything. You're good.'

'Yeah – thought I spotted you.' Joe's face brightened.

'It was great, how you played for that crowd, the calm of it, the melody.'

He nodded, his words eager. 'That was me, that was. I said we needed to chill it all out for that time of day, edge people softly into things. We had a bit of an argument about that.'

'Well, I think you called it just right.'

'Thanks.' He smiled at her and Libby liked the way that made her feel.

They journeyed companionably for a while before Libby spoke again. 'Are there checks – I mean, does the van get checked before it's allowed in?'

'Well, it did the first time, y'know those bomb detector things being swept under it and all that, but they know me now at the vehicle gate. It's a different entrance to the main one. It'll be okay.'

Soon enough they approached the sun and moon gate and Libby knew that next would come the deliveries and trucks entrance, situated, she guessed, a bit further down the road. She ducked as they drove past the steward who had laid a hand on her back and spoken in soothing tones. Anger flushed through her. She wouldn't be flicked away from the festival when she hadn't done a thing wrong, it wasn't fair, and she had to keep her focus on finding Dawn. A plan. That was what she needed. But all she could think was that Dawn had been so obsessed with getting a free pass to Sanctum and so heading there would be her best starting point.

'You probably think I'm over-reacting a bit. Dawn's a grown woman after all; she can look after herself—'

'No, not at all. You're looking out for your friend. I'd do the same. And it is weird they've chucked you out. You're hardly a troublemaker.'

No, she had never been one of those. Not with a mother like hers.

There was a pause and then Libby spoke quietly, not really sure why she needed to say this: 'My mother – she died a few weeks ago. At the end, though, her last words were . . . hard to hear . . .'

It was so sudden the way Libby was dragged back to that sickroom, the curtains half-drawn, sunlight only a thin strip on the worn carpet, the scent of rot, of effluence under the freshly laundered sheets, the air freshener plugged in at the wall pumping out bursts of a cloying artificial lily smell. The flowers used at funerals. Her mother's claw hand had dragged her down, pulled her close to feel the wheezing, foul breath on her cheek as a kind of fevered kiss but there was no such affection in what she had said, those last words barbed and ready to tear into skin, designed to dig in, to cling, to scar.

'You . . . were . . . my biggest mistake . . .' Another heave of the chest, another rattle of air. 'I never . . . really . . . wanted you . . .'

Her eye had latched on to Libby's, the white of it blurred mostly red, a demonic gaze almost, not her mother, Libby had told herself, not her mother. The cancer had finally eaten through to her brain. It had fizzed like acid through those parts that stored compassion and love so that what spoke to her from this bed was not the woman who had raised her. But Libby knew this to be a lie. The eye that swivelled to her, a hellish red, was her mother's: the gaze was clear.

'That was it,' Libby ended, not looking at Joe. 'She lay back and closed her eyes with this kind of happy smile on her face. Died about ten minutes later.'

'Oh, Libby, that's . . . I'm so sorry . . .'

Libby did not want to look at the pity on Joe's face because then she would have to see herself as he did – a woman whose own mother hadn't loved her. Most mothers loved their children, even if life was hard, even if the children did horrible, terrible things. What had Libby done wrong? How gross, how deeply disgusting was she, that her own mother had called her a mistake? She picked at the skin around the thumbnail until a bead of bright blood welled up.

'See, what I'm trying to explain is that I've got to get my head around the fact that the last thing my mother needed me to know is that she never wanted me . . . but Dawn? Dawn's *always* chosen me. Ever since school, our first day in the comp, when she came bounding across the playground to introduce herself, ever since then she has chosen me, no matter that I'm awkward and quiet and I don't wear fashionable clothes or care about selfies. *She has always wanted me.* I know, without any doubt, that if she were here, if she were me right now – she would go back and find me, no matter if it was an overreaction, no matter if it seemed silly or whatever. She would go back. I have to do the same for her.'

Then Joe's hand was on hers, stopping her from tearing at the skin on her thumb anymore, the warmth of his palm, his rough guitar-playing fingers. He didn't say anything else but his touch told her that he understood. The two of them simply sat as he drove and Libby's vision blurred with hot tears.

Ahead of them a basic metal gate opened, no brass moons and suns to smile upon them here, a wave from a guard, a crossing of the threshold and it was disturbingly easy to return, to be back inside the festival once more.

As Joe and the rest of the band bustled equipment into the van, Libby took her chance to slope away, deliberately not saying goodbye to Joe, not needing him to feel he had to come with her in whatever it was she was about to do.

'Wait!' The word was a strangled whisper. Someone touched her elbow and she turned to see Joe at her side. 'I can't let you go off on your own. I'll help.'

'Joe. It's okay – really. Two of us sneaking round is going to look suspicious anyway, especially if one of us is the handsome lead singer in the festival's hot new band . . .'

There was a beat as Joe smiled. 'You think I'm hot?'

Libby blushed. 'No, no, no,' she hastily corrected herself. 'That's not what I said. I said I think *your band* is hot.'

Joe kept on smiling anyway. 'But I'm a part of that band so . . .'

'Hey!' a voice shouted over to them brusque with authority. 'Is that your van? You're going to have to move it, mate . . .'

She could wait for Joe to come back. It probably wouldn't take him long to move the van and then together they could find Dawn.

'Just give me a sec,' he had said as he rushed off.

But this was her responsibility. She didn't want to think of anyone else, she didn't want their opinions on what she should do, when, where and how. And she didn't want to have to wait even a second longer than she had to.

Looking around, she tried to get her bearings. She was next to the lost property tent, and she realised that she was in the staff backstage area behind the Moon Stage, the one they had visited when Sal had taken them on their VIP tour. Pulling her cap down to shade her face from any inquiring glances, Libby ignored any warning voice in her head and focused on how she was to get to Sanctum and find her friend.

But that focus splintered like old wood when she saw what was in the box in the doorway of the lost property tent.

There on top of a pile of bracelets, odd shoes, plastic cups, a washbag, a battered teddy bear and a book with crumpled edges was a phone, face down, its case instantly recognisable: rhinestones and a decal of Dolly Parton, high hair and wide lip-sticked smile.

Dawn's.

Chapter 32

Dolly Parton smiled at her as something cold and slithery coiled in Libby's stomach.

Dawn's phone was not a piece of technology, it was an extension of Dawn's hand. It was the way she saw the world, the way she remembered it, how she functioned as a person. It was never out of her grip and, when it had to be put down, it often went into its own little sling that she wore like a bag, no other belongings needed because the phone was everything – her wallet, her camera, her life neatly stored in one piece of rectangular plastic.

Seeing it amongst other people's lost junk made Libby feel as if the world around her was tunnelling in too close to breathe. She took a few quick glances to either side and then the phone was in her grip and she was walking away from the tent with purpose, because that was the trick, wasn't it? If you wanted to get away with something, you had to do it with confidence so no one would bother to stop you.

Hardly even taking in her surroundings, Libby headed to a spot where she could let her legs crumple from under her and sit on the ground, Dawn's phone in her grasp. The grass was hot and scratchy under her bare legs and Libby was shocked to see the time on the phone screen telling her it was now evening.

The day had rushed past her: she had got up around noon and been kicked out before most people had even considered lunch, then she had been stuck in Edna's shop for far too long. Despite the late hour, the heat was a smothering embrace that made her T-shirt stick to her back in damp patches.

Dawn would never lose her phone.

It didn't matter how wasted she got, it didn't matter if she was drunk or high, if she had been really excited or in a massive rush – Dawn never let that phone out of her sight, Libby knew. The rhinestones glittered in the sunlight, a little flash of Morse code, a warning.

Getting into it was easy. Libby knew that the fingerprint sensor had been acting up over the last month and so Dawn had gone back to a code, a swoosh of a pattern that Libby had seen enough times to be able to copy.

She began to search for clues, though she knew there wouldn't be any – the festival deliberately didn't have a mobile signal so it would be fruitless to search through Dawn's call log or try and open her social media apps.

She was about to give up when she opened her gallery of photos and videos, not really expecting to see anything new, just a bunch of the silly, goofy poses they had struck at various times in the festival, Dawn's face daubed in glitter, Libby's sweaty fringe stuck to her forehead, both of them laughing even when they were trying to be serious, all of them familiar to her.

But there was one last video that Libby did not remember.

It lasted only three seconds. Dark, blurred, Libby had to stare at it for a while for it to make sense. Dawn herself did not feature but she could see a leg sticking out, the yellow paint on her toenails, the VIP tour flip-flops still on her feet and the tie-dye edge of her minidress just making the shot. It seemed as if Dawn had been in a room somewhere, a dim, gloomy place: bare floor, bare walls, an open door looking out on nothing but night sky. There was something about the video though, about the rushed way it had been taken, the daze to it, the muffled gasp that she could hear come from Dawn that made the cold finger of unease trace a warning across the back of Libby's neck.

She checked the date stamp: 01.43 a.m. that morning. As Libby herself had been awake and worried in their tent, Dawn had been . . . wherever that was, that murky, austere place. She played the thing over and over again, searching for something, anything to tell her where her friend had been. No helpful clue to that at all, but instead she found something else.

A shape.

A shadow.

She played the video again. There, Dawn's leg twitched. There, the half gasp in her breathing. There the slightly less dark slice of doorway opening out only to a starred sky and the shadows of a field. And there in that doorway, the jerk of a figure just about to enter, tall and broad-shouldered, one leg forever stuck in a pose that looked as if he was about to stride in . . .

. . . and what had happened then?

Libby really needed to know.

She stood and her heart beat so fast that for a second her vision almost blacked out, the dark spots swimming over her view like poisonous jellyfish. She steadied herself and took a breath of warm, stale air that seemed to dry out her throat. The sun was low in a sky that was an open oven mouth, and the air smelled of wood smoke but also there was the faint scent of scorched grass, of metal overheating, of meat about to turn, of drains that hadn't been bleached. There was a crisp packet crumpled at the base of a nearby bin and Libby could see more litter, bits of paper, snack wrappers left abandoned too, an air of carelessness in this staff area. The noise of the crowd was beginning to coalesce into something now beyond beast-like. The festival-creature had shrugged off any pretence at animal form and had become mythic, a roar made up of many hoarse screams from people left out too long in a sun that had made them arid and mad.

Libby knew what to do. It was too hot to overthink; she was afraid that if she did her brain would fizz and steam whilst much-needed pistons snapped and melted. She needed to leave, get to a place where she had signal on her phone and call the police, show them the video, where she could crank into action the machinery of authority, which could roll out and over this festival, flattening it all until she found her friend.

Beside her a man cleared his throat and then said, in a familiar and confident voice, 'Hello, Libby Corrigan.'

Abel Blake. Libby spun around, still holding Dawn's phone. She desperately tried to come up with a reason why she was here, snooping around where she had no right to be and not chucked out on the road like Ma Blake had wanted.

She pressed her lips together. Living with her own mother had taught her that sometimes, it was best not to say anything at all.

The sun at his back made his face a shadow. 'What are you doing here?' His tone was smooth, no slicing edge of anger or irritation.

Libby decided to fight question with question. 'Where's Dawn?'

'Dawn—?'

But Libby found she couldn't stop now she had started. 'She disappeared last night and hasn't come back and then your mother threw me out, out of the actual damn festival for no good reason, and I think I'm going to ring the police pretty soon—'

'Wait, wait, wait, wait . . .' Abel took a few careful steps towards her, arms outstretched. 'My mother – Ma – threw you out?'

'Yes!'

'Well, I don't know anything about that and I can only apologise.' Uncharacteristically, Abel lost the confident gloss to his tone. 'Ma – she's not a well woman anymore. In fact, she's quite ill and the medication, it's pretty strong . . .'

Libby thought back to the woman who had gripped her arm and hauled her through the festival, hair wild, eyes wilder, a fevered intensity to every word spoken. Yes, she could believe that Ma Blake was ill . . . but it didn't mean she trusted Abel.

'Where's Dawn?'

'Ah, now – that's something I can help with. In fact, we've been looking for you, but your tracker told us you were in what appeared to be a patch of woodland just outside the gate and, of course, I didn't know that Ma had thrown you out. Again, sorry about that. But Dawn? Dawn's fine, she's safe. This has all been a massive misunderstanding.'

'Where is she?' Libby was so sick of those words.

'At Sanctum.'

Libby frowned. 'Why there?'

'Your friend got a bit . . . overexcited, shall we say? She was caught trying to sneak into Sanctum. She'd got herself in quite a state, and then she fell into the river trying to hop onto the stepping stones.' That certainly sounded like Dawn, Libby had to admit. 'She was a bit of a mess so we gave her somewhere to sleep it off and I think she lost her phone in the whole chaos. Our team did try to find you, but it seemed Ma got there first.'

This all sounded plausible, Libby had to admit, but, despite that, she couldn't throw off that chill finger of unease at seeing the last video on Dawn's camera roll. There could be an innocent explanation. The picture could merely be showing someone moving to help her, to get her out of whatever mess she had got herself in. However, Sal hadn't mentioned any of this when she escorted her out and, it seemed to Libby, Sal was the kind of person who knew everything that went on at the festival.

When Abel came closer again, his face was open and sincere, eyes kindly watching her, his hands palm out as if she might spook and canter away. She wasn't sure that she wouldn't.

'Take me to her,' she said and heard the wobble in her voice though she crossed her arms and planted her legs firmly, trying to at least look as if she had more confidence than she felt.

His next words knocked that out of her, as if she were a soggy cardboard box that had been stamped flat.

'There's another reason we were trying to find you though, Libby. Well, *I* was trying to find you. Not because of Dawn. I think you were given those free tickets for a reason. You see, you're not Libby Corrigan.'

'Wha—?'

'You're a Blake. You're Libby Blake.'

Chapter 33

Ma Blake, Twenty Years Ago

Fat drops of morning rain fell on Ma as she stood under the oak tree in the middle of the stone circle.

This was the final day before the festival.

Silas had not returned.

She had not slept. For a while she had lain there as her brain had whirred over everything like a cricket chirping incessantly in a field, but then, in the early hours, she had quietly got up, so as not to wake Abel, and tiptoed down to the kitchen, avoiding the creaky floorboards she knew so well. Once there she had made herself a cup of tea and read her book on local folklore. Outside the wind had thrown itself against the windows as the sky lightened to an angry morning.

She already knew the stories, however. Many years ago, she had told them to Abel, his watchful face taking in the tales, his frown as he asked questions, whilst Silas played with trucks and sang songs to himself, ignoring them both. But, even though Silas would not agree, the tales were important. Across the country, these stones and stone circles had all kinds of meaning: they were gateways to the otherworld, cursed places that could turn a person mad, blessed places that could heal.

An offering.

Mud squelched under Ma's foot. Once the sun had risen she had walked straight here, to the circle with the oak tree in its middle. The rain had lessened but it wasn't the promise of a break in the weather; this was merely a breath being taken before the next onslaught. Ma stopped, not quite sure what to do next. She wanted to ask, to beg even, or plead, but she wasn't a woman used to doing those things.

She was past feeling foolish.

The rain pummelled the hood of her coat. One day left. From where she stood she could see the bedraggled stage, its backdrop leaning slightly due to the wind, the sun-painted curtain loose of its moorings on one side and flapping wildly. A few volunteers tried to fix it. People would still come in the rain; this was Wales, after all: if people stayed inside every time there was a downpour the entire country would be a nation of shut-ins, but there would be fewer of them to spend their money on-site. The magic, and the profit, would disappear.

A son gone.

A festival ruined.

Their land taken from them by debt collectors.

Dropping to her knees, Ma did not know what to do next. Perhaps she should have brought an offering for the Grey Sisters, those pitted stones around her. Food, jewellery, the lighting of a candle, these were the kinds of things deities supposedly liked.

A whispering came to her on the wind. Quiet voices, mumbling things that she would never be able to properly hear, the words dipping away from her like flotsam on a sea. That sound burrowed its way into her head, gave her brain a rhythm it had not had before, so much so she felt herself swaying in time to it.

Shifting her position as water dripped from the end of her coat, Ma felt a sharp slicing pain in her knee and wobbled forward, one hand bracing herself against the muddy earth. Sitting back in shock, she saw a rip in her jeans and through that the deep jewel red of blood against the muck. Where she had been kneeling a twisted shard of metal lay half buried in the ground, some bit of old farm equipment left out here by mistake. Her first thought was one tinged with annoyance – she would have to go and get a tetanus shot because the metal looked rusted.

Her second thought was . . . stranger.

Offerings to Old Ones were maybe food or gold or lit candles but her mother had told her stories where those gifts were much darker. Blood. Ma touched the cut on her knee and contemplated the smear of red on her finger. Sacrifice. Pain. The words almost said themselves in her head:

Grey Sisters, I ask you. Make the festival a success.

Ripping the hole in her jeans she daubed the blood onto her hands and pressed her palms into the earth, staying like that for a few beats. What would anyone think, looking over at her from across the bridge – this madwoman muttering to herself and kneeling in the mud in the middle of the stones? That self-consciousness did not last, however, It felt oddly comforting to be almost prostrate, bleeding and desperate, in a place where perhaps others had pleaded and begged through the centuries, asking for help, hope, salvation from a ring of stones steeped in stories. Belief, the kind as strong as cobwebs, stickily hard to erase.

The whispering swirled around her.

In the end she stood.

Waited.

She wasn't expecting it straight away; in fact, if she was honest with herself, she wasn't expecting it at all but as she stared at the rain she thought it looked a little lighter, the hard, fat raindrops of before now more of a drizzle.

Coincidence, of course.

But it wasn't just the sky brightening above her as she limped back to the front porch of the farmhouse. Her mood lightened too.

A son could reappear.

The weather could lift.

Their land could be saved.

That feeling soon fled when she saw who it was on the path that led from the road, walking towards the house. Silas. It would have been a blessing, him returning home so soon, not dazed on drugs in a squat somewhere. But he was not alone. There at his side, him supporting her most of the way was Tess, head bowed, feet dragging against the ground. Ma watched them walk closer, blood from her knee running down her shin, and she studied Tess properly, realising that things were even worse than she had imagined.

Much, much worse.

Chapter 34

Ma Blake, Twenty Years Ago

The girl had no more energy left to scream. The only sound that came from her was a harsh rasping gasp, her face slick with sweat, hair matted and damp.

Ma had never done this before.

She had lost track of the hours since she had run to meet Silas walking their path, half holding, half dragging Tess with him. A woman in the early stages of labour.

Ma gazed at the knife. She might have to use it soon.

Morning had become afternoon and then darkened into evening. From the chair by the window, Silas clutched his head in his hands. He had sat that way the entire time, only raising his head to look at her with a helpless expression she knew so well from childhood, that beseeching of his mother to fix all of this, to make it right.

She wasn't sure she could.

Tess made an awful, ragged grunting sound, her eyes not focused on anything, her colour too pale, her breathing too laboured.

'You have to keep pushing, Tess,' Ma said, trying to keep her voice calm. 'If you don't push, your baby will die.'

Tess tried to sit up, her arm reaching for Ma who moved to her side, brushing the hair from her feverish forehead. The girl spoke in jagged shards of sentences: 'This baby . . . I have to . . . I'm scared of . . .'

'No, no, no – nothing to be scared of . . . your baby will be fine, just fine. Both of you will.' These were things that Ma was expected to say, so she said them.

'No!' Tess's eyes blazed for a moment. 'I can't be here, I can't be . . . here . . .'

Her words were cut off by the fresh wave of pain that made her throw her head back against the pillow.

'Do something.' Silas stood, clutched his hands into useless fists and took a step forward. 'Ma, for God's sake! Do something!'

The fact Silas was the father had been a shock. It explained why the girl had been so adamant she speak to him that day when she had knocked on the farmhouse door. Due to Ma's own efforts to keep the two of them apart, though, it seemed Silas had been in the dark as much as her. No wonder the girl felt as if she couldn't be here; there had been too many secrets, too much bad feeling.

There was also too much blood.

'Why haven't you taken her to hospital?' Ma had asked as she had run to them on the path.

'Tree's down by the farmhouse gate. Can't get a car through.'

'How did you get here then?'

'No, you don't understand. She was here, on our land – I found her in our old bothy.'

When Ma had grabbed Tess's hands they had been so cold they hadn't felt like human flesh. All that time, those weeks she had been missing, she had been in their bothy, that tumble-down shelter on the outskirts of their farm, living God knows how, probably dying there if Silas hadn't found her.

'Ma – do something!' Back in the bedroom Silas came over to the bed, dark shadows under his eyes, his hair a tangled mess.

She had done this kind of thing before, of course, for many of the animals on the farm over the years – the tugging, the pulling, the rush of blood and fluid, the welcome mewl of life. But never a person. Never to save her grandchild.

'Push!' she yelled at Tess, but Tess was now almost beyond hearing.

When Ma brought her hand away, it was red with blood. The room smelled heavy, like an animal's lair, and the musk of it made her dizzy for a second. Blood. Something was wrong. She pressed on Tess's stomach, trying to get the baby to move but she knew she did not have much time left. The baby would die in the womb and Tess along with her, probably.

'Push!'

There was the crown of the baby's head, Ma could see it but Tess didn't have much left to give and the child seemed to be stuck.

The knife waited.

She had learned with these things that she should do them quickly before she could think too much about it. The knife in her hand, the quick slicing movement, cutting the flesh of the perineum so the baby had more room and in that moment she thought she heard once again the Grey Sisters whispering. They were with her, five hands on her hand, their old magic keeping the baby safe, her kin.

Slithering, a gush of blood, and one last guttural yell from Tess as she pushed the child out of her and into Ma's hands.

No cry.

Silas rushed to Tess, hardly awake on a sweat-drenched pillow. The baby was a strange bluish colour and still, so, so still. Ma rubbed at its little limbs and swiped the mucus from out of its mouth and nose.

Not it. *Her*. A girl. A still, pale doll of a baby. Blake flesh and blood.

That whispering swirled around her and Ma could see the stones from where she stood, through the bedroom window, the five of them fingers breaking through earth and reaching out to her under a dark night sky. Not knowing if it would work, she breathed into the baby's tiny, perfect nose and mouth and pressed with fingertips on her chest. All the while, as her deft hands worked, she listened to that whispering and she offered up her own prayer to the Grey Sisters:

Let the baby live.

A hitching hiccup, a flailing of arms and the child took its first breath.

Ma slumped to the floor with her granddaughter in her arms and she hushed her as the baby took great gulping ragged yells of fury at this new world into which she had been thrust.

Elizabeth. That was her name, the name of Ma's own mother. A good, strong name, for a strong woman.

'Hello, Elizabeth,' Ma said softly as she rocked her and wrapped her in her cardigan. And, at hearing her name the baby quietened, her eyes no longer squinting in rage but limpid and huge, gazing into Ma's own. 'Hello, little one.'

Chapter 35

Backstage at the festival, Abel stood in a dying summer sunlight as the evening shadows began to stretch and Libby got to grips with what he had just told her.

'I'm a . . . what?'

'A Blake.'

There were prank shows, Libby knew. She hadn't ever watched them because her mother had liked a strict set of programmes each evening and the television had never been allowed on in the day because too much staring at a screen caused wrinkles. But Libby knew that the makers of these shows went to elaborate lengths to create bizarre situations in order to trick their hapless victims. She opened her mouth to say something, anything, and closed it again. This had to be one of those shows. Dawn disappearing and her being chucked out of the festival – there must be a secret control centre somewhere and a presenter waiting to jump out and tell her this was all a joke.

Ta-dah!

She waited. There was a distinct lack of 'ta-dah'!

'Look. I know you must be confused and you're going to have a lot of questions. I didn't mean to spring this on you, but well—'

'Silas Blake is my father.' This was not a question, this was

Libby holding that fact to the light, shaking it out for size and finding it moth-ridden and full of holes. Abel had told her the basic facts as he knew them.

'Your mother, I mean Tess, your real mother – she gave birth to you here at the farm. This land is a part of you. But then she disappeared with you the next day and I never knew what happened. I don't know all the details about how you ended up in your new life. I don't know how much Silas was a part of it all, but I'll find out . . . He's a complicated man . . .'

Complicated. Like a tough jigsaw puzzle with pieces missing, where you try to create order but find only gaps that cannot be filled. Silas had told Abel everything, only a day ago, and Abel explained it to her. It had been Silas who had made sure she was picked that night at the club for those free tickets. He had been monitoring her and knew Dawn was her friend, so it was easy enough for him to be put in charge of sending out the free festival tickets for certain businesses. Dawn had already registered for the Solstice newsletter, so he only had to make sure Dawn's email was one of the ones that got the notification of an invite to the opening of a new club.

He then must have been there that night to make sure Libby's hand got the correct stamp to win. It seemed Silas had taken all that trouble to track her down, had even now confessed it all to Abel, but was unwilling to face her for some reason. Could that reason be whatever happened to Tess?

'Tess Sanderson is my mother. The woman from the missing poster?'

Abel, backlit by the late evening sun, was a biblical saint – the kind who appeared suddenly in a story about ordinary people and then violently upended their lives with a dire proclamation. 'Look, it's not my place to try and explain it all to you because it's not really my story to tell. I think Silas . . . well, I think he's lost his nerve to talk to you himself despite getting you here. Tess had problems of her own and the two of them together, her and

172

Silas, they were just . . . an unhealthy combination, you know? They brought each other down. He's not a bad guy, my brother and he'd been trying to make a go of a clean life: helping me with the festival, putting the hours in, staying away from temptation and then suddenly, one night, I came back from the fields and she was in our spare bedroom giving birth. Silas was a wreck. Ma was nearly out of her mind. I remember you though. Your tiny little red face, your angry cries . . . and then the next morning you and your mother were gone. Silas was frantic. I'd never seen him that way before, nor since. He swore he had no idea where Tess was and I did try but . . . it's hard to find a person who doesn't want to be found . . .'

Or if *someone else* doesn't want them found, Libby thought.

'This can't be . . . I don't believe it . . .'

'I know this is hard and I've rather sprung it on you—'

'There's no evidence for any of this. I should just . . . what? Believe everything you say?'

'I know, I know – it's all so . . . I don't know how to explain . . .'

A seat. That was what Libby needed. A comfortable seat and a cup of tea and she needed some cool, clear time to deal with this . . . this mess of rats that had been dumped on her lap and she had been tasked to untangle their tails. One wrong move and sharp teeth would sink into her flesh.

'Libby?'

She snapped back to reality. Despite the heat and the grimy film of sweat on her skin, there was now a cold core deep in her stomach that made her want to crouch over. It was too much to take in and such a lot had already happened, Dawn disappearing, her being thrown out of the festival and she felt like she had lost control, those rats in her lap writhing horribly . . .

She took a breath.

No. She couldn't let shock take over.

Perhaps there was one bit of evidence. Libby remembered a hidden photo fluttering to the floor from behind a painting as she had cleared out her mother's belongings from the flat. Two windswept women in their twenties, one of them her mother. The other? Hair over her face, shy smile – well, it could very well have been Ma Blake.

Abel moved closer so that when he ran a hand through his blond hair the strands of grey glinted at the temples. His eyes looked as if he had rubbed at them many times, sore and blood-shot. 'Ann Corrigan went to school with Ma and the two kept in touch in the years afterwards. Because of Ma's . . . illness . . . I've got access to her bank accounts and what none of us knew is that every month since the festival began she has sent a sizeable sum of money to Ann, and I mean – I can't help but think that was for you. I wish she'd told me. God I wish they both had. I don't know all the facts. I'm catching up here so I don't know if Silas has always known where you were, or how Ma knew, or why he got you those free tickets. I would hope he's trying to reach out in his own way.'

Reach out. Libby hated that phrase – 'I'd like to reach out' – because it was so vague. Someone could reach for you but it didn't mean the reaching was going to come to any good: they could just as well be reaching for your neck to throttle you.

Abel cleared his throat. 'But I do want to say this. You're a part of the Blake family now and that means something to me at least. I don't have children and I'm not getting any younger. If you want, you have a future here with us, with me at least, with the festival. You're our blood.'

Suddenly she saw that sickroom and her mother's final moments in a new light, a flicking of an optometrist's lens so that the whole thing came into sharp focus. Her mother's last words saying that she had regretted having her were perhaps nothing to do with Libby herself. Ann had been paid to take care of her and motherly love can't simply be bought.

There was a headache building above Libby's browbone and she was sticky, her mouth dry, her mind a broken mirror flashing shards of sharp-edged information at her. Silas her father. Ma her grandmother. Abel her uncle, holding the festival out to her, the whole fiery sun in the palm of his hand. In the space of a conversation she had gone from having no relations left to being part of the most famous family in the country. She was at the top of the biggest funfair ride she could imagine, the kind that was about to send her into a screaming plummet.

'You don't even know me.'

'I'd like to change that. And, in time, I'd like you to see that you have kin here, and that there's all of this waiting for you.' He waved a hand behind him, meant to encompass the fields, and trees, the Wyrd Wood, the food trucks and people, Sun and Moon Stages, tents and circus performers, stuffy toilets and people singing along to songs at the top of their voices, sweaty, glittered and sun-drunk.

Libby let that thought shine in her mind. Being a Blake, apprentice to golden boy Abel, learning the ropes each summer until she could take her place, the new ringmaster of this whole show, so different from her previous quiet life and her days shelving well-handled books in the library. A family who wanted her, who did not immediately pick out her flaws like cheap thread as her own mother had done, wishing to see her unravel, but who wanted to help her, to teach her. The kind of family she had never had, and never imagined she would. It was a thought she could swing into like a trapeze artist but when she plunged forward the hand that stretched to catch her was Dawn's; it was always Dawn's.

'What are you thinking?' Abel reached as if to take her elbow but then changed his mind, his arm frozen oddly mid-gesture.

Whether or not she was really a Blake and what she wanted to do with such information, well, those tangled rats in her lap would have to screech for a while longer because there was something more important than all of that. There was Dawn.

'I'm thinking that I have a friend I need to see. And I'm thinking it's time you took me to Sanctum, or wherever she is, so I can find her.'

Chapter 36

Beyond Libby was the river.

The sun finally gave up for the day and a gauzy twilight began to rise from the horizon in a purple smudge. The heat remained a tight piece of cling film tucked across the fields and the feeling of a cool breeze was now only a dream. Even standing still was a heavy-limbed effort.

Abel had already gone across, the stepping stones rising for him as if he even commanded nature itself. Libby stared at the clear water rushing past, intent on its own course, little flurries of white as river met the rock.

She paused.

Across the water was the farmhouse, its white limewash and dark slate roof, light spilling from the kitchen window and onto the porch where they'd had brunch with Dawn and Silas in his sunglasses, hiding his eyes as he watched the daughter he had never wanted to know until now. Maybe. Shielded by bamboo screens in preparation for Sanctum, Libby knew there were the stones, the Grey Sisters in their eternal circle, the oak tree in their centre. She could hear a light kind of music coming from them, mixing in with the drumbeat starting up in the Wyrd Wood beyond, the two tunes sinuously wrapping themselves around each other, making something new and disorientating.

Abel waited, standing on the riverbank. Still Libby did not move, did not step onto the first stone. He had told her that Dawn waited at Sanctum, having now recovered from her misadventures the night before, the river water dry on her clothes, the headache from her debaucheries already dulling, eager to see Libby, to apologise for causing such a fuss. There was no reason to not trust him. He was Abel Blake, a public figure, shining son of Solstice.

If he was to be believed, he was her uncle.

Yet she remained on the opposite bank. She was a computer in need of a hard reset after all she had been told, a system update was waiting and it needed a restart to get it all up and running, but there was no time for that because Dawn was waiting for her, her impetuous, reckless best friend. She wished Joe was with her. Someone to hear the story too, someone to stare at incredulously and shrug as if to say: 'Hey, weird things happen. You're Libby Blake and Dawn is fine.' Someone to slip a hand into hers as she crossed the stones, to catch her if she slipped.

One tiny hop-jump and she was on the first one. It was flat and smooth, almost impossible to fall from but for a heart-thumping second she imagined Abel's fingers flicking at the remote control in his pocket, for the stones to drop away from her and for her to plunge into the water. It looked deep and swift, though she could probably swim it if she had to.

Another few hop-jumps and she was in the middle of the river.

She was a Blake. Dawn was fine.

She wished she had a hand to hold.

Abel did not move but, as still as a hunting heron, he watched her skip across the final few stones to reach the other side.

'Welcome to Sanctum,' he said as the stones sank like mysterious water creatures going back to their lair.

Libby was acutely aware that if she wanted to leave, she would have to ask someone to raise them again, or swim, or head out for the other path that led around the farmhouse to the road. It didn't feel like she was trapped – no, it didn't feel like that at all – but even so, she cast a look behind her as she followed Abel towards the stones.

They rounded the screens set up to prevent prying eyes from across the river seeing Sanctum and a glowing archway greeted them, a sister to the one at Wyrd Wood, made of intertwined twigs and branches upon which hung big fat gold bulbs like bubbles.

Other figures dressed in robes detached themselves from the gathering shadows and rushed towards them, material flapping at their ankles as if they were tattered demons.

'Excuse me a moment. I have to look the part.' Abel stepped away from her and the figures surrounded him. In the glow of the archway bulbs, Libby could see them smiling, offering up different masks and cloaks and unbuttoning his white shirt, the courtiers to their king. Each bit of material was a shimmering gold that almost rippled in the light, a mix of silks and jacquards, embroidery and velvet.

A few minutes later, not Abel but a figure from myth stepped out from the middle of the group. Gone was the linen shirt and instead a heavy cloak had been fastened around his bare shoulders and on his head a golden helmet that arched around his eyes, the top of it spiking out into sunrays, each one tipped knife-sharp. He looked like the kind of leader who dressed for a battle in which he would never fight but watch from a safe hill somewhere.

He opened his arms wide so the cloak hung in all of its glory. 'It's ridiculous, isn't it? But it's what the punters want. Bit of theatre.'

The figures swarmed Libby like moths, and she could feel fingers plucking at her band T-shirt, fastening something onto her wrists, pulling at her hair.

'Hey!'

'If you want to enter Sanctum, you have to be properly dressed. Those are the rules.'

And, though she protested, the moth people butted and nudged her towards a barn at the one side of the farmhouse with plain slatted walls and a rickety double door left ajar. Inside there were a few safety lamps dotted around and amongst the old farm machinery and tools hung on the walls there had been an attempt to soften the place into a suitable dressing room for the staff running Sanctum that evening. Velvet throws had been draped over hay bales and a few tall mirrors were stood at intervals. There were even one or two battered old dressing tables set up with stools, a range of brushes, pots and hair straighteners scattered on top.

The moth people in their fluttery robes were all wearing masks decorated in golden swirls and were either deeply in character or deeply rude, Libby couldn't work out which. They answered none of her questions or entreaties to hurry and so it was simply easier to give herself up to them.

Behind a screen embroidered with huge peacocks, their wings outstretched in a fan of lush blues and greens, Libby took off her cotton T-shirt and shorts and over her head went such a cool silk robe that the shock of the chill brought out goose bumps on Libby's skin. Somehow the material did not warm with her body heat and each movement brought slithery wintry strokes to her arms and legs.

She refused to change her hiking boots.

When she came out from behind the screen something was placed on her head and she touched it, tracing her fingers over a small tiara made of the same spiked sunrays as Abel's mask but on a more delicate scale. Then she was plonked onto one of the stools and once again she tried to tell them that she was in a rush, tried to bat away the brushes and pencils coming for her face, but the moths did not give up. Libby sighed and closed her eyes. Feathery brushing touched her cheeks and eyelids. There was the warm breath on her skin of the person in the mask as they came close to view their work, to smudge something away, sharpen something else. Then she was led to a mirror.

A glimmering person stared back at her. Otherworldly in gilt robes, a crown on her head, gold swiped across her eyelids and temples in one mask-like band. *Absolutely ridiculous*, her mother's voice told her. *Absolutely beautiful*, a smaller voice offered instead.

The double doors opened and Abel stood in the middle, the soft glow of candles and fairy lights making him a dark-cloaked silhouette.

'Everyone done?' he asked. 'We ready?'

Chapter 37

Of course, no self-respecting Sun King would be without a staff. Abel's was a huge carved chunk of wood. On it were swirls, patterns and creatures that Libby couldn't make out in the rapidly dimming light, topped with a bright golden disc that spun in its holder, happy sun on one side, pensive moon on the other.

Abel strode through the archway, thumping this staff on the ground, his cloak billowing, and Libby lifted her robe to stop it tangling up at her feet as she hurried after him.

In front of them was a scene straight out of a fairy tale. The light had faded even more as Libby had been dressing and the time was now nearly ten o'clock in the evening. The Grey Sisters were bathed in a glimmering light, candles placed in front and around them as people milled about, dressed in the same strange way as Libby and Abel – filagree masks, capes and dresses made out of gold net, satin and silk, their costumes turning them into actors in a scene, not festivalgoers anymore and certainly not the sweaty, unkempt people Libby had wandered amongst over the last few days in the field across the river. Here there was a sense of calm, and of space. No crowds elbowing each other, no feeling of being crammed in: the people here had been hand-picked, the invitation a privilege.

But it was the oak tree that made Libby stand and stare, the shining fulcrum upon which the whole of Sanctum whirled. Around its trunk fairy lights were wrapped so tight it looked as if the tree had risen on a pure magic beam from the earth and each branch had more of those gold bulbs hanging from it, but these weren't simply lights. Libby could see people reaching up to unhook them from the boughs, lifting them to their mouths to drink.

'Stand with me. You're kin.' Abel gripped Libby's arm as she went to move past him, into the crowd to begin searching out Dawn. Then he clapped his hands together once, loud and assured, before raising his voice. 'Midsummer's Eve. The shortest night of the year. A time when the realm of night and its shadows are pushed back. But here at Sanctum it is also a time for rebirth, for renewal. Those of us who work on the festival ask humbly of our gods and goddesses . . . or our witches turned to stone . . . that we may have another successful year, that this land continues to hold and nurture us. But it is not just about the festival. No, we are at the midpoint of the growing season and we, all of us, are little plants growing. We have much to do, to become the people we should be. So here, amongst the stones, under the mighty oak tree, is where you shed your old perceptions of yourself – tonight! Cast off like snakeskin who you think you should be, whichever box society has shoved you into, cast it off and rise with me into the glorious dazzling possibility of *you*, the one that has been deep within you all along, the one waiting to bask in the sun.'

Libby couldn't help but be caught up in the moment, even as a cooler voice in her head sighed at the clichéd ideas. The shimmering lights, the ancient stones, the man next to her in his robes and helmet and staff with his booming, confident voice . . . the whole thing could have risen like smoke from the mists of time, all of them trapped now within the past and this magic circle. She was a part of it too, if Abel was to be believed. She was a Blake. One day she might be running this very festival, the one wearing the spiked helmet, her own voice ringing clear. But it wasn't really the festival that she focused on. No, her focus was the farmhouse behind them, the glow coming from the window and the promise of something far more dazzling than Solstice – family. Even if Ma was ill, even if Silas was secretive and closed, this was the bright new prospect of being part of a new family, one that would, perhaps, love her.

'This tree . . .' Here, Abel gestured to the oak in the middle of the stones. 'The oak tree is sacred to so many people, the Celts included. Witches are said to dance under its branches – hear that, my Grey Sisters?'

There was a ripple of soft laughter.

'And of course, oak is sacred wood burnt at the summer sacrifice back in those ancient days.' Another gesture from him and fires sprang up at a safe distance from the tree, making Libby gasp. The firelight made the gold of Abel's mask glint, his eyes hidden dark shadows, the angles of his jaw suddenly sharper and more wolf-like. He smiled and it looked more like a snarl. 'Sanctum was always Ma's dream and I'm sorry she can't be here tonight, but she is with us in spirit. For you. We have chosen you out of all the people at this festival to step up and go a little bit further. We know you can. Tonight you will offer up a pledge that these hours will bring a truer knowledge of your own wants, your needs, your desires, that you will look yourself squarely in the face exactly as you are and you will not just *accept* it, no . . . you will *embrace* it. You will enter into whatever happens tonight and allow it to guide you, to lead you to the right path . . . into yourself and back out again, emerging as a better, stronger person.'

There seemed to be areas set up in Sanctum designed to help in this process of self-enlightenment. A big brass gong, the kind used for sound baths in wellness retreats, stood over to one side and smaller rustic canvas tents were dotted further out from the stones, presumably for more private one-to-one coaching.

Abel lifted two bulb-shaped glasses that had been waiting on a wooden stump nearby, one of which he pressed into Libby's hand as he raised his own. 'To the Grey Sisters!'

'To the Grey Sisters!'

'To the oak tree!'

'To the oak tree!'

'To Sanctum!'

'To Sanctum!'

Abel tilted the glass to his lips and drank deep, emptying the whole thing in one swig. Libby, half hypnotised by sweet smoke and strong words spoken by a charismatic man, did the same. The bitter, tepid mixture tasted faintly medicinal with a tang of soft earth recently damp from fresh rain.

It was a mistake.

She knew this after only minutes as the scene around her began to take on a gauzy quality, migraine-tinged and out of focus.

'What was in the drink?' she tried to say as she grabbed Abel's arm and missed. He was now a ghoulish mask, hollow-eyed and smile too wide. Words came from his mouth but they were flies, zipping past her too fast for her to understand. Then those fly-words became bigger black blobs in her vision and she found the ground under her palms, the dry grass sticking up between her fingers, and she couldn't say anything else. Her brain had lost its connection to her body. It was screaming at her to get up, to stick her fingers down her throat and throw up the liquid she had drunk, to do something, anything because this was all so terribly wrong and she had made such an awful mistake in allowing Abel to trap her here.

The world reeled in sickening swoops and then the only thing to do was to tip into the waiting darkness.

Chapter 38

There was something firm behind her, Libby realised as her consciousness swam up out of the black.

She tried to move but her limbs were leaden things, too heavy to lift. Around her swirled light and smoke and shadow, figures dressed in glistening fabric, dancing to a music that seemed more of a heartbeat coming from the earth itself. Through the thin silk of her robe she felt rough bark and realised that she was propped against the trunk of the oak tree.

She was still at Sanctum.

Out of the depths of her brain she tried to pan for more information, bits of shimmer in the murk, but she could not remember why she sat here or why she could not move. Thoughts darted away when she tried to swipe at them.

Directly across from her was one of the Grey Sisters, the worn smooth curve of it like a bent spine, candlelight pooling in its crevices, those rough pitted places in the stone.

Then it moved, a subtle straightening at first, like a hunched woman stretching out her back as the stone became flesh and long hair and the moss became a face with a haughty and watchful expression. This melted into a deep sadness as she locked eyes with Libby.

The drink. Libby blinked, telling herself this was a mirage, a hallucination. She had taken that drink and there must have been something in it. The Grey Sister shrugged off her hard carapace and began to walk towards her as other masked people danced together and laughed, their heads thrown back with wild glee and the flames from the fires that had sprung up at Abel's command seemed to writhe closer and closer. In another spot there were raked coals and people lining up to walk over them, moving over the hot surface with a studied calm, their arms out to their sides as if performing a balancing trick.

A whispering came to her. Sibilant sounds and mutterings that seemed to drug her further so that she couldn't stop her head from lolling as the fires and people and woman made of stone bulged and twisted in her vision.

Then a face loomed into view. A person spiked like the sun's rays, glinting like armour, half metal, half man.

Abel.

He had done this to her. He had given her the drink. He had drugged her.

She tried to move again but her arms and legs were broken plastic things that would not even twitch. Abel's face swooped in, his mouth opening but Libby could not hear the words because the whispering took and smothered them. Hollows for eyes, his face was distorted into a grimace as he reached towards her, his hand unnaturally large, the palm big enough to swing at her and make her topple but instead she felt fingers brush her sweaty hair from her forehead.

Then he was gone.

Where two standing stones had been were now two women as the Grey Sisters came to life just for Libby. One was a face and figure Libby had only ever seen on posters with the word MISSING above her head in big block capital letters. Tess Sanderson. There was her tired stare, with a hint of bolshiness behind it, her ratty hair scraped back in a ponytail, and she wore old baggy clothes. She sat at a small round table made of a tree stump, a teapot and two delicate cups and saucers laid out on it. Opposite her was the woman who Libby had thought of as her mother until today: Ann Corrigan. Sparse of hair due to the cancer drugs, she was dressed in her best silk nightgown with sprigs of flowers patterned on it, hooked up to her IV drip, the needle patched by a plaster on her arm. She lifted the teapot, opened the lid and swirled the contents before looking at Tess.

'Shall I be mother?' she said, and Libby heard that as clear as anything, the words like breath in her ear. She wanted to laugh at the bitter absurdity of it all but the corners of her mouth would not lift.

Ann offered her cup to Tess and they chinked them together.

The edges of Libby's vision darkened and curled in on itself and it wasn't Tess or Ann or Abel she thought of as she fought to stay awake – it was Dawn. She hoped that she was in fact safe somewhere, that Abel had been telling the truth, but it wasn't just blackness creeping up on her, it was despair too. She had been so utterly stupid, so gullible. She had failed to find her friend and now she was stuck here under a tree in the middle of a stone circle where once witches had killed a man, his blood seeping into the roots of this oak . . .

. . . but darkness choked out any more thoughts.

Now she stood. Up and out of the black pool in which her consciousness had swum, she was on her feet, an arm supporting her at her back and she would have smiled if she could have got her mouth to work because clearly someone was helping her, hopefully out of this stone-ringed fiery level of hell. She flicked her eyes to catch a glimpse of her rescuer.

Abel.

He did not look at her. His helmet had been discarded some-where, his blond hair was ruffled and there were glistening streaks on his face.

He began to drag her along, him at her side, holding her by

the waist and taking most of her weight, her feet scraping at the earth, her legs useless. She wanted to stop because as bad as it was being propped up against the oak tree, helpless witness to a barrage of drug-induced, hallucinations at least she had been surrounded by others. At least there were witnesses.

Where was she being taken?

Once again she tried to have command over her own limbs, to dig her toes into the ground, and she thought she was yelling, that her open mouth was screaming for help but she couldn't have been because each face they passed did not turn her way. Abel smiled at some of them, as hands clapped on his shoulder and patted his back and he waved at people Libby could not see in the smoky gloom.

The whispering she had heard before took on an angry hiss and she wished those stones really could come to life in the way she had imagined, each one a vengeful witch ready to swipe Abel aside, find Dawn and hold her safe.

The farmhouse came into view as Abel hauled her out from Sanctum's archway, its kitchen window glow a beacon. Libby was a boat lured onto the rocks by shining lights and it was here that she fully understood the extent of the mistake she had made by following her uncle across the river this night. Abel's arm around her back was a thing of iron, she could not escape it and so she could only watch as the front porch came nearer and nearer, a zoom shot over which she had no control. When it came to the steps, Abel let her crumple to the ground and then changed position to get behind her, hoisting her up from her armpits so her ankles bashed on the wood of the steps, little jolts of pain.

And then she had to be hallucinating again because she found herself on the floor and there were tiny faces everywhere, on every shelf, on tables, on chairs, lined up against the skirting boards, each one howling at her, each one a mad expression of either warning, or frenzied delight.

She closed her eyes and all was black once more.

Chapter 39

Ann Corrigan, Twenty Years Ago

Miles away from the Blake farm, Ann Corrigan opened her door to find a wreck of a woman whose eyes were bloodshot and swollen. Mud was streaked across both hands, blackening her fingernails, and her boots were partly unlaced. Sunrise had barely lightened the morning sky.

'Clara? Clara Blake?'

'Ann, please, you have to—'

'Come in, come in, you look like death.' Ann caught Clara's arm and supported her as she staggered up the stairs and into her flat. 'What are you doing here? What's happened?' That was when she realised that Clara was holding something in the huge blanket she had bundled in her arms. She saw it wriggle and then a tiny arm flailed free and there came a whimper that made Ann grip the doorframe.

'Is that a baby?'

Three times life had kicked Ann Corrigan down. Three times she had failed.

First the modelling. A path to sure-fire superstardom, her agent had promised her, a permanently sweating middle-aged man with shifty eyes who had got her a couple of jobs, each one requiring fewer and fewer clothes until one day he disappeared with her earnings and a good chunk of her dignity. She had been in her early twenties.

A failure.

Second, the marriage. The choice had been good: Mark was rich enough so she could concentrate on getting her modelling career back on track without having to worry about other work and for a while things had gone well. Until they hadn't.

Failure.

Oh, but her third failure had been the worst. So she wasn't to have a glittering career, so she wasn't to have the perfect marriage, but a baby would have fixed it all. Women much more unworthy than her had them all the time and she had been able to see it, how she would, at last, succeed at something. In her imagination she had pictured herself the glamorous mother with a well-behaved child holding her hand, people marvelling at its perfect behaviour and how it looked just like her: absolutely beautiful.

It had become a gripping sensation in her ribcage – this need for a baby, to prove to the world that she could win against it for once, to prove to herself that she could too. Something that was totally hers, made in her image, that would love her the way she was meant to be loved . . . that would be a little bit of her left to live on. But life, unfair again, had given her a womb that would not hold fast to a child.

So here she was, newly divorced with much less money than she had imagined due to some surprisingly astute clauses in paperwork she hadn't even read, though she had signed. Careerless. Childless. Less in all ways. And that was simply wrong. A woman like her, with her face, her figure, her practised smile in the mirror, she should have been . . . so much *more*.

The baby in Clara's arms gave a soft cry and a ghost cramp twisted once more in Ann's stomach at the sound. It had been just over a year since the final loss, the one that made her vow not to try again.

'Oh God, I know, I know, I should never have brought her here. I'm so sorry. I just can't think of what else to do. I can't think, I can't . . .' Clara's words faded away.

But Ann could only focus on the little chubby fist that had broken free of the blanket, how tiny the fingers were.

'I don't understand.' Ann muttered, not taking her gaze from the child-shaped lump mostly hidden in swathes of cloth.

Clara collapsed into a chair and Ann felt like she should have been doing something, patting her friend on the arm, or making a cup of tea, but all she could do was stand and continue to watch that small fist as it waved in the air. She was barely awake, her eyes gritty and dry, her throat sore, her hairline feeling oily and tight. There was another snuffling cry.

Clara spoke quickly. 'I . . . I would never normally ask but . . . how do I explain? Oh God, he'll know I'm gone soon. I have to be quick!'

Ann tried to work out the last time she had seen Clara. They had grown up together in a muddy little ditch of a country village in the backwaters, Clara's family running a dingy little smallholding that scraped a living and Ann the daughter of the minister of the local chapel, her father as grim and cold as the chapel's stone walls. As soon as she had turned sixteen, she had fled the place and her parents, running to the nearest city which, in her mind, was going to be a shining place full of glittering opportunity. Clara had married and moved to the bigger farm with her husband and two boys but they still met up once or twice a year as Ann had waited to be discovered, for her real life to start, the one that should have been a success.

She turned to the kitchen in the corner of the living room. The landlord had called it open plan, but Ann knew that in this case that just meant short on space. She hadn't changed it since, the

Formica worktops cracking a bit with age, the cupboard doors creaking, the white plastic sink stained with use, no matter how hard she scrubbed it. Not that she did any scrubbing. She had never been meant for that kind of drudgery. Only a few days before she had walked out of her third job that year, at a department store. Bloody place. It was not for her to assist others: she should be the one being assisted. She was meant for better things, always had been.

But then came that snuffling cry from the blanket in Clara's arms and suddenly Clara stood, rushing to Ann. 'Take her. Take her. I can't stay – he'll know. For God's sake, take her!'

Ann held up her arms as if she were being robbed at gunpoint. 'Clara, I think you need to sit down. I'll make us some breakfast and you rest. You look ill.'

But Clara would not sit down and now, this close, Ann could smell her, the musty scent of her unwashed hair, of fresh mud and stale sweat. She stared at the blanket, its red trim fraying and faded, a troop of tiny stitched elephants on it, each trunk holding another's tail.

'Take her, please!'

'Clara!' Ann snapped. 'What is wrong with you? You turn up here with no warning, I mean, the sun's not even properly risen yet – and whose baby is that? What happened? Have you been in some kind of accident?'

A low keening sound came from Clara and she hunched over the baby, her hands shaking as she adjusted the blanket. 'I'm so sorry, I'm so sorry,' she muttered and this wasn't to Ann, but to the child, it seemed. Then Ann saw her visibly pull herself together a little, stand taller, regulate her breathing and push her hair from her face. 'Ann, this is my granddaughter.'

'Your granddaughter?'

'Yes. She's not safe at the farm. I can't explain—'

'Silas?'

There was silence. Clara's eyes darted around Ann's flat as she bit her lip. Ann knew a little about Clara's youngest son, the drugs and the trouble he had caused over the years.

'What about her mother?'

'Her mother's gone. She won't be back.'

'I don't get it. You and Abel could bring her up—'

'No! She's not safe. *He* can't keep her safe and I can't either. No one must know she exists. *No one*. Take her.' This time Clara caught Ann unawares, plonking the baby in her arms and the weight of it tugged at something deep within her. 'It would work. This is . . . fate. You tried so hard and now . . . people will just think you did another round of IVF before the divorce.'

The baby was newborn, Ann could tell by its scrunched-up, wizened little face, eyes blinking at her in that wise way very young babies often had. And there it was, that yank in her ribcage. Life had been unfair and she had endured so many failures: modelling, marriage, motherhood but here was her chance to grab at something still. Here was the face that would love her, that would grow up to be just like her. Anyone could do it: motherhood. She could do it well. Yet it had been taken from her again and again, and if there was something Ann immediately wanted, it was what she couldn't have.

'This is crazy,' she said, not taking her gaze from the child.

'It looks like we can make the farm work so I'll send money each month – you won't go without. All you've got to do is keep her as your own. Keep her away from us. Please.' Clara's voice beseeched her as the baby blinked again, slower this time, falling into sleep. Clara was already moving backwards to the door. Now that her arms were empty, she clasped her hands together, bits of mud falling from her boots as their laces dragged on the carpet.

'Money? Each month? How much money?'

'Whatever you want. There's going to be lots of money, so Abel says. You won't have to work or worry about . . . anything. You can send me your bank details.'

It was crazy. It was what she had wished for – a life in which she was given her due. Now that sounded fair. All she had to do was look after the child.

'Her name is Elizabeth,' Clara said.

Ann didn't like that name at all, but she could work with it.

In the days to come, Ann would spend a lot of time staring into her new baby's face and realising that it was nothing, *absolutely nothing*, like hers. The wizened newborn wrinkles didn't smooth themselves out into mini versions of her own perfect nose, lip and chin. This was a completely different person to her, one who cried when she wanted her to be quiet, who stayed awake when she wanted her to be asleep, who soiled the brand-new clothes into which she had just been changed. In those days to come Ann would realise that what she had wanted hadn't been *a* baby, what she had wanted was *her* baby, a child of her own flesh and blood. This poor substitution would have to go back to Clara.

But by the time those days came a month had passed and her bank account suddenly had more money in it than she had seen since she had got divorced. That money paid her rent, bought her some lovely outfits, kitted out the child. It meant she would never have to attempt a dull nine-to-five job ever again, would never have to rely on a husband, or deny herself a few of life's little luxuries. The baby was a docile thing, a good sleeper, generally quiet, very obedient. It would be an easy life. And, after all of her failures so far, that was what Ann Corrigan truly deserved. That, was – *finally* – fair.

Chapter 40

The next face Libby saw when she woke up was that of Ma Blake.

Libby found herself slumped in an armchair in the corner of the farmhouse kitchen. Someone had draped over her a blanket patched with ragged crochet squares and she pushed at it, her drugged movements weak. At a huge wooden table was Ma, her head in her hands, hair hanging down, wearing a pair of faded cotton pyjamas, her feet bare.

'You took no heed,' she said, her voice cracked and muffled, not looking up.

Libby realised that there was something in her lap, a small earthenware bottle, bulbous and fat, narrowing to a tight neck with a face carved on the side. Then she properly took in the kitchen for the first time and saw that these bottles were everywhere, on surfaces and the floor, shelves, chairs and windowsills. Hundreds of glassy ceramic eyes watched them, hundreds of mouths stretched into laughter that tipped into screaming.

'You took no heed and now look what's happened. Just like your mother.'

Libby licked at her dry lips and forced a word from her throat: 'Tess?'

At hearing this name Ma raised her head but her gaze was

a pinball bouncing from bottle to bottle, darting away from Libby. She had a sick cast to her skin and her hair was lank and unwashed. 'I wish she'd stayed away from my boy. None of this would have happened if she'd stayed away.'

'Wha . . . What happened to Tess?'

Because in all of this, there was someone who was a hole in the story, a person-shaped cut-out on the page interrupting the sentences. Tess. If, as Abel had told her, Tess had disappeared with Libby as a baby and then Libby ended up with Ann Corrigan, it wasn't hard to guess what had become of Tess. Libby did not let herself think the word 'dead', but it cast a cold shadow in her mind anyway.

Ma's eyes slid to Libby, managed to hold her gaze for a second before dropping away, her mouth a tight line.

'I tried to keep you safe. But you've ended up here anyway. No heed, no heed, no heed, no heed . . .' Ma groggily rose to her feet and swiped at another bottle from the table where they were lined up in rows, a little troop of fat soldiers ready to go into battle. 'Here,' Ma said as she lurched towards Libby, brandishing the jar, 'take, take, take . . .' She pushed it into Libby's hand and then crumpled next to her to sit on the floor at the foot of the armchair.

The ceramic was cold against Libby's skin and her next words poured out in a stinging rush that brought tears to her eyes, 'I want . . . I want to leave . . . please . . .' She tried to stand but her arms were useless lumps of meat that would not obey her.

Ma patted her knee. 'Everything will be fine.'

'No . . . please . . . let me leave . . .' Libby found some strength in her arm muscles and pushed herself up only to find her legs buckling beneath her. She slid out of the chair to the floor beside Ma, tears on her cheeks. 'I have to find Dawn. Please . . .'

'My granddaughter,' Ma said and put her head on Libby's shoulder, the two of them in a grotesque mimicry of family affection, one clearly turned mad, the other drugged and desperate to escape. 'Blake blood in your veins.' Here she grabbed Libby's arm and dragged a dirty fingernail along the faint blue tracery under her skin, pressing too hard. 'That's the problem.'

'Silas is—?'

Ma cut across her, 'This is all his fault, is what it is! I couldn't fix him, couldn't help him – he didn't want to be helped and now look at the mess he's created. *You.*' The hand that had been on her arm suddenly gripped her chin, twisting Libby's face so she was almost nose to nose with Ma. 'Oh, but you're beautiful. You were as a baby too. My beautiful Blake grandbaby . . .'

'Please . . . let me go . . .' Libby wrenched her chin out of Ma's hand and tried to get to her knees.

'Abel will sort all of this out, don't worry. He's my good boy. He's my good, good boy. Silas I've lost, but Abel, Abel is . . . everything . . .'

Libby couldn't stop to work out Ma's words. She didn't know who to trust, neither Silas nor Abel, but her priority was getting out of this farmhouse and getting back across the river. Dawn wasn't here, had never been here possibly and the only thing she could now do for her was raise the alarm. But that meant getting her body to work. Clumsily tucking her legs under her, she pushed the stupid silk robe she was still wearing out of the way and tried to put some weight on her foot so she could stand. Her limbs were taffy-soft. She paused, breathing heavily.

'I don't think there are enough.' Ma too was on her knees, scrabbling for the bottle that Libby had dropped. 'I should have made more. We need more . . .'

This was her family, Libby thought as she gave up on trying to stand and instead began crawling to the front door, so painfully slowly it was as if her personal video was playing at a glitchy lower resolution. The Hallowed Blake Family. And what a family they were. The maddened matriarch surrounding herself with her weird jars. The youngest son who probably knew more than he was letting on about the disappearance of the mother of his child and the eldest, Golden Boy Abel, who had just drugged his niece. Welcome to the fold.

One hand in front of the other she shuffled on all fours towards the door, dragging herself more than crawling, keeping her eyes on the handle, a round brass thing worn to a dull shine by the touch of many hands over time. She could use that to pull herself up and then all she had to do was twist it and she was free. Except she wasn't. She was one young woman in the darkness, who would then have to get across the river and find help at the festival.

How long the drugs had been in her system she did not know but she could feel a certain command return to her, more trust that when her brain told her legs to move they actually would, not just twitch helplessly. All she needed to think about was the door. That was the only thing that mattered and she could deal with the rest when it happened.

There was the sound of sobbing behind her. Libby did not stop to look back because that would be a stupid thing to do and her mother . . . Which mother? The dead one? No they're both dead. The one in the sickroom bed with the rasping voice . . . Ann Corrigan? Yes. She had not brought her daughter up to be reckless.

'Don't leave me!' Ma scurried to her, blocking her route to the door. 'You can't leave me! I'll come with you. Keep you safe – wait! We'll need these.' Here she reached over and scooped up an armful of those strange bottles with faces and began forcing them onto Libby, shoving them into the crook of her elbow, piling them in front of her like a macabre obstacle course.

'Stop!' Libby pushed them away, sending them rolling out across the floor, their faces spinning.

'No. You don't understand. I have to help. I . . . just have to . . .' Then she put her head on one side, a bird listening out for predators. 'Have you heard the whispering?'

'The . . .'

'From the Sisters. I heard them that night, so long ago now and I've been waiting ever since, for them to talk to me again but . . . nothing . . .'

Libby remembered flashes of being drugged and propped under the oak tree, the sibilant hissing of words she had not been able to hear properly. In her imagination, the standing stones had stretched and shrugged and became women she knew, as well as a witch with eyes the colour of firelight and hair like smoke.

She shoved Ma out of the way and into a table leg, which sent more bottles crashing to the ground, one cracking in half. A foul, musty smell wafted to her. Among the mess of earthenware shards was a concoction both sticky and gritty, of a dark earth-like consistency with what looked like hair in it, long and grey at the ends and something else, a small white crescent moon of a thing which, with a sick feeling in her stomach, Libby realised was a fingernail.

'Ugh!' She raised her gaze to the door once more, trying to keep her focus as halting, dragging steps came up the porch steps from outside.

The doorknob rattled, turned and then two people stood on the threshold, one supporting the other.

Silas and Dawn.

Chapter 41

'Dawn!' Libby managed to stagger to her feet but her vision blurred and blackened for a second as she swayed.

Dawn could not reply. Her head hung at an awkward angle and the only reason she was upright was because Silas was supporting her. She still had on her tie-dye minidress but one of her flip-flops was missing and there was glitter smudged across her cheekbones and bare arms, along with streaks of mud and a thin trickle of blood coming from her collarbone. Silas was a Grim Reaper dressed in faded black and scowling, the muscles in his neck straining from Dawn's weight.

Dawn was dead. She had gone missing, just like Tess had gone missing years ago, and now she was dead. This huge overwhelming thought made Libby stagger back to the armchair, her feet tangling in the crochet blanket she had discarded earlier, shoes crunching on small bits of broken bottle. Dawn had died somewhere alone and frightened and Libby had not been able to find her and it had been him, the shaven-headed screw-up of a brother standing in front of her. He had had something to do with it because otherwise why would he be here with her – now? She knew that was a jump, to think Silas had killed her friend, no matter if his own girlfriend had disappeared. But then Libby noticed what was in his other hand: a stubby knife with a wooden handle and a sharp-looking blade.

'What the fuck?' Silas said as he allowed Dawn to slowly slip from his grasp, propping her up against the wall next to the door.

'She took no heed. I tried, I tried, I tried and here she is anyway . . .' Ma's fingers fluttered against each other, tapping out a disjointed rhythm as she too got up off her knees, using a chair for support and standing behind it. 'Silas, I—'

'Shut up! Let me think . . .' Silas rubbed at his shaved head, but Libby could only stare at the knife. Had he stabbed Dawn? She couldn't see any blood apart from the graze on her neck.

Next to Libby's foot was a longish piece of earthenware from the bottle she had broken, the ceramic forming a sharp point, and she managed to fumble and pick it up, her body beginning to obey her a little more. She wasn't sure if it would make a good enough weapon but anger and fear and adrenaline took over anyway, all those emotions fizzing into her brain, mixing together to create an unholy chemical potion that awkwardly launched her from the armchair and towards Silas . . .

. . . just as Dawn coughed and then gave a snuffle.

'Get the fuck back!' Silas, his gaze flicking to the piece of pottery in Libby's hand. He brandished his own knife and so Libby froze but could not stop staring at Dawn who wriggled a little, opened one eye, gave Libby a woozy smile and then fell back to sleep.

Libby faltered with her pottery weapon, the fact that Dawn was not dead putting a wobble into her onslaught. She had to be smarter, now she didn't have only herself to worry about.

'I've called the police,' Libby said, keeping her voice firm, no tremor to reveal the lie in her words. Her phone was with Dawn's, back with the rest of her clothes in the barn where she had changed ready for Sanctum.

Silas smiled, a tight dead thing. 'No, you haven't.'

'I phoned them before . . . before you got here. I phoned them then.'

'Well, they should have been here by now then, shouldn't they? Sanctum's finished for another year. Why are you even here?'

If Sanctum had ended, then Libby had been passed out at the farmhouse much longer than she had first thought. Hours and hours and hours. It had been around nine in the evening when she had crossed the river and Sanctum was meant to last until beyond midnight. She glanced out of the window – it was still dark at least but that was really no comfort. Hours and hours in which both Abel and Silas could have done anything, could have prepared for anything, anything at all, whilst she had been asleep under a crochet blanket in a room full of jars with faces.

'I know you're my father.'

This piece of news stilled Silas, his face watchful. 'What?' He stayed where he was, blocking the door, but the sharp edge of aggression in his voice softened for a moment.

'Abel told me. About you and Tess and how she's my mother—'

'I don't—'

'How you found out where I lived and then rigged it so I'd win tickets here. I know – I know it all.'

'Rigged . . . what?' Silas frowned.

'There's a lot that needs explaining, isn't there, Silas?' Ma cut in, smoothing the face of the bottle she held in her hand. 'Abel will help though, when he gets here – Abel will sort all of this, yes? Nothing bad is going to happen.'

Libby turned on Ma. 'Abel drugged me, Dawn's a mess on the floor and Silas is holding a knife! Bad stuff has already happened!' She definitely heard it this time: the tremble in her voice that gave it away, how completely out of her depth she was, still light-headed from the drugs and washed out from the heat. She tried not to move her eyes too suddenly because when she did the room moved in a strange jelly-like way, a bubble trapped under glass.

But she wasn't the only one shaking. Opposite her Silas lowered his knife, his voice one of croaked disbelief. 'You're my daughter . . .?'

'Let's wait for Abel. Abel will explain,' Ma said again.

'There's no time to explain everything.' Silas shook himself into action. 'Hell, I don't even know what's going on here but you both have to come with me – now,' he said as he bent to help Dawn to her feet once more.

'Stay away from her. We're not going anywhere with you. Stay back!' Libby waved the earthenware shard in what she hoped was an assertive, aggressive way.

Silas paused. 'God, just then . . . you sounded like her. Like Tess.'

A woman she had never known, who was probably dead somewhere and had been for twenty years, killed most likely by the man in front of her.

'Just let us go!' Libby pleaded.

And Silas might have. She could see it in the relaxing of his frown, the way his gaze took on a mistier quality, thinking back to the woman he had loved all those years ago, and all she needed was some more words, a bit more time and that front door behind him could be something she could run out of, dragging Dawn with her.

A doorway now filled by the figure of Abel.

Chapter 42

A fallen Sun King surveyed the scene in front of him.

Gone was the spiked helmet and heavy cloak Abel had worn all evening and instead he had put on a fresh white shirt, though it was unbuttoned and the sleeves had been rolled up. Gold paint remained daubed around his eyes, strange tribal markings that made his face a mask in the low light of the kitchen's lamps.

'Ah.' Abel looked from Silas to Libby and then finally to Ma. Dawn didn't even warrant a glance.

'Abel – what's going on?' Silas strode forward, the short blade of the knife still in his hand. Abel regarded it warily.

'You'll explain, won't you, Abel? This can all be sorted out—' Ma had been sat at the kitchen table with lots of those odd ceramic bottles gathered towards her but now she stood, her chair teetering, caught at the back of her knees. Her eyes were wide and beseeching.

Abel sighed and walked into the room, closer to Libby. 'You weren't meant to be here,' he said to Silas. 'You were meant to be away from home tonight.'

'Changed my mind.'

'And you just had to go snooping, didn't you?' He gestured at Dawn who was now groggily awake and trying to move.

'I found her at the bothy. Had to cut her free because someone had tied her up. Good job I had my knife. What was she doing there, Abel?'

Abel raised his eyes. 'Moping about that place does you no good.'

'You didn't answer my question.'

'She tried to get into Sanctum without a ticket. Fell in the river, high on something. I put her there to sober up, somewhere out of the way so she wouldn't cause any more trouble.'

'Doesn't explain why she was tied up. And this? Her?' Silas waved a hand at Libby.

'Well, this is your daughter. Thought you might like to meet her.' Abel slammed a hand on Libby's back, pushing her stumbling towards Silas as if he would open his arms and enfold her in them, a stereotypical father-daughter reunion hug.

Silas didn't move, disbelief freezing him. 'After all these years? You found her and didn't tell me?'

'Well, I didn't find her.' Abel turned to Ma with a hard glint in his eye. 'Ma's always known where she was – isn't that right, Ma?'

At this Ma let the chair fall backwards with a clatter. The effect of this new revelation was instant as Silas swung around to her, his gaze one of utter pain and betrayal. Ma stuttered, 'No, wait – I mean—'

Lurching closer to the kitchen table, Silas was almost hoarse with the repressed violence in his tone. 'You knew where she was – my daughter – for how long? And you never told me?'

In contrast to Silas's storm, Abel was cool waters. 'Years, it seems. She's known for many, many years. She's been paying someone to bring her up.'

'What? That can't be . . .' Galvanised by this information, Silas moved in a jerky way, lurching towards his mother as he took Ma by the shoulders. She tried to wriggle free, bottles rolling to the floor, a few cracking open.

'I was keeping her safe! Silas, you have to understand!'

'Keeping her safe from who? From me? Is that what you think of me?' At this, Silas's face crumpled.

Libby could hardly keep track of what was going on but that wasn't even important – what mattered was that both Abel and Silas's attention was distracted and they had both moved from the open doorway. There was a chance for escape. She tried to slowly creep a little closer to Dawn, not really sure how she was going to get her friend out with her, but she could see some of the old Dawn in the eyes that stared back at her: a girl who was scared and still groggy but had some of that familiar fire in her gaze, searing through the confusion.

Ma did not speak. She glanced from one son to another, biting lips that were already cracked and dry. Nearest to Libby, Abel folded his arms across his chest and watched his mother with an expression that was almost curiosity.

'Where was Tess, Ma?' These words Silas spoke in a quiet voice, as if he was afraid to ask the question. His hands still on her shoulders, he gave her a shake. 'What happened to Tess?' Ma stayed silent. Her eyes were hollows of pain as she beseechingly reached out a hand to her youngest son. 'I'll find out anyway. What did you do to Tess?' This last question was punctuated by a more violent shaking before he lost control completely and raised his arms as if he wanted to throttle her. She cowered back against the sideboard and set all the little jars there trembling as if they were as scared as her.

Just in time, Silas pulled himself up short and took a deep breath. Libby edged another fraction closer to Dawn, bringing her behind Abel as a stale breeze came from the open doorway and a night that had already been broiled for too long. Ma and Silas locked gazes and what passed between them was years of misunderstandings, hurt, betrayal and anguish. There was no way through that tangle of emotions and nothing either of them could say.

Then Silas turned abruptly and fixed Libby with a glare. 'You.' Marching over, he grabbed her by the arm. 'You need to leave. With me. Now!'

Libby, startled by Silas's sudden movement, tried to wrestle her arm free, her other hand still clutching the shard of pottery. 'Let me go!' Somewhere in her beleaguered brain she knew that leaving was most definitely a thing she wanted, but not with him. She wasn't going anywhere with any member of the Blake family ever again. On the floor, Dawn tried to sit up and tackle Silas's legs but her movements were kitten-weak and just as ineffectual.

Through the scuffle came the sound of slow hand clapping.

Abel.

He smiled as he applauded, clapping three, four times and then let his arms fall back to his sides. 'Excellent . . . excellent. Just excellent. Entertaining as all this has been I'm on a bit of a schedule tonight and the performance is dragging on now so we need to skip to the next part . . .'

And with that he snapped into business-like movements, taking hold of Libby's other hand, the one holding the cracked bit of earthenware. It was sudden, powerful and swift, the way Abel grasped her hand in his. Too stunned to realise what was going on, Libby could do nothing but watch as Abel's hands held hers and plunged the makeshift dagger into Silas's side.

Ma screamed.

Chapter 43

The world became fuzzy, like the kind of felt toys Libby had played with as a child, the little Velcro houses and trees that she had stuck into position, carefully making a safe, soft little world. Her ears seemed to be full of the stuff, wadded tight.

Then the fuzzy felt figure of Silas slumped into her.

Her hand was warm and she looked down to see her wrist slick with blood, her fingers holding on to the blade that was now sticking out of Silas's shirt, the material already sodden with red.

His head thumped against her shoulder and she staggered to hold the weight of him, not fuzzy felt at all; there was no way she could Velcro this man back into his spot, neat and firm.

Libby whimpered and that weak noise brought all the other sounds rushing back at her: Ma's wailing, Dawn's incoherent mumbling and the beat of her own heart, so loud it seemed to thud in her head.

She had stabbed a person. Abel had forced her, his fingers tight over hers and she had felt how easy it was to punch something sharp into flesh. Silas attempted to put a hand on her shoulder, leaving smears of gore on her arm as he lifted his head to stare at her.

'Run,' he managed to gasp before slumping down as she tried to hold him, letting go of the makeshift dagger but not pulling it out, her knees buckling under his heaviness.

Then she was being pushed aside by a frantic Ma. 'No, no, no, no, no,' she cried as she gathered her son to her, her hands fluttering around the wound on his side but not too near it, the pottery sticking out from him as more blood spilled over it. 'Abel, what did you do?' Her face, when she turned to him, held none of the vacancy Libby had seen in it before. Now she was pin-sharp, her eyes focused and clear. 'What did you do?'

Abel was the only one left standing, the rest of them toppled bowling pins scattered around him. 'Me? Ma – she grabbed my arm! Look, she used a bit from one of your bottles, she'd been holding it this entire time. I tried but I couldn't stop her.' There was a false note to his voice, a bad actor repeating poorly memorised lines.

Ma rocked Silas whose head lolled to one side, the clarity in her face clouding over like breath on glass. Libby, too, was on her knees, palms flat against a dusty floor, leaving bloody handprints against the tiles.

'No, that's not—' But Libby cut herself off when Ma turned her head to her, a gorgon who could strike with one look. Abel bundled up some tea towels and passed them to his mother.

'Here, keep pressure on the wound. Don't take the blade out, he'll bleed too much.'

Ma hardly glanced at the wadding Abel gave her, instead she gently eased herself out from under Silas and laboriously got to her feet, heading for Libby. Before anyone could stop her she had lunged forward, grasping Libby by the throat with both hands. The two of them crashed back against the wall by the doorway, Ma's face almost pressed against Libby's so she could smell the sour edge to her breath and see the burst blood vessels in the whites of her eyes.

'You. You hurt my boy.' Her fingers dug into Libby's neck,

cutting off the air so that Libby clawed at them, desperate to breathe.

'Ma, get off her!' Libby heard Abel's voice but it was Ma's face that filled her vision, her eyes that she locked on to, trying to find the reasoning woman behind the madness and anger.

Prising a few fingers up a fraction allowed Libby to gasp out some words, all the while keeping Ma's gaze, willing her to believe what she said. 'I . . . didn't . . . do it. He did!'

There it was. Something flickered in Ma's look and, to Libby's relief, her hands loosened, sliding down Libby's neck to her shoulders, still pinning her against the wall. 'I swear.' Libby rubbed at her neck. 'It was him. He grabbed my hand.' She wasn't sure but she thought she saw Ma nod, a tiny fleeting motion with her head. That could have been her imagination though, hoping for some kind of helpful telepathy between her and this woman but all Ma did was push her roughly away and return to Silas. Kneeling, she pressed the cloth to his side using both hands, seemingly ignoring everyone else in the room.

Watching them was Abel, with an interest as if this were a favourite television programme he had been looking forward to all week. Scrambling over to Dawn, Libby grabbed her forearm and pulled at her, trying to get her to stand.

'Dawn, come on!' she yelled in frustration, manoeuvring herself so she could try and drag her up by the waist.

Abel's voice came, cool and clear, an icicle waiting to fall: 'Are we done, everyone? Ma, stop being over-dramatic. Silas will be fine – he'll lose a bit of blood but, once I've sorted matters here, I'll call an ambulance. Okay?'

'I won't say anything. I won't say anything about tonight. I promise, just let us go. Please!' Libby hated herself for pleading, she hated the wobble in her words and the way her muscles weakly refused to lift Dawn.

Abel did not reply to her but he gave her the charming charismatic golden boy smile, a ringmaster waiting with a flourish to welcome an audience into the circus. Then he swiftly grabbed her ponytail and began to drag her out of the door.

The shock of it struck Libby dumb until her feet went from under her and she slammed onto the ground, hitting the small of her back hard enough to make her cry out, sliding, sliding, sliding over the kitchen tiles and then the rough wood of the porch floorboards before her body hit the steps, each thud jolting the air from her lungs. She found herself on the grass as the farmhouse tunnelled away from her like an arty film shot. Dawn was still in there. She tried to twist, to reach upwards to yank herself free. Certain clumps of her hair were tearing from her head, she screamed, long yelping sounds that ended in cries.

'No one's going to hear you!'

And she knew Abel was right because there was the roar of the festival beyond the dark, sliding river, the sound that she had thought of as the rumbling warning growls of a huge mythical beast.

All the fires and lights in Sanctum had been extinguished so when Abel stopped under the oak tree there were just the dark stones waiting for her. Libby couldn't stop the terrifying gulping sound she made as she clutched at her head and felt a wetness that she was sure was blood.

Abel knelt next to her and flicked on a hurricane lamp, noticing the red on his fingers, brushing off the clumps of her hair that had come out as he had dragged her.

'Blood,' he said, pensively. 'I've got a little story about that.'

Chapter 44

Ma Blake, Twenty Years Ago

It had only been a few hours after Tess had given birth and the farmhouse was quiet and sleeping.

Ma didn't know why she had woken.

The house was dark, steeped in the earliest hours of morning. Ma had stripped the sheets on Tess's bed and laid fresh ones, the girl asleep and breathing normally enough but Ma knew they would have to get her to a hospital soon, if only to have her butcher-like stitching redone. Infection could set in quickly.

Throwing off the covers she turned on the lamp and tiptoed over to the drawer she had cleared out and lined with soft blankets. In this makeshift cot she expected to see soft skin and a tiny mouth in perfect pink.

It was empty.

The fear that grabbed at Ma's heart made her almost bend double and she ran, slamming the lights on as she did so, first to Silas's room and then to where she had left Tess sleeping.

Empty again.

It had to be a nightmare, she thought, as she checked and found Abel gone too. This had to be a terrible dream and she had to

213

still be asleep. How had three people and a baby disappeared in the night and left just one, a frenzied woman in her nightdress, alone and confused?

'Silas! Abel!' she yelled, over and over as she took the stairs at a run and found the kitchen deserted.

She forced herself to stop for a second, to take a breath, to listen to the whispering that was never completely out of hearing. The Grey Sisters would help her. After all, they had given her a granddaughter, they had helped the child take her first breath – they would not swipe that away as fast as it had happened. Would they?

There it was. An odd faint glow in the front window. A glimmer in the darkness outside.

Pushing her feet into her boots, she was still putting her arms into her raincoat as she dashed out onto the porch and headed for the light coming from the stones. A downpour had begun again, and the wind pummelled her, sending spattering raindrops down her neck, up under her cuffs and in her eyes.

A hurricane lamp had been set up under the oak tree in the middle of the stones, its light illuminating the branches like a terrible Hallowe'en decoration.

There was a man sat on the ground. Ma staggered to a halt, expecting to have to drag Silas back in, her son who was now a father himself, completely unprepared and unsuited for the role. She thought of the way Elizabeth's tiny fingers had curled around hers and she vowed to make a proper father of him for her. She strained to catch sight of her granddaughter.

'He won't understand.'

Abel.

'I . . .' Ma's brain fumbled to catch up. She had been ready to deal with Silas, not Abel.

Her oldest son's days and nights had been completely taken up with festival preparation over the last month. This was the final night before the festival began. It had only been yesterday morning that Ma had stood almost in this very spot, in the early dawn light, with blood running down from the cut on her knee. Tess's labour had taken a whole day and Abel had come back very late, after the sheets had been changed and mother and baby had been asleep.

He had not said much, had sat and listened as Ma had told him the day's events, picking at a plate of food she had made for him, his face stern, golden hair unusually limp. She had thought it due to stress about the festival.

She had been wrong.

'Silas won't understand.'

In the light from their hurricane lamp, Abel's face became strangely angular, throwing shadows over his eyes, giving a devilish tinge to his expression. Something in his voice made Ma approach him cautiously, though he hadn't even turned to her and was speaking as if to himself.

'Where's the baby? Where's Silas?' she asked.

'He couldn't sleep, fussing over . . . *her*. I told him to go start clearing the path.'

'In the dark?'

'He wanted to.'

That was a good thing, though, Ma told herself. Silas had been worrying about Tess and the baby. He knew they needed a hospital and so that path needed clearing. He could set up some lights, drag the tree out of the way. That was maybe not sensible; after all, he could have waited until it was light, but it was . . . understandable.

'So where's the baby, Abel? Where's Tess?'

Ma realised she was using the kind of voice needed to calm a frightened animal, yet Abel was unnaturally still, his own words devoid of any kind of emotion. She could feel her heart thump in her throat, that muscle in her chest already knowing what was wrong here.

A shape moved under the tree.

Abel was such a good son. Abel was her golden boy, not sullen and scowling like Silas. He looked after her. He looked after the farm. He was trying to save it. Her son was the light of her life.

But light casts shadows.

Ma had never investigated those shadows. There had been nothing to see in them, she had always told herself.

Nothing in Abel that she had ever allowed herself to see.

But she could not turn away from this, the shape under the tree as it moved again in a jerky, spasmodic lurch.

Ma's feet moved her forward. All too soon she could make out that the shape under the oak was a person, was a woman, was Tess, her face a swollen mass of bruising and blood, her body curled up on itself even as she hauled one arm out and weakly tried to drag herself away. In her other arm she clung to her newborn.

Ma let out a cry. 'The . . . the baby . . .'

And then Abel's voice, not a flicker of emotion in it. 'The baby's mine.'

Chapter 45

Libby did not want to hear any more.

She was living it, that moment under the tree. She was lying probably on the exact spot where her mother had lain, bruised and beaten, holding on tight to her baby – to her, Libby. With Abel standing over her.

Her real father.

Every time she had tried to crawl away whilst Abel had told her of what happened to Tess, Abel had kicked her, in the side or the stomach. She coughed and tried to listen to what he said next because she was not going to die here under this tree by the hand of this man; she was going to stay alert and listen and try to find any way she could to get out alive. Whatever it took.

'Don't pass out on me.' Abel lightly slapped her cheek. 'I need you awake.' Water sloshed in her face, enough to get up her nose and make her gasp. 'I need you to know your part in all this. It makes you a better gift if you understand.

'It was Ma who told me the stories. The myths and the super-stitions. I remember listening to her, to those tales, and being captivated by . . . the power of them, the way that power could be harnessed. Maybe the festival would have been successful anyway. I mean, I'd worked hard on it but it was *such* a success; it raked in *so* much money, more than I'd ever hoped for . . . all because of that spilled blood.'

Libby's hands were gritty with dry soil as she lay still for a moment under the tree. Abel seemed to think Tess's death had been some kind of sacrifice – the type of thing that only existed in ancient stories – something that had caused the success of the festival. It was absolutely and without doubt . . . unhinged. Abel's golden boy image had been a mask, just as shiny as the helmet he had worn earlier that evening, bright enough to dazzle everyone from seeing the rot underneath. She wondered if her mother's bones were buried under this tree, if its roots had grown fat on her decomposing flesh.

It could have been the blood rushing in her ears but Libby thought she heard a dry whispering sound, like women's voices talking low and she glanced at the dark slabs of stone in a circle around them. The Grey Sisters. If those sisters were on any side tonight, then their story would suggest that they had to be on hers. She half expected them to lurch into action, like her hallucination earlier that evening, ready to wreak a moss-covered vengeance on the man who held her captive.

Abel knelt next to her, the glow from the hurricane lamp flickering until he thumped the lantern on the ground so it sputtered and then the light steadied, a golden circle in the dark. Around them was the litter from the finished Sanctum party, extinguished fires, creamy white candles with hard wax drips abandoned on the grass, looking like strange mushrooms. Neatly folded under the tree was Abel's cloak and, on top, that sun helmet with the spiked rays, placed like a decapitated head.

He spoke again: 'Ma, she wasn't wrong about those stories . . . she *knew*. And she made sure I did too, each bedtime, telling me the tales. Blood magic. It's special, what you're going to be a part of. After all, it's not an understatement to say the festival really could do with a miracle. It's grown too big and the cracks are starting to show. The money's running out and there's nothing left over for repairs, for staff . . . it's starting to be a bit of a mess. That's where you come in . . .'

Move! Libby told herself even though there was a sharp pain in her side, her whole scalp throbbed in angry pulses and it felt as if her body was at least three times heavier than it really was, a bloated, leaden mass that she could barely command. Abel didn't need to kick her this time, instead he calmly pressed her back, his knees digging into her thighs to hold her down as he reached behind him to bring out the object he had stuffed into the back of his jeans.

It was Silas's stubby knife.

'It was me, not Silas, who rigged it so you got free tickets. I got a tip-off that Ma had squirreled you away and I knew I needed you here. I need blood. Your blood, in particular. If Tess gave us Solstice as we know it, if her blood gave us that success then yours, her daughter's – what could yours give us? That kind of blood magic is . . . well, Ma would say it's sacred. It's powerful, is what it is.'

Libby watched the knife. Her whole world, her whole life, narrowed to its blade. There was no point protesting anymore, no more use for 'No!' and 'What?' and other ineffectual words like those. Whether she liked it or not, she was in this madness, pinned down into it by the man who loomed above her, the one she had first thought of as uncle and now knew to be father. The man who wanted to kill her so her blood would feed this tree, these stones and the festival. It didn't matter how nightmarishly unbelievable all of that was – *he believed it*, and that was all that mattered. She had minutes to save her life. Bucking and writhing, always wriggling and shifting, she made it hard for him to keep a grip on her as she kept moving ever so slightly sidewards.

If the Grey Sisters weren't going to show up and save her then Libby would have to make do with what was lying on the grass, nearly within her grasp.

Abel focused on her. 'I saw it, y'know. How your eyes lit up at the idea of being a Blake. Being a part of all of this. I don't blame you – it's quite the prize. I shouldn't have strung you along, I guess – but, well, it was interesting to watch, couldn't help myself. You were so gullible.'

He made the word an insult but, Libby thought, twisting in desperation, being gullible just meant you trusted someone, that you trusted what they told you. That wasn't terrible, it wasn't something to be ashamed of. It was beautiful. And, as she tried to bite Abel's hands until he slapped her hard in the face, it hadn't been about the festival. Not really. What had made her eyes light up had been, not the idea of money, but the idea of family. A family that might love her.

More whispering, from throats as dry as summer-scorched leaves, and in her head Libby made the sound a spell, an incantation, a weaving of words that would bring protection. But she knew the only way to be saved was to save herself and so she continued to turn and kick, to thrash and wriggle.

Abel thumped her down hard onto the ground. 'The festival is *everything*. Your death will ensure that it carries on, thanks to the Sisters . . .'

The Sisters. The low whispering became louder to Libby; the stones did not move, did not become flesh and bend to help her but she felt them there around her, the women who had fought back against a man they hated. They watched.

He grabbed her jaw, squeezing it as if he wanted to force words from her before jamming her head upwards, stretching her neck ready for the knife. 'You will make the perfect gift to them. And you should thank me, for making your boring little dull existence special . . .'

Abel raised the knife and Libby took her chance now both his hands were full to wrench her own arm free and reach out, almost making her shoulder pop, to finally get hold of what had been out of her grasp on the ground next to her. Her last chance.

At the same time a shape appeared behind Abel and Libby, bruised and nearly concussed, thought for a second that perhaps she had been wrong – that the Sisters had risen up for her, that it had begun, the first stone woman to come screeching for Abel. There was a wailing scream and the shape launched itself at Abel as he, shocked and confused, half turned to fend off this new attack.

But this was no mythological creature, this was no story made flesh, this was Ma Blake who lunged at her son, trying to push him off Libby but succeeding in only making him topple . . .

. . . straight into the gold helmet's sunray spikes that Libby had managed to thrust in front of her.

221

Chapter 46

The two women, the stone circle and the oak tree watched the man flail.

'I couldn't let it happen.' Ma crouched on the grass, her knees tucked up under her chin, her eyes wide in the lamplight. 'Not this time. I couldn't let it happen again.'

Libby scrambled backwards, out from under Abel's weight as he tilted from her and listed to the side, his shaking fingers fluttering at the spikes that had pierced him through the shoulder. She didn't know whether to laugh or scream or cry and so the sound that came out of her was a strangled half-gulp as she got to her hands and knees in the dirt and breathed raggedly.

Abel Blake had tried to sacrifice her to the Sisters and now he was speared on his own helmet.

Sacrifice.

Sisters.

Speared.

The thoughts slid from her, ice-slick and she could not get them to stick. Above her the night sky did not look so black anymore. It had lightened as if it were material being stretched and held against a lamp and she realised that this was now Midsummer Day, the longest day of the year, sunshine winning against darkness for everyone . . . even for her. She was breathing, she was alive, she had not been split open and left to bleed into the roots of the oak tree that rustled above her head.

She had to escape.

Nearby Abel gargled something incomprehensible, unable to sit up, unable to do much at all except arch his back and flail at the spiked helmet sticking out from his shoulder.

'He'll live,' Ma said, raising her head from her knees to look at her oldest son. There was a flat certainty to her voice, a disappointment almost.

They both saw it at once.

The knife, dropped in the scrubby grass at the foot of the tree, the blade meant for Libby, to slice clean lines in her skin and peel back her flesh so she could drain quicker.

They both moved for it.

But Ma was fast, she scooted over in a half-sprawl, half-crawl and slammed her hand down on it, just as Libby tried to do the same, finding her face inches from Ma's as they both crouched on either side of the weapon. Ma did not let go and though her hair swung over much of her face, though the light from the hurricane lamp cast odd shadows, Libby could see her fierce expression, one that would have suited a baring of teeth, a warning snarl.

Libby backed away.

Ma remained still.

This woman had helped her, Libby reminded herself. She had pushed Abel from Libby and saved her life, though perhaps she hadn't meant to send him straight into the sharp points of the sun helmet that Libby had been holding. Flicking her glance to Abel, she saw him prostrate on the ground, his chest heaving, grunting incoherently in pain. She had done that. To Ma Blake's son. Yesterday she had never stabbed anyone and now here she was, working her way through the Blake family one by one.

But Ma now held the knife.

Libby backed away some more.

223

But Ma did not spring at her. Instead she picked up the knife and studied it, testing its weight in her hand, letting her fingers wrap themselves around its smooth wooden handle.

There came a shout.

From the doorway of the farmhouse a shape appeared, weaving unsteadily towards them, the voice so hoarse at first that Libby hardly recognised it.

'Stop!'

It was Dawn, wobbling on her feet, a figure rushing towards them, and Libby saw Ma startle, saw how her grip tightened on the knife and for one awful moment thought that she was going to leap towards Dawn with a flash of steel glinting in the lamplight.

But before she could get any closer, Dawn's ankle gave out and she crashed to all fours, the same as Libby and Ma, all three of them clambering around in the dirt. Just another two, Libby thought, just another two women needed and they would have the full Grey Sisters set of five. The stones waited in their circle.

Libby tried to rush to Dawn, but Ma crawled over to her, surprisingly swift on hands and knees, her fingers digging into Libby's chin as she wrenched her face close. Bracing herself for a cold blade to slip in between her ribs, Libby gasped, her eyes locking on to Ma's, her hot breath on her cheek, certain that this in fact was it, the moment that had always been waiting for her, no matter what she did. Like one of those Choose Your Own Adventure stories, each option she picked led her back to a knife pressed against a skin, her sacrifice, her blood spilled, no matter how she turned the pages.

Ma spoke: 'Run to the festival. Get help for Silas. Get out.'

Libby blinked, not quite believing the words.

'Go!'

With that, Ma pushed her, sending her stumbling towards Dawn, and Libby hauled herself up onto her feet, tired of scrambling around on the grass, her walk breaking into a run and, across from her, past the stone circle, she saw Dawn get up too.

They crashed into each other, a mess of tears and streaks of blood, some their own, some not, and Libby stuffed her face into her friend's neck, hugging her tight enough to convince herself that she was real, that she hadn't lost her. But there was no time to hug and cry and try to work out how they had got themselves into this nightmare; there was only the moving forward. That was all that counted.

No one paid any attention to Abel. Not Ma, who stepped back, far too close to him. Not Dawn and Libby, too busy incoherently trying to talk and hug and stand all at the same time.

So Abel seized the last of his strength and his opportunity. Swaying, he got to his feet, the sun helmet sticking from him like a terrible burr, and snatched the huge wooden staff that had been laid nearby with his cloak, moving with more speed than a man speared in the shoulder should have been able to muster.

It was done in seconds.

Perhaps he had been swinging for Libby, to finish the job he had started, perhaps he was too blinded by pain to think anything at all but when he lunged forward it was Dawn who saw him first, who pushed Libby out of the way and held up her arms as if that could shield them both.

It was Dawn who then crumpled to the ground.

Chapter 47

Libby was inside a huge bell and someone had just struck it hard.

Her whole head rang, hollow and reverberating, as she pulled herself over to Dawn, her thoughts trembling and then shivering apart. Over to her right she saw Abel once more on his knees, Ma standing over him, kicking the staff from his grasp. It was almost an inventory, the way Libby shakingly searched Dawn's body for injury. There were her feet, blessedly unhurt and not bloodied so Libby scanned the rest of her legs from calves to thighs, telling herself everything was fine, everything was okay because Dawn was okay. Libby could barely breathe for relieved sobs until she crawled closer.

Dawn was not okay.

Not fine.

There was a lot of blood, her blue and pink hair now red and matted at the roots, but that wasn't even the worst thing, the worst was the way she lay, head on the grass, her face pale, eyes closed. Not moving.

Someone again struck the bell in which Libby's head was trapped and she saw the whole scene blur around her.

Dawn was not dead. She was not. If she kept thinking it, if she kept muttering it to herself then it would not be so, because

Dawn being dead was so large a concept she could not see a way around it and it would topple on her, crush her to nothing.

No. Dawn was not dead.

Gently she touched her friend's face and the relief when Dawn fluttered her eyes open was a blast of cool air over her entire body.

'Here, take this.' Libby heard a ripping sound and Ma shoved a bunch of material into her hand. 'Take it! I'm so sorry, I'm so sorry.'

The staff had connected with Dawn's skull and Libby could see swollen flesh at her temple, her hair hiding the wound. She didn't know how long they had before too much blood was lost and there was so much of it already, running down Dawn's face and neck, staining the strap of her dress. She pressed what she realised was part of Ma's long skirt to the spot and Dawn's hand joined hers, shaking and slippery. Tying the material around her head, she saw her friend staring at her, but she couldn't say anything despite the way her mouth opened and closed a few times. When something like this happened, usually a person could make one phone call and help would be on its way, sirens blaring, blue lights, noise and colour and the reassurance of other people knowing what to do but here, in the gloom, there was just her, a murderer and his mother.

And then Ma was behind Dawn, lifting her under the arms with Libby's support so all three of them stood. 'Go. Go now. Across the river – get help!'

There was no way Dawn could walk with her, Libby thought, watching her sway. But it was as if Dawn could read her thoughts because she caught her hand with the one not pressed against her head, gripping it hard, and her tight-lipped expression when Libby stared at her was one of total determination as she forced out the words: 'Don't . . . leave . . . me . . . behind . . .'

Libby paused. There were two options. The darkness of the path that led around the farmhouse to the main road, versus the glittering lights of the festival across the river. People. Help. The path might be quicker but there was no guarantee there would be anyone on that road when they reached it or how long they would have to walk before finding aid. The route to the festival, however, was a shining thread in her mind: river to wood to security tower or whoever would stop for them on the way. Thousands upon thousands of people, people who did not want to kill her, all capable of help.

'The . . . road . . .' Dawn managed to force the words out, but Libby shook her head.

'No. This way.'

Dawn did not argue, which was a bad sign. She let her head hang, giving way to the pain and shock. Why Abel had taken her was a mystery, maybe to act as a lure, bait, to bring Libby more easily the river and into his power: 'Your friend is here, come and see your friend.' Or maybe Abel had told the truth and Dawn being Dawn had tried to get into Sanctum without a pass, and he had seen his opportunity and grabbed it. Libby would have to wait until Dawn was more coherent to ask.

She took her weight, Dawn leaning into her, as they both staggered towards the river. Libby had a firm arm around Dawn's waist, keeping her up, hauling her on, her own muscles trembling from the effort, pain firing in her side where Abel had aimed his kicks, her ankles weak and wobbling. She expected to fall, she expected not to be able to see where she was walking and for her foot to find every bump and rabbit hole. To guide them was the sprinkling of festival lights across the water and the sky had lost its velvety darkness as the purple-grey promise of sunrise appeared behind a distant hill.

Solstice was a festival that never slept. The Moon Stage pumped out dance music until the early hours but this was now the morning of Midsummer Day, Libby realised. It was the most important sunrise of the whole celebration, where people stayed up to greet the dawn, willing it to rise with music and smoke.

She could hear the thump of huge bass speakers from her side of the river.

It was only when she reached the water that she knew she had made a mistake.

'Shit!'

There was the water, a fast-flowing rush of sound below them. There were the steps cut into the bank ready to walk across the stepping stones . . .

. . . that hadn't risen.

Libby remembered how Abel had made them magically appear as if he was a low-rent Moses, not parting the water but making a path anyway. He must have had some sort of remote control on him, the kind of thing she should have been clever enough to have taken for herself as he had rolled in agony on the ground.

'The stepping stones!' she screamed behind her, hoping Ma could hear.

A shape moved against the lamp glow amongst the Grey Sisters, like a wraith. If Ma had heard, she made no sign and there was no responding shout.

They would have to go back, she thought, the arm holding Dawn up already beginning to numb. She wasn't sure she had it in her. Dawn had been right – they should have taken the path to the road and now she had used all of her energy dragging her this way only to find they would have to retrace their steps. It would take too long. Dawn would be limp and cold in her arms by the time they managed it.

A worse thought slithered into her brain: perhaps Ma had changed her mind, a mind that had already slid into madness anyway. After all, she had nearly throttled Libby back at the farmhouse when she thought Libby had hurt Silas. Perhaps she was waiting for them, lurking in one of the pools of shadow, ready to jump out with that knife that Libby had stupidly left with her. So many mistakes. Dawn slipped in her grasp and the trees rustled their disapproval to each other.

She did not want to go back, to the Sisters, to the tree with the bones of her mother underneath it. She did not want to look behind her as Dawn buckled a bit more at the knees, taking Libby with her, her sheer force of will keeping them both upright.

The wraith shape flitted again.

'Please, Ma – please . . .' Libby muttered.

With a faint whirring sound, out of the water rose the stepping stones, Libby's pathway to salvation. There was no hesitation – she crossed the river.

Chapter 48

The Wyrd Wood was a theatre set now empty of its actors.

'Help!' Libby shouted in a hoarse, ragged voice.

But there was no one to hear. Libby let Dawn slide to the ground and dropped to her knees with her. The walk across the stepping stones had been rough for both of them. The stones themselves were flat and wide and not too far apart but had never been designed for two people to cross together and never for one of them to be almost carrying the other.

Dawn's face was a terrible grey photocopy of the original, toner low. Blood streaked down it and the material wrapped around her head was already sodden. She mumbled something Libby could not catch.

'We're going to be fine.' Libby tried to believe her words.

People could do extraordinary things when under great pressure, when adrenaline kicked in and fizzed through a person's blood vessels making them forget pain and fear and the natural laws of what a body could feasibly achieve. She got to her feet and then she helped Dawn to stand. All she had to do was walk; she didn't have to lift a car or run into a burning building or drop from a great height. All that was required was for her to put one foot in front of the other.

So she did.

Dawn did not speak again and, before she got very far into the wood, Libby had to stop and put her head to Dawn's mouth to check she was breathing, tapping her cheek to make her open her eyes, and pressing her hand to her head to secure her make-shift bandage.

Time. She did not have much of it.

Not just the fact that Dawn was slipping into unconsciousness, but also the figures who stalked at her heels. Ma. Abel. There was no guarantee that they wouldn't have followed her, that Abel hadn't already killed Ma and wrenched the spikes from his shoulder in true action-hero style, ready to come after her and finish the job. The sacrifice. Her upside down from the oak tree branch, her blood draining into a thirsty earth.

'Help!' she called again but there was no one to hear her, only the trees who, if they did whisper secrets to each other, root to root, had no words for her.

Everyone had packed up and left, presumably to watch the sunrise over at the main stages on this most special of mornings: Midsummer Day. No dancers to whirl her into a gavotte, the scattered cushions empty, the hand-drawn carts selling sweet nuts and coffee shuttered and parked in groups together. Even the fortune teller in her painted wagon had a chalkboard hung over the front steps with the message 'Gone to seek my fortune elsewhere' on it. *You don't fit.* That had been what the woman had told her in that wagon. *You don't fit.* And, of course, she had been correct. Libby did not fit, not with the woman she had called her mother, who had regretted ever taking her in, not with her biological family the Blakes either, only interested in her blood, and not in this festival, this beast strung with fairy lights and flags, the beat of its speaker-heart and the roar of its crowds.

She wanted out of it all. Her old life, the Blakes, the festival, the lot.

Shivering, she hoisted Dawn up a bit more, her arms aching, and hauled them both over to the steps of the fortune teller's wagon where they rested for a minute or so. She realised it was the first time she had been cold in days. The silky material of her robe flapped the wet patches of blood against her skin like damp, chill kisses and she felt the shivering twist deeper into her core.

In her head there was an hourglass and the sand inside it was fast sliding out to pool at the bottom with a dry hiss. Every tree trunk had its own shadow lurking alongside it, Abel himself about to jump out; every sound became his footsteps running over the bracken-strewn ground towards them; each light seen between the trees was the glint of fire on a knife.

She should have tried to find her phone. It might have been back at the barn where she had got changed before Sanctum and there might have been a signal that side of the river near the farmhouse, but she had gone racing off instead, spurred on by Ma telling her to go, so eager to get herself and Dawn out of Abel's grasp.

Had that been a mistake?

Heart hammering so hard in her throat it made her feel dizzy, Libby could see the entrance of the wood, that arch through which was framed an almost hellish scene of firelight and bodies in the red-orange glow, an unholy crash of sound muffled a little by the branches above her head.

Up. Up. They needed to keep moving.

When she tried to get Dawn on her feet again, the two of them crashed to the ground once more, this time Dawn too heavy a weight to try and heave back up. Her head lolled awkwardly.

'Dawn!' Libby tapped her cheek urgently. 'Dawn!'

No response. She could almost hear that dry ticking sound of hourglass sand sliding away from her as Dawn's eyes did not flutter, though she could see the weak rise and fall of her chest.

For a moment Libby considered the worst: leaving Dawn behind so she could run on and get help. She couldn't drag

Dawn by her heels and she didn't have the time anyway: she needed to get help fast. She didn't even know if she had done the right thing, bringing Dawn with her, and she wasn't sure what the rules were for head injuries, whether she should have left her broken back there on the ground near the oak tree. No! There was no point thinking that. There was so much blood though, slick and sticky, it was on her hands and clothes, in her hair, on the grass as Libby tried to stop Dawn from keeling over to the side. Too much.

That hourglass sand hissed.

Dawn opened her eyes.

What had she been thinking? There would be no splitting up; the two of them would move together, escape together, crawl together, and, if it came to it (though it wouldn't, it wouldn't) they would lie down and die together too. Whatever happened, they went together. They were a team.

They were family.

Up. Up.

Each breath seemed to come from glass-studded lungs, but Libby steadied the two of them as they swayed in their own personal storm wind. In front of her the festival thudded and thumped; it roared and cheered and swooped and swirled and they stumbled into the fiery heart of it all.

Chapter 49

Later, Libby would know why. She would read how the budget cuts, the squeezing of funds, the scarcity of security, the lack of stewards on duty, the shoddy fencing that had allowed too many people to gate-crash – she would understand how all of those things had created the scene in front of her. It would be rational.

But there, that morning as she tried to find a way through the crush of people, there was no reason to any of it.

When she had left with Abel yesterday evening, the Sun Stage had been winding down and the Moon Stage about to rise. The heat had been suffocating, the speakers had been loud and the crowds had begun to swarm in like midges sensing something delicious to bite. The sense of order had been fraying, though there was still a feeling that the crowd remembered it was made up of a group of individuals who could look out for each other, humans who remembered their humanity.

The horde in front of Libby waiting for the sun to rise remembered no such thing.

Midsummer Day was almost upon them. The longest day of the year, to be welcomed in with cheers and celebration . . . but this festival had been left out too long in the sun. It had turned brittle, withered down to a wild and foul-tasting core. As was the design for this part of the event, both stages blasted music across to each other, both of them tribal pounding beats, a call and response that seemed jarringly out of sync at times, the music snarling up and twisting together. The sound of it sent Libby's feet tripping and stumbling too as if the music jerked her own puppet strings and tangled them around her legs. Sustain – the strip of food trucks in the middle between the two stages – had been cleared away and so people filled the whole of the space, as lasers beamed across the tops of heads and smoke swirled.

The immediate help Libby expected to rush to her did not appear. Two bloodied young women staggering into the throng should have caused some consternation: one dressed in strange silk robes, the other with gore-matted hair. Libby had anticipated hands reaching for her, faces full of concern, immediate aid.

That did not happen.

Perhaps they thought her part of the show.

Libby tried. She grabbed people's arms, she shouted at them, tried to get their attention but she was one tiny voice, one tiny figure amongst too many all crammed in. No one could or would hear her, no one bothered to take any notice of yet another drug-and-sun-addled girl, dressed madly for the occasion, even with the blood smeared all over her. Many of them had their own warpaint. They shouted too and screamed and danced and there was a new wildness to their flailing, a new abandon in the way they stomped, not caring who they stepped on. A lurching seasickness swept through them all. They swayed and rocked into each other, knocking some off their feet, carrying others with them, and from above the movement would have looked like rippling, but a ripple was gentle. It was a soft undulation of water and this . . . there was nothing gentle about this at all.

The maddened gleam of violence shone.

'Please!' Libby yelled, grasping on to the arm of yet another woman who was whisked away and then an elbow smashed into her neck and the sudden pain made her stumble into the people behind who in turn gave her a shove into someone else. Fingers dug into her spine and she couldn't get a big enough breath, her ribcage a shrunken vice. All the while she kept a tight grip on Dawn whose head lolled, her eyes closed once more.

Over to one side, people tried to swarm up the bright strips of material that covered the security tower, their bodies spider-like as they climbed, a few slithering back down. Others were intent on creating mini mosh-pits amongst everyone, pockets of quicksand in which the unwary could sink all too quickly. A few even began attacking the Sun Stage, trying to tear off some of the boards that hid the struts and using them as planks on which to crowd-surf. One member of the security staff, a broad-shouldered man with long hair, grabbed on to one of these boards, trying to stop it being carried away but was almost instantly surrounded and, though no punches were thrown, there was that strange dancing bob of men about to strike, of working up that courage, gripping on tight to their prize. The security guard let go with a shrug and backed away, just like his companions who seemed to all be heading for the security tower.

The tower. Sanctuary.

But that was when she spotted a familiar Mohican hairstyle. At the back of the Sun Stage, groups of people had clotted together, a mix of staff and performers watching the chaos unfold, unsure what they could do, and amongst them was Sal, a recognisable silhouette due to her distinctive hair.

Capable, organised, knowledgeable Sal. That was who Libby needed.

A mini beacon had been set up at either stage, meant to look like the big version burning on the hill. These smaller bowls of flame were secured high out of reach on plinths that looked solid, but they were too much of a temptation for the people already beginning to either scale or hurl themselves at them, setting the structures trembling. At the edges of this hellish scene, people scurried in the shadows, possibly those who had once run the food trucks now packing up and heading out before the crowd began to spill like fire across to them, or other festivalgoers repelled by the dangerous wild abandon of what was building to some kind of deadly crescendo.

Getting to Sal seemed almost impossible, a sea of people through which she could not swim, their flailing limbs tangles of seaweed waiting to wrap around her and bring her down. Libby kept her head ducked; she wiped the blood and dirt from her eyes and she kept her grip on Dawn, shoving people out of her way, squeezing through, ducking under, elbowing, trying to breathe and also keep those breaths calm and measured. As she pushed on through the people a rough cheer rose from off to the side.

One of the panels from the stage was now being crowd-surfed across raised hands, a man lying spread-eagled on his back, arms and legs waving, sticking his tongue out and spraying everyone below him with beer. There were more, life rafts of painted MDF, floating above their heads, being carried across the crowd in a baffling fluidity. Libby saw one head towards her and even did a desperate calculation: down here they were liable to get stuck, or trampled on, or she would lose her hold on Dawn. Up there on one of those boards . . . maybe they had a chance. But that was a wild thought, stupid and desperate – she would never be able to get on one of those things with Dawn too and, even if she did, they weren't boats, she wouldn't be able to steer it in the right direction. They were more likely to get chucked off, fall and cause themselves more damage.

The crowd remained a sea she could not part. The only way was through it.

And, finally, help came in the form of a beleaguered security guard somehow stuck in the current nearby, a tall man in his fifties with long hair and a beard who looked a bit like the kind of Jesus figure she had seen in Bible pictures, if Jesus had dressed in sweat-wicking polyester and had gone to the gym instead of handing out loaves and fishes. Jesus spotted her struggling and for the first time she felt as if someone really noticed her, even though the man was covered in sweat, his T-shirt sticking to him, his eyes bloodshot.

'Shit! You okay?' He yelled the question.

'My friend's hurt!' she shouted. 'Help us get to the stage!'

She didn't need to add more. The stage was safety. He nodded and grabbed her arm, hoisting her along, using his bulk to shield them from the majority of bumps and buffets as around them people danced or fought or fled. She was aware of her own yells, pushing others out of the way, their faces passing her with wide open mouths and huge eyes like the kind of carnivorous fish that lurked in the deepest parts of the ocean.

Above them the sun began its first preparations to rise, an intense orange-pink aura over the hill in what was now a grey, cloud-streaked sky.

She could only watch the nearby bowl of fire to one side lurch as the crowd surged into the scaffold tower it perched upon. The whole structure began to lean and she turned her head towards the Sun Stage. There were no bands for this final bit of Solstice, just two DJs, one on either stage, pumping out the strange thundering beats that accompanied the death of night and the birth of the longest day. Abruptly, the music cut out with a whine from the speakers.

'Libby!' That yell, it was a voice she recognised.

The lasers and smoke made her vision cataract-cloudy, but Libby could see a familiar face peering out from onstage.

'Joe!'

Adrenaline flooded her bloodstream as the fire bowl lurched again and this time it fell not in slow motion but hideously fast, splashing people below with flame. Screams made the crowd jittery, a human wave surging towards her and so she moved fast, dragging Dawn with her, right to the huge blockade of the stage.

It was too high for her to climb.

Trashed safety barriers lay beached underneath it, the wall a sheer cliff of smooth material, nothing to get a purchase on. The crowd-wave surged again, sweeping them closer to being crushed against the stage.

'Here!'

There were faces peering down on her – Joe and Sal. Arms reached down, two people above and two below, as Libby and the security guard got the half-unconscious Dawn up first before Libby herself grabbed on to Joe's waiting hand. The golden glow of an emerging sun began to set fire to the edge of the sky as she was half-pulled, half-pushed onto the middle of the stage.

She had made it.

'Help her, help her, help her!' Her knees gave out as she sank to the floor and gathered Dawn to her, brushing her hair out of her face, her skin clammy and cold. People rushed to them. She heard the shouts and instructions from those who knew what to do, who could save Dawn's life. The security guard who had helped them was also dragged up and onto the relative safety of the stage. Everything, the screams of those on fire, the yells and whoops of others, all of it hollowed out to muted echoes as Libby only heard the panicked bird-pants of her own breathing loud in her ears.

Safety. Help. Other people taking over. She could let her beaten body sag into exhaustion.

Her silk robe drenched in blood, her arms sticky with it up to her elbows, she pushed back her matted tangled hair with her one good arm and surveyed the scene below her: the smoke writhing, the upturned faces, mouths stretched wide in glee or fear and beyond it all, though she could not see them, were the river and the white farmhouse, the oak tree and the grey circle of standing stones that had stood on that spot long before anything else.

The first sirens could be heard as the sun rose on Solstice.

Chapter 50

Ma Blake, Twenty Years Ago

Under a night sky and the branches of the oak tree lay a badly beaten Tess cradling her newborn baby. Abel stood over her. Ma's mind reeled.

'No.'

'The child is mine, Ma. Silas doesn't know.'

'How did . . .?'

'She was off her head on something one night. She wanted it.'

Those words slipped from him as easily as if he was saying 'Good morning' to an elderly neighbour but the terror . . . the degradation they suggested. Ma's body refused to move as she looked at the man before her, the man she had brought up, the person she had created.

'But how do you know the baby is yours?'

'She said she'd worked out the dates. She was sure about it.'

No. Abel did not do this kind of thing. Abel did not do . . . whatever he had done . . . to his brother's . . . whatever she was to Silas. Abel had girls fawning over him. He didn't need to do something like that. He was the charmer, the leader of the pack, his smile as sunny as the one on the backdrop of the newly erected festival stage.

Tess managed to stretch her hand out towards Ma and for a second their gazes locked. In that look Ma should have seen that there were no excuses left for Abel, but she chose to briefly close her eyes and take a step back. As she did so, Abel stood and casually walked over to the beaten young woman clinging to her baby.

He paused.

This was it, Ma thought. This was where he was going to explain what had really happened, that he hadn't just dragged Tess out to the oak tree and beaten her so badly she couldn't even speak.

Slowly and deliberately, he stepped on the girl's trembling hand, crushing her fingers into the mud.

'No!' Ma ran to the girl, to the baby, shoving Abel away. 'Have you gone mad? What are you doing?'

'What you taught me.' Ma gaped and so Abel continued. 'Myths and folklore and superstition . . . ways of asking the land for things – isn't that right? She's the perfect opportunity. If we want the festival to work we need an offering for the Grey Sisters – like in the stories. Actually, it kills two birds with one stone because then Silas'll never have to know the baby isn't his. I'm not prepared to lose my brother over some slut.'

It wasn't Abel's voice, she told herself. It wasn't Abel. This couldn't be happening. This wasn't the kind of offering she had ever meant. Blood, yes, blood could be involved, like she had done earlier, using her cut, but that was just a little bit, freely given. It wasn't . . . this . . .

Ma crouched under the oak tree, the one knee stiff from where she had cut it early that morning. With shaking fingers she searched out Elizabeth's little face, wrapped in a sodden blanket, and she almost gasped with relief when she heard a tiny, weak cry.

'Let me have the baby,' she begged, not sure if she was asking Tess or Abel.

'Don't worry, Ma – I have it all planned out so you don't have to do a thing. I'm going to bury them here. Tell Silas she ran off in the night with the brat.' He pointed to the spade he had brought with him. 'And then we'll know, once it's finished, that we've done everything we could to make the festival a success.'

It was as if he was informing her of the items he needed to add to a shopping list. Ma looked at him, her brain whirring through all the words she should be saying, the ways she should be taking control of this situation that had spiralled so horribly away from her. However, all she could do was wait. She was waiting for the Abel she knew to reappear – for him to explain that this had all been a mistake, that she had misunderstood, that he was not to blame for this at all.

But the Abel she knew had been a fantasy of her own creation.

'I'll do it,' she said, intent on sending him away, keeping him far from the baby that Tess would not give to her, her grip tight despite the blood and swelling and the way her one arm looked oddly bent. Ma carried on, the desperate words spilling from her: 'You go help Silas clear the path. That way, he'll never suspect you of being involved, yes?'

Abel considered Ma for a beat and then came closer to Tess who had stopped trying to crawl away, her chest heaving in erratic choking gasps for air. Crouching near her, he gazed at her in a dispassionate way, as if she were a bug that had landed on his windowsill, one he hadn't yet decided to squash. Ma tensed, on edge and ready to push him away from the baby if she had to. The seconds stretched and he continued to stare.

Then his face became a sudden blank. 'Fine. The offering's been given. You clear up here.'

The shock of his sudden decision made Ma almost slump with relief. With those words he didn't even look at Ma before he walked away, leaving her with the broken girl and the baby and a black night lit by one single lamp. Ma lifted her head to the rain that pelted her as she knelt next to Tess and tried to think, aware she was taking gulps of air as if she were drowning.

Of course, at first she thought about dragging the both of them, Tess and her baby, back to the house, about calling an ambulance and the police, knowing they would be able to force their way through the path that was probably half cleared by now. Of course, she thought of that first.

But when she moved, it was only to take the baby from Tess's now unresisting arms.

Holding her inside her raincoat, Ma wiped the water from Elizabeth's face, and saw how pale her cheeks were, how cold her skin was to the touch. The baby gave a sad half-cough, half-snuffle and Ma wanted to whisk her away instantly, tuck her into her dry, warm blankets in Ma's bedroom once again, safe and snug.

Of course, she needed to get them *both* to safety.

However, there was no trying to get Tess to stand because the girl was nearly unconscious, a dead weight, one that Ma couldn't manage whilst holding Elizabeth at the same time.

Time was not on her side. The path would soon be cleared and her sons would return. One expecting to find Tess and his new daughter waiting for him and the other expecting them to be gone.

Ma let Tess slump back onto the ground under the oak tree and let out a yell of frustration. She could not think a way out of this.

She knew what she should be doing: calling that ambulance, calling the police, handing her son over to the authorities to be branded the monster she was sure he wasn't, because he was her son. She knew him. The festival would fail, the village would still hate them and they would end up God knows where, with her left to make monthly visits in prison to the boy she had thought would go so far in life.

Abel had made a mistake. That was it.

He was devastated by it, too ashamed to face what he'd done, leaving her to deal with it. Even now, out clearing that path, he was racked with guilt. This mistake should not be allowed to ruin everything. She would not let it. That was her job as a mother, to protect her boys, even from themselves.

A switch flicked in her brain, turning out the lights on any bright, good thoughts. Only darkness was left.

Next to her Tess lay dying, Ma knew. If she didn't get her to a hospital soon then her chance of surviving even the next hour was slight. Ma knew what the sound of that laboured breathing meant. She had heard it over the years from animals who had caused themselves injuries that meant they had to be put down.

If the girl recovered, she would talk. She would tell of this night. Ma could not let that happen.

But on the wind that swirled around them came another sound. A whispering. The sound of five women once known as witches, talking in low voices, an incantation. Ma could feel the stones around her, leaning in, watching what was about to happen. So the thought that came to her wasn't really hers, it was theirs.

Her blood yesterday morning had not been enough.

The land required more.

The Grey Sisters required more.

Ma moved with the hurricane lamp, a deep pain throbbing in her injured knee, searching the ground near the stones until she found it – the spade Abel had brought out with him. She tied the blanket into a sling around her waist so it held the baby firm to her chest.

The oak tree rustled its leaves above her head. Huge and sacred. Stories had been weaved about it for centuries, enchantment wreathed around its bark and hung from its branches, glistening like dew on berries. Tomorrow would be the longest day and this Midsummer's Eve – she could feel the electric tinge in her teeth of old magic in the night air. The whispering wrapped itself around her.

Her light found the dark shape under the tree, found the face with big pleading eyes. Dying. She wished she could have been surprised, by the pain, by the cruelty of it, but she was not. It would be a mercy to the poor creature; she had done it for many animals over the years.

This, however, was not grubby farmyard work. This had to be something different. It was sacred. This was older than her, as old as the land that waited in silence for her to act, to save herself and her family. She raised the spade above her head, ready to bring it down with one quick, hard swing.

This was an offering.

Chapter 51

Once again, Ma found herself standing under the oak tree in the darkness with a knife in her hand, a body prone at her feet.

Twenty years had passed since then. Twenty. Her hair had greyed to a silver white, her muscles had stiffened in the mornings, her eyesight blurring at small print. Her boys had grown into men. In the years after handing over her granddaughter to Ann Corrigan, Ma had hoped that whatever was twisted in Abel would straighten itself out over time, that running the festival and the adoration it brought would be enough, that there would only ever be one set of bones under the tree.

She was no more innocent than him. Worse if anything. The monster, when it does what it does, it barely understands, barely even recognises the damage it causes, but its creator, the person who stands back and lets it happen, who clears up after them – well, that person is worse than a monster.

That person is a mother, maybe.

She had been the one to end Tess's life. Abel had beaten the poor thing so badly that she had been unlikely to survive but it had been Ma who had smashed the edge of the spade into her skull. At the time she had told herself it was an offering. The myths and stories, the superstitions and folklore had taught her that. The land only understood blood and so blood she had given it, hoping for a miracle.

Instead she had been cursed.

She had got what she wanted. The storm had ceased, the weather had then held and the festival had been a massive success, had been the start of something that grew and grew each year, a parasite, a tick, gorging itself on the body of the farm.

It had not been enough for Abel.

She had no longer been able to lie to herself. Her golden boy had dazzled her but she couldn't keep up the pretence of his shine any longer, especially after washing Tess's blood from her skin. No longer could she hide from it, the cold star behind his sun, which chilled her to the bone.

The idea of Sanctum had been hers, meant as a counterbalance. A more private, healing kind of space where festivalgoers could soothe their troubled souls, could work through the pain that held them back, could turn away from the darkness that beckoned and stay in the light, on a safe path. Its site was where Tess's bones lay under the oak tree and she hoped that the good done there every year, the healing that went on, would go some way to compensate for the horror Ma had let happen – had taken part in.

The witches' bottles offered little in the way of protection, but she couldn't stop herself from making more of them, finding the process strangely soothing, filling the kitchen with them, and then the living room and then on through all of the rooms of the house, each bottle a protection spell for every festivalgoer, every member of staff who crossed paths with Abel.

She didn't think he had ever done anything like what Tess had endured since that night . . . but she couldn't be sure. And so the jars popped up everywhere, on windowsills, in corners, on tables, on top of books, next to vases. Silas had grimaced and told her it was crazy but then Silas did not understand anything of what happened that night. He had gone out to clear the path of that fallen tree and then, when he had come back, exhausted and covered in sawdust, all he had found was Tess and his child gone, vanished like a terrible magic act. Of course, by then Ma herself had disappeared too after roughly burying the body, planning to go back and dig a deeper grave when she had a chance. She had gone with the baby straight to Ann Corrigan, the first person she could think of who she had a chance of persuading to upend her entire life and take in a stranger's child.

Of late, she had found that she could not stop herself from checking on Elizabeth, or Libby, as Ann called her. Once a month, every month for the past year she had left the farm at dawn, driving to Ann's home, sometimes Ann sneaking out to meet her, to give her updates whilst the girl slept on in her bed, or inviting her in if Elizabeth had stayed with her friend for the night. She had needed to know, to be certain that the girl was okay, that nothing terrible had befallen her, and that need had grown stronger as she had realised just how ill Ann Corrigan had become.

'Ma.' Abel dragged himself over to the oak tree and sat with his back against the trunk, his one hand reaching out to her. 'Help me, Ma – please!'

It was ingrained in her to grab his hand, to tend to his wounds, to pull him up and nurse him back to health. If she had been that tree there, that instinct would have been etched as rings inside her trunk. But she did not move.

There was only one person to blame for all of this. Her. She was his mother. She had created him, her monster. She had filled his head with wicked folklore and she had killed a girl to save him from going to prison, to save her home.

The bottles she made, they were to protect others from her too. What she had done, it hadn't been an offering; the land did not require blood, never had done. It required nothing, absolutely nothing from her. It was just land.

'Ma?' There was a tremble in his voice that she had never heard before. Abel the charismatic, the smooth, no crack in his veneer.

What had she done to form this smiling beautiful horror? What kind of poison in her womb had created this man who beat a woman nearly to death because her death would be useful, who had viewed her as merely an object? What had Ma done wrong?

She had to do better.

Tess's bones lay under the oak tree but all these years, the girl had been at her side. No matter how many bottles she made, how well Sanctum worked, how much money she donated to charity and put in Ann Corrigan's bank account each month, no matter how kind she was to every person she met at the festival, none of it made any difference. There Tess was in the corner of the kitchen, eyes wide, blood bubbling. There she was backstage, watching the band, her arms limp, her head hanging to one side. There she was in the passenger seat of her truck, at the table at mealtimes, at the end of her bed, breathing in her ear. No amounts of whispered pleading apologies in the dead of night helped.

She had to do better. For her.

'Ma? Ma! I'm bleeding . . .' There was a childlike whine to Abel's voice, but Ma did not respond.

Instead she walked away, to the shed behind the farmhouse and got what she needed, keeping Silas's knife in her hand and checking in on her youngest son first. She gave him water and pressed more material to the wound in his side and, though he was weak, it looked like he would make it until the ambulance came. There was nothing more she could do for him. She had ruined his life too.

By the time she got back to the oak tree she could see that Abel had been trying to get to his feet but blood loss was beginning to weaken him. The polished side of the fruit that he had always shown to people had turned to a soft black bruise and there was a new harsh grit to his tone.

'For fuck's sake – help me to the house. Call a fucking ambulance!'

Again, she did not respond. She *had* called an ambulance, from the ancient kitchen phone fixed to the wall, but it was for

250

Silas. He was the only one who would need it. She didn't want to talk to Abel anymore. She didn't need to try and understand him, nor did she want to coax, manage or persuade. She was done with all of that. Since the night she had killed Tess she no longer heard any whispering from the Grey Sisters, but the stones in a circle around them, they had had the right idea. For some men, there was no saving. There was no changing. Eurig Swain, the man who had hunted them, he would never have stopped, would never have given up, and so there was only one way to save themselves and other women like them.

As she had done once before, twenty years ago, Ma raised the spade above her head.

Across Abel's face flashed the realisation of what his mother was about to do and he reached out to her, opening his mouth to speak, but she did not look at him as she swung the spade down hard and his words choked off in bubbles of blood. She swung again, just as hard, and again, until he stopped moving and then she swung one last time to make sure.

The land would have its blood after all.

What she had killed was not her son, because the son she had known had been a figment of her own imagination, what she had built him to be in her head so she would never have to face the truth. But there, on the ground at her feet was her true son. There was no coming back from what he had tried to do tonight, to her granddaughter, to the woman who had once been baby Elizabeth. There was no coming back for either of them.

The knife was for her.

She rolled up the sleeves of her shirt. The stones around her could be hunched women, leaning in. The wind sighing in the trees could be the dry whisper of throats cracked with moss. She dug the knife into her forearm near her elbow and dragged it down to her wrist, her flesh tougher than she had expected. Then the other arm, as best she could. Unlike Silas back at the farmhouse she had no one to press wadding to her wounds and she hoped that when the paramedics came for him she would already be cold, her cuts efficiently done to let out life faster. She lay back against the trunk of the tree next to the body of her son and let her mind blur. This was more than death.

It was an offering.

Chapter 52

It was the fifth time she had watched the news report but Edna Kirk kept the television on anyway.

The clock showed midnight but she was used to being awake long past that hour. The flat above the shop was quiet and lit only by the lamp in the living room, its tattered velvet shade the colour of trampled grass.

The first report had come in that day at breakfast time, which for Edna was usually around eight o'clock before she opened the shop at nine. But the shop that day had remained closed, as it had done for days and it would stay so until she handed over the keys.

She had won.

This, though, reports of deaths and chaos and blood – she had not expected her actions to lead to this at all. When she had spotted Ma's truck that day almost a year ago, she could never have guessed that it would all end up here.

It had taken many years, but she had got the upper hand eventually.

On her television the video footage cut to drone pictures taken that morning, wide-angle aerial shots of the farmhouse, the ring of the stone circle and the oak tree in the middle as the fulcrum of that wheel. The blue police tent was a bulbous flapping growth upon the tree trunk. Two people dressed in white coveralls could be seen coming out of it, their hoods tightly pulled around their faces.

The news reporter spoke over the pictures: 'It seems that there has been a murder-suicide at the standing stone circle where Sanctum was reported to have taken place earlier that evening. There is no confirmation on the identity of those dead and we have had no word or official statement from Abel Blake.'

Edna had always woken early. As the years had lain over her like layers of rock on a cliff face she had needed less and less sleep, often to be found watching reruns of *Murder, She Wrote* so late into the night it became morning.

She always kept the curtains open. Her own glow of lamplight was dim enough that she could see out into the dawn street, watch the odd fox creep across the road, note the lights in windows, fewer and fewer each year as people deserted the village, torches on sinking ships succumbing to black waves. And who could blame them? The festival had choked all life from the village.

And the people responsible? The Blakes. The three of them but especially her – Ma Blake. She could still remember the way her face had scrunched up in anger that day years ago, when she had told Edna that she would ruin the village for daring to voice its opinion on her precious festival.

Ah, but who had been ruined now?

One morning a year ago, as the sun rose, Edna had been awake to watch a truck drive past.

Ma Blake's truck.

Ma Blake who had not been seen for years now, who, so the gossip went, had become ill, or mad, or both and now hardly ever left the farmhouse and never went to the festival anymore.

What was Ma Blake doing driving around in the thin light of dawn?

Her mother had always told her that 'curiosity killed the cat' but that had always seemed like a stupid saying to Edna because what curiosity got you was a whole heap of the best treasure ever: secrets. She knew what everyone said about her and they were right. There was nothing that went on in this village without Edna Kirk knowing about it. Because secrets were trade, they were better than the paltry money she had made from the shop; they were insurance for future favours down the line.

She kept an eye out for that truck.

Once a month, for six months, Ma Blake drove by at dawn. Once a month, for six months, she came back again as regular as clockwork in the late afternoon.

In the end Edna could not restrain herself. Jessica Fletcher, the intrepid amateur detective from *Murder, She Wrote*, would have done exactly the same thing as her. And so, on the seventh month, she made it down the stairs, grabbed her keys and her coat and drove after the truck.

Liaison, Edna guessed. A little bit of illicit passion. A romantic interlude. After all, Ma's husband had been dead over a decade and she got to meet all sorts of exciting people at the festival, lots of the fancy London crowd. Edna had hoped she wasn't going to London and that Ma's secret tryst was a lot closer to home. She didn't have enough petrol. Or snacks.

Shadowing Ma's car had proved easy enough. There had been hardly any traffic on the roads, even once they had left the village, and so Edna had been able to keep a good distance away.

In the end, of course, it hadn't been a man; it hadn't been romance, or lust at all. It had been a whole new puzzle. That was what Edna had been presented with that morning, watching as Ma hadn't even had to knock on the door of a Victorian terrace an hour or so away from Grey Sisters. A woman about her age had already been waiting on the doorstep, her head shaved, wearing silk pyjamas and the sickly pallor of someone seriously ill.

And then Ma had gone in and the door had closed.

Edna liked a puzzle. She did crosswords and wordsearches, powering her way through puzzle books each night as sleep edged out of her grasp. And so Edna had worked on it, watching and waiting even after Ma herself had driven away again that afternoon, until her surveillance had paid off. Until she had seen a young woman return to the house, presumably from work.

Until she had seen the young woman smile.

She smiled like Tess.

Once she had seen that, all the other things clicked into place – her age, the copper sheen to her hair just the same as Tess's, the Blake chin on her, the whole mix of her face which, when looked at in the filter of this new realisation immediately got Edna's brain whirring. It took another trip to find out the girl's identity, skulking after her to her place of work, a library where the staff handily wore name badges. She had felt exactly the same as when a key crossword clue had fallen into place and suddenly all the other words tumbled in, the grid almost filling itself.

Libby Corrigan. Tess's daughter.

And the father? Well, the father could only be Silas.

For some reason, Ma wanted to keep all of this secret.

Edna didn't care why. That wasn't the point. The point was the power of the secret itself, one that if Ma wanted to continue to keep then she was going to have to offer something as powerful in return.

And Edna had known exactly what she wanted.

In the end it had been Abel who had given it to her. Ma was ill, he had told her. She couldn't be disturbed and she wouldn't be talking to anyone, he had said, standing at the gate to the farmhouse, a huge thing now with a metal box and a button you had to press to get anyone's attention. A crackled conversation via a grille and then there he had stood.

Once she had told him what she had seen, Edna had got his attention all right.

So here she was, three months later in the flat above the shop in which she had lived for more years than she cared to count. The shop that now belonged to Abel Blake, who had paid handsomely for that information she had given him there at the gate and paid for her to keep her mouth closed.

Curiosity might have killed the cat but what it did for Edna was get her out of this godforsaken village. It gave her a long string of numbers in her bank account, which she could use to get very far from here, away from the Blakes and their festival.

It had given her power.

On the television the news reporter, standing presumably outside the festival gates though it was too dark to make them out, spoke again: 'However, I'm getting reports that there may be more fatalities as yet to be reported. The final night of the festival and its iconic morning celebration of the sun fell into chaos as the crowd spiralled out of control. Please be warned, the following video may be upsetting for some viewers.'

The picture showed shaky footage from someone's phone. Smoke, shouts, people blurring into shot and then a stage with figures scurrying about in its shadows. Two blood-soaked girls, faces camouflaged by gore and grime, were pulled onto it, one in a silk robe supporting the other with a cloth bandage around her head. They swayed for a moment, bedraggled, wild-eyed, gazing around at the madness playing out below them until their legs gave out and they crashed to the floor.

Of course, it had been a shock to see Libby turn up at her shop, but Edna had hidden it well. There had been a part of her that had wanted to tell the girl to run, that no good could come of her being anywhere near the Blakes, but instead all she had been able to do was give her Tess's missing poster, a little clue to her real mother. There hadn't been much more she could do for the girl. It hadn't been any of her business and she hadn't wanted to get on the wrong side of Abel. No time like the present to learn to keep her nose out of things that weren't her concern.

Edna switched off the television. The deaths, of course, the deaths were regrettable, but they had been nothing to do with her. That had all been Solstice's fault. When you played with fire, as the Blake family had found out, you very often got burnt.

Chapter 53

One Year On

There were gaps in Libby's memory. Holes, like a gum abscess, the surrounding area sore to the touch. She worried at them none-theless, her brain a probing tongue, as she gripped the steering wheel and tried to concentrate on the road.

She had passed her driving test only a few days ago and the car was new with its polish and plastic smell. A train would have worked just as well but somehow it seemed important to drive, to be able to leave in the car if it all got a bit too much. It wasn't a long journey.

The past year had been, not a whirlwind because one of those simply picked up stuff and swirled it around, dumping all of the broken pieces on the ground afterwards for people to pick over. There was nothing of her old life left to salvage. No, this past year had been a nuclear blast, in the zone where everything turned to ash.

She remembered dragging herself up onto that stage, her clammy blood-soaked gown clinging to her, she remembered the way the bowl of fire tipped and fell and the people underneath it tried to scatter but couldn't get far. She remembered the screams and how she had fallen to her knees as the wail of emergency sirens had pierced the cacophony around her. She remembered how hard she had gripped Joe's arm as he had pulled her onto the stage and how she had managed to ask for help for Dawn, through a jaw that had begun to shake.

And then?

Nothing. The abscess.

Later, Joe told her that she had been awake, that she had kept a hard hold on Dawn even as help arrived, smoothing hair back from a face too still, too pale, the eyes closed. She could imagine it. The terror in her voice, the ragged fear. She could imagine the gaze of those staring down at her, foreheads creased in confusion. She could almost see her own bloody handprints on the stage floor.

She could not remember any of it.

Perhaps it was easier for the mind to simply pluck out that infected tooth, to leave only a throbbing absence, the ghost pain of what had been there.

Her first memory was being given a paper cup of water and she had gulped at it greedily until the liquid made her cough and her heart hammered as she spat it back out. The last drink she had taken had been from Abel and that moment she had gone straight back there, to Sanctum, to the firelight glow that had glittered in his eyes as he had handed her the drugged cup. She had tried to tell them about what happened at the standing stones but her words would not make sentences anymore and her thoughts jumped around too much to be coherent. She had slumped onto the ambulance stretcher.

Back in the car, Libby tried to manage actually being in control of the vehicle as well as concentrating on working out the directions, ending up doing neither of those things successfully. A horn blared as she swerved into a roundabout exit despite not being in the correct lane.

'Sorry!' She raised a hand at the driver behind her who was only a shadow figure.

It was summer. She had got used to the chill of winter, the softness and protection of a thick jumper in those colder months when she had woven her new life. This heat meant she would have to peel off layers again and it wasn't a prospect that she relished.

'Umm . . . maybe remember to indicate?' Joe sat next to her in the passenger seat, gripping onto the handle above the window like he was an unwitting participant in a rally car race. In a way he had been, not just for this car journey, which she had to admit was not showing off her best driving skills, but for the entire past year. They had moved in together only a month ago, boxes piled in the hallway ready for when they had time to work out which bits of each other's life-junk they wanted to keep.

Little plastic bobbleheads of Dawn's Holy Trinity – Dolly, Beyoncé and Taylor – nodded at her from the dashboard where she had stuck them. Her brain would not give her the picture of her friend's still body being carried out on a stretcher. That was probably for the best.

She hadn't done any of the interviews. The picture of her on the Sun Stage covered in blood, her gold robe tattered and ripped, had gone viral before her story was even known. There was even a shaky video of her being hauled onto the stage by Joe and Sal, of her wobbling steps to the edge and the gasp of the person filming it: 'Is she . . . is that . . . blood?' Then the whole thing cut out as fire tipped into the crowd and a panicked screaming began.

Deaths.

Injuries.

The nearest hospital had been kept busy. The fire itself had caused only wounds and burns and had been quickly put out, the shock of it and the appearance of the emergency services serving to jolt the crowd into a more subdued, smoke-stained mood.

Journalists had jostled for her story. With Ma and Abel dead and Silas holed up first in hospital and then in the bothy on the farm, there had been no one else from which to get the details. There was a clamour for those details, for each drop of blood, for each twist of the blade, for every kick Abel had aimed at her and for each lie she had been told. The fall of Solstice's golden boy. The darkness behind the mask.

Of course, that made Libby Blake the new pretender to the crown.

The crown didn't interest her. She'd had a year in which to do so and still hadn't legally changed her name to Blake. Neither Blake nor Corrigan had wanted her and in some moments she did consider making up a whole new surname, a fresh start created by her and her alone. So no, Solstice and the festival held little appeal for her anymore.

But the land did.

There was a lot of it, those rolling fields upon which there had once been a security tower shaped like a bright rocket, a stage reigned over by a sun and another reigned over by the moon, a wood filled with magic tricks and acrobats and fortune tellers in their caravans handing out futures like cracked gems. There had been sleeping tents crammed together and people, so many people, sitting, standing, lounging, drinking, laughing, fighting and around it all that fencing with those huge brass gates built as if the festivalgoers were about to enter a magic kingdom.

The magic had gone and Libby did not want it back. But the land – oh, the land was a different prospect. She had plans for that.

Glancing at Joe, she flicked her indicators, completing a perfect right turn, which made him smile but clearly not quite feel confident enough to loosen his grip on the handle. There it was, that one street in the village where she had first arrived by mistake a year ago. There was Edna's old shop.

And there standing in front of it was a familiar figure.

Chapter 54

'Libble-Lobble!'

Dawn ran over to the car and waited until Libby was nearly out of the driver's seat to crush her in a hug. They always hugged each other hello and goodbye these days because they had both learned that the goodbye could suddenly, and without warning, become much more definite. Dawn's hair, now a regular blonde, smelled of apples and she wore a pair of dungarees with a vest underneath, the kind of outfit that would make Libby look like a children's TV presenter but on Dawn looked edgy and carefree.

The first few tense days after Dawn had been taken to hospital had seen Libby teetering on a tightrope of fear. Dawn had hardly been breathing when they had carried her into the ambulance and the head injury she had sustained had plunged her into a coma, a deep black pool from which Libby worried she would never emerge.

On one of those days in the hospital room, Libby decided to play a selection of terrible Dolly Parton cover songs into the headphones placed over Dawn's ears and, third song in, Dawn had opened her eyes. It was no coincidence. 'I don't remember the music, but I do remember feeling really annoyed, like there was an itch in my ear that I had to scratch.' So, it was now legend. Dolly had saved Dawn's life.

Dawn released her from the hug. 'In Dolly we trust.'

Libby knew the response, 'Praise Parton.'

'Joseph,' Dawn said, nodding at Joe. The use of his full name was a new thing, only begun after he and Libby had made their romance official and decided to live together. Libby imagined that very soon Dawn would take on a stern expression, clamp a hand on his shoulder and take him to one side to issue the age-old warning from father to prospective son-in-law, perhaps even throwing the phrase 'my boy' in there for good measure.

Edna's old shop was a shell soon to be completely repurposed. It had taken a while to sort out the Blake finances but Silas had kept worrying at them like a sharp beak on a tough piece of gristle. Silas should have been heir to whatever was left of the Blake inheritance but all he wanted was his small safe space in the bothy, now given a rudimentary makeover to make it sanitary. He had no appetite for legal paperwork, land or money; too much of a temptation to buy substances that would only send him down a dangerous path. So he signed it all over to Libby as Abel's daughter. Fields, farmhouse, oak tree, standing stones . . . and, bizarrely, this shop. One of Abel's last actions had been to buy it from Edna for reasons unknown.

When asked, Edna had shrugged and said, 'I didn't care why he wanted it. Glad to be shot of the place.' She was currently living on a cruise ship, having worked out it was cheaper and better value for money than buying another property. She sent Joe lots of pictures of cocktail glasses artfully arranged in front of spectacular sunsets.

Grey Sisters Activity Centre. That was the plan. Libby could picture it: a place with a café and shop, showers and changing rooms, offering guided hikes up into the mountains, cycling routes and other suitably sporty activities. All it would take was the purchase of the houses on either side, which seemed to be easy enough. Libby had the money to do it.

'Remember to keep a job open for me if I fail my degree,' Dawn said, smiling at Libby.

'You're not going to.'

Dawn gave her a mock-panicked stare. 'Anyway, if I do, I'm planning to blame the near-life-threatening head injury. It might get me a pity pass.'

It seemed, for once, that Abel had been telling the truth. Dawn, in her inebriated state, had slipped away from Libby that night at the festival, intent on getting Sanctum tickets. The closest she had got to it, however, was a dunking in the river when she fell in whilst snooping around. Security had fished her out but then Abel had taken it from there, remembering her from the brunch they had shared earlier that day and taking his opportunity to lure Libby in with the prospect of finding her friend. If Dawn hadn't tripped and landed in his lap, it was unclear how he had planned to snatch Libby ready for her fate under the oak tree. They would never find out now.

One thing had played on Libby's mind: what Silas had said as he had walked away from them after brunch that morning on the farmhouse porch. YOU NEED TO LEAVE. At the time she had thought them the words from the note but that note had turned out to be nothing. So what had Silas actually said?

'Bloody hell.' Silas had scowled. 'I can't really remember. Probably I was telling you both to hurry up because I needed to leave . . .'

As Joe and Dawn got into the car for the final part of this journey Libby stopped to take another look at the village, some of the windows in those houses and shops boarded up, some with their curtains firmly closed. It had a dusty air of neglect, a feeling that it was a shelf in a collection no longer cared for. But with the activity centre could come new cafés, other shops selling sports gear, or little souvenirs, and maybe those windows would gleam with a new light.

'*They cut us off on purpose.*' That was what Edna had told her, that day they had arrived in her shop. The Blakes had created this ghost town and now Libby was going to breathe life into it, if she could.

The massive brass gates were gone. Libby, Dawn and Joe got out of the car, the village far behind them. There was fencing but it wasn't painted in bright swooshes of colour, instead it was plain and grey and had health and safety signs attached to it. The beast-like sounds of the festival were replaced by the softer grumbling of diggers chewing up the soil.

Most of the land Libby had found herself in possession of had been sold off, enough to fund her two projects: the activity centre and this.

'I don't quite . . . see it yet . . .' Dawn nudged her hard hat into a more fashionable angle and pushed a wellie-clad foot into the mud. 'There's just string and some bollards.'

She had known the name for this place ever since the idea for it had ballooned into her mind like a beautifully formed glass bauble. The Tess Sanderson Clinic. Holding the festival again was never an option; it felt too much like dancing on someone's grave – Tess's. That string and those bollards marked out where the foundations would soon be laid, the walls of separate rooms and hallways, a place for rehabilitation, where people could find the peace and support to try and get themselves clean. The kind of place both Tess and Silas had needed. Most of the guests would be fee-paying, but there would always be money set aside each quarter for people who could not afford those fees yet needed the help just the same.

'Here it is.' Libby walked over to a spot towards the back and threw her arms open wide. 'My library.'

Dawn sighed a little too loudly. She didn't understand. She

thought Libby was being . . . well, boring, safe old Libby again, going back to the job she knew, too scared to try anything different. But Dawn was wrong. This was in no way the same job, this was to be a space in a building she had commissioned, helping people she would choose to be admitted, filling the shelves of the library with the kinds of books that would help them during what might be a difficult stay, where they could get lost in stories. Libby wanted to be surrounded by those tales that, once read were set, known things that would not suddenly flip and change like life could. Like hers had.

It wasn't going to be her entire world. She and Dawn had already mapped out their six months of travelling that they planned to do together before Dawn used the degree Libby was sure she would ace with flying colours to get a brilliant job some- where important. Joe's band had been approached by someone who had seen them perform at the festival, who wanted to manage them, on the strict proviso that they rethink their band name. So the future was an exciting thought, one filled with sunshine and new countries and even newer contracts. It was a balloon and it needed a ribbon attached to a weight. That was here. It was this clinic.

You don't fit. That had been her fortune, handed to her in a painted wagon not too far from where she stood now, and she finally understood. No, she didn't fit. As the wrong child, she hadn't fitted with her mother, neither had she fitted in the festival, nor with Abel her father, who had only wanted to use her blood. But she could carve out her own space, somewhere shaped snugly around her, where she did fit, fitted exactly, because she could create it herself and share it with the people around her who mattered: Dawn and Joe.

After Libby had caught up with the project manager, the three of them took a path through the mud and digging and piles of cellophane-wrapped building materials to another gate at right angles to the one through which they had entered.

It led to the wood.

This would all remain exactly as it was. These trees, the river and the land beyond it; the farmhouse, stones and bothy would not be sold.

The space between the trees was shadowed, cool and quiet. The roots connecting trunks probably remembered a time when sequinned acrobats tumbled over them, when there were fairy lights and stilt-walkers and the pattering of many feet dancing to strange music. Now there was only a hush.

They paused at the river.

'We can go with you . . .'

'No. I'm fine.'

'We'll be right here.'

And then Libby made stones move to her command, watching them rise from the water into the now familiar path. She handed the remote to Joe who nodded and kept it in his grip, raised a little and ready to be used at a moment's notice.

There was one last person to see and they were waiting for her on the opposite bank, still and watchful.

Chapter 55

There was no hug. Silas's face, angular and sharp-featured before, now seemed more hollow than flesh. He did jerk oddly, his one arm moving as if almost to shake her hand, a weirdly formal greeting for two people who had been through so much together.

'We'll get this over with.' Silas made it sound as if this were an unpleasant medical procedure upon which they were about to embark.

It was merely ink on paper.

They walked uphill, Libby shortening her stride so Silas could keep up. He put his hand to his side, a ghost instinct for a stab wound now healed. Once he had been released from hospital he had made it clear that he would recuperate, alone, at the bothy. He rarely answered emails or his phone and, in the past year, Libby had probably spoken to him a total of ten times, always about the sale of the land.

There had been a DNA test. No one trusted Abel's word that Libby was in fact his daughter and so they had let science make the final call as to which Blake was the father. For a week whilst waiting for the results, Libby had allowed herself to duck from under Abel's shadow, maybe not his child after all, his maddened

269

blood not running in her veins. But no. In this one respect, he had been telling the truth.

'You'll want tea.' Silas opened the door to the bothy he had made home and stamped his feet on the mat, little crumbs of earth shaking off into the thick coir. That was something she had noticed about him: he hardly ever asked questions. His sentences were always statements, firm in intent, no possibility for disagreement or confusion. She wondered if it was a new thing or something he had always done.

Her uncle. She knew very little about him, only that he had tried to help her that night and had been abandoned bleeding on the floor of the farmhouse for his good intentions. In one evening he had lost his mother and brother but more importantly he had lost who he thought they were, their memories now tarnished by what had happened to the woman he had loved under that oak tree twenty-one years ago.

Libby wasn't sure gaining a niece was any kind of recompense.

The bothy was clean and neat but simple, the sofa by the fire old and sagging, the table and its one chair scuffed, the wood heavily marked. A half-open door gave a glimpse of a bed with the plain white cover thrown back, the pillow dented from Silas's sleeping head. Spread on the table were papers, a pen laid on top. Silas handed her an enamel camping mug, the tea in it like a muddy puddle.

'How are you?' Libby began flicking through the paperwork, trying to look as if she had any idea of the details written within, some final documents to do with a trust set up to manage the money left over from the land sale.

'Good enough.'

'I don't . . . I mean, this money is yours. I don't need—'

'You'll take what's offered. It's only right.' There was nowhere for him to sit so he stood at her shoulder as if they were posing for a Victorian family portrait.

For a while there was only the sound of rustling paper. Libby signed the final one and then put the pen down, twisting the cap around as she glanced up at Silas.

'You know I'm going to visit, right?' Libby said as Silas reached over and shuffled the paper into a neat pile. She saw his hand pause, noted the callouses on his tanned skin, the scrapes on his knuckles as if he had got into a fight, though the only person left to fight on the farm was himself. He didn't say anything. 'You know you're not going to get rid of me. I'm going to turn up at odd weekends and make you open the door and bring you things that I've baked, which is going to be awful for you because my baking is horrendous. I'm going to make you do polite chitchat and you're going to have to offer me tea and tell me how your day's gone. Just so you know, I don't give up easily either. So even if you don't open the door I'll just sit outside it and . . . I don't know . . . sing really loudly or something . . .'

Here Silas smiled, a slow thing that softened his gaze and made him duck his head slightly as if embarrassed to be caught in any kind of joyful expression. Then he turned suddenly and walked over to the small square-paned window that gave him a view of the farmhouse and the stones.

'Thank you.'

'Well, I wouldn't thank me yet, like I said, my baking is hideous—'

'No, thank you for the clinic . . . for naming it after . . .'

Tess. After Libby had made her statement to the police, and Ma and Abel's bodies had been taken away, the ground under the oak tree had been dug up and her bones finally found.

Libby knew this wasn't a time for words. They would come, she hoped. There would perhaps be a time in the future when she could sit here with Silas and he could tell her about the Tess he had known. Her mother. But it would not be soon. Silas was too buried under suffering right now. The weight of it hunched his shoulders and bowed his head, a mix of guilt and anger and shame and he could not unclog his throat to even begin to speak. Libby would have to wait. She could do that. All those months spent in that sickroom with Ann Corrigan had taught Libby well in the art of patience. She could sit in silence with him for as long as he needed until his voice came back to him.

Patting his shoulder, she stood and then left. She had one last thing she wanted to do.

Six stones. An oak tree.

Libby stood under the branches and gazed over at the farmhouse, imagining all the little eyes of creepy earthenware pots staring back at her, locked in their four walls. If it had been up to her it would have been demolished by now, the land scraped clean like a surgeon's knife clearing pus from an infected wound. But Silas hadn't wanted it touched and so there it stood, its curtains closed, left to moulder.

There was a new Sister in the ring of stones. A smaller crooked one, too new to have any moss furring its edges though it did have initials carved into it: TS. Finally a marker, a heavy rock of a full stop indicating the end of Tess's story.

If, on the breeze, there came a sound of whispering, an insistent murmuring that could, if listened to closely, be a kind of incantation, then Libby ignored it.

At the base of Tess's stone was a bunch of yellow roses, tied with twine. Silas's handiwork. As Libby reached out to prop them up once again from where they had fallen, she gasped and yanked her hand away, blood beading on the tip of her finger from a sharp thorn.

There was a moment when she thought about letting a drop fall, when she heard Abel's voice talking about blood magic and she wondered what kind of wish Tess would grant, how it would be fitting at last to give her some power, the woman who had been so badly treated by the Blakes. The bead on her skin was a perfect red dome. But if she knew one thing about the future she was building for herself, it was that there would be no more blood shed in this circle.

She sucked her finger and left the stones to their whispering, to talk only to themselves.

No more offerings.

A Letter from Louise Mumford

Thank you so much for choosing to read *The Festival*. I hope you enjoyed it! If you did and would like to be the first to know about my new releases, then you can follow me on X: https://twitter.com/louise_mumford

Readers are the reason I get to do a job I love and so I cannot express enough my appreciation for their support and enthusiasm. This book is based on the horrors of massive music festivals but, rest assured, I always enjoy any literary festival I attend. Bookish people are the best!

I hope you loved *The Festival* and if you did, I would be so grateful if you would leave a review. I always love to hear what readers thought, and it helps new readers discover my books too.

Thanks,

Louise

Sleepless

Don't close your eyes. Don't fall asleep. Don't let them in.

Thea is an insomniac; she hasn't slept more
than three hours a night for years.

So when an ad for a sleep trial that promises to change her life
pops up on her phone, Thea knows this is her last chance at
finding any kind of normal life.

Soon Thea's sleeping for longer than she has in a decade, and
awakes feeling transformed. So much so that at first she's
willing to overlook the oddities of the trial – the lack of any
phone signal; the way she can't leave her bedroom without
permission; the fact that all her personal possessions
are locked away, even her shoes.

But it soon becomes clear that the trial doesn't just want to
help Thea sleep. It wants to *control* her sleep . . .

**An unputdownable, gripping psychological thriller for fans
of *The One*, *Behind Her Eyes* and *Girl A*!**

The Safe House

She told you the house would keep you safe. She lied.

Esther is safe in the house. For sixteen years,
she and her mother have lived off the grid, protected
from the dangers of the outside world. For sixteen years,
Esther has never seen another single soul.

Until today.

Today there's a man outside the house. A man who knows
Esther's name, and who proves that her mother's claims
about the outside world are false. A man who is
telling Esther that she's been living a lie.

Is her mother keeping Esther safe – or keeping her prisoner?

The Hotel

Four of them went to the hotel

Four students travel to Ravencliffe, an eerie abandoned hotel perched on steep cliffs on the Welsh coast. After a series of unexplained accidents, only three of them leave. The fourth, Leo, disappears, and is never seen again.

Only three of them came back

A decade on, the friends have lost contact. Oscar is fame-hungry, making public appearances and selling his story. Richard sank into alcoholism and is only just recovering. Bex just wants to forget – until one last opportunity to go back offers the chance to find out what really happened to Leo.

Ten years later, they return one last time

But as soon as they get to the hotel things start going wrong again. Objects mysteriously disappear and reappear. Accidents happen. And Bex realises that her former friends know far more than they are letting on about the true events at Ravencliffe that night . . .

Acknowledgements

I would like to thank my fantastic agent Kate Shaw for her unwavering enthusiasm for my books and her hard work on my behalf. Thanks also to my brilliant editor Audrey Linton who has been such a delight to work with and really brought out the best in the story. Thanks to all at HQ, every person who goes into the making of a book: copy-editing, proofreading, cover design, sales and marketing. Huge thanks to Lisa Milton for setting me off on this journey.

Massive thanks to the readers. For all the amazing bloggers who read books, shout about them and leave those all-important reviews – there are too many of you to name individually and I don't want to miss anyone out – but I love each and every one of you. To everyone who turns up to library talks and bookshop launches and who recommends one of my books to a friend or a book club, your support means the world to me. Thank you to all of the bookshops who stock my book too, and to Griffin Books in particular for being such a cheerleader.

Thanks to my family and friends who put up with me disappearing into my imaginary worlds at inconvenient times. My sister Caroline, Mart, Cath, Ffion, Aidan, Gwen and the 'Coven' (Em, Fi, Liz), Chris K, Dan, Will, Dennis and someone else . . .

think his name might be Chris too . . . but anyway, he's merely my friend's husband so we don't need to worry about him . . .

My much-loved mother, Carol, died as I was editing this book. She was a powerhouse. Because of her I knew from an early age what being a strong, independent woman looked like. Because of her I know the lyrics to far too many Tom Jones songs.

A huge thank you to my husband Jason. For each book, he reads my messy first draft and still thinks I can write. That's love for you.

Dear Reader,

We hope you enjoyed reading this book. If you did, we'd be so appreciative if you left a review. It really helps us and the author to bring more books like this to you.

Here at HQ Digital we are dedicated to publishing fiction that will keep you turning the pages into the early hours. Don't want to miss a thing? To find out more about our books, promotions, discover exclusive content and enter competitions you can keep in touch in the following ways:

JOIN OUR COMMUNITY:

Sign up to our new email newsletter: http://smarturl.it/SignUpHQ

Read our new blog www.hqstories.co.uk

𝕏 https://twitter.com/HQStories

f www.facebook.com/HQStories

BUDDING WRITER?

We're also looking for authors to join the HQ Digital family!

Find out more here:

https://www.hqstories.co.uk/want-to-write-for-us/

Thanks for reading, from the HQ Digital team